OVER THE EDGE

Above him, maybe a foot or so, Cooper saw the girl's legs. It'd be great just to shoot her. Forget the plans he'd made for her earlier. He was too damned tired for that anyway. But he couldn't shoot her, at least not to kill.

Beth dug in her poncho for the Swiss Army knife, the blade no more than two inches long. What now? Tweak the son of a bitch's nose with the bottle opener?

A hand closed over her boot, dragging her backward and slamming her elbows against the rock. The man's other hand grabbed the ledge and his face appeared, only inches away.

"Okay, that's it." He blew tobacco breath in her face. "You're coming with me now, or else I'm gonna blow off a chunk of your pink little—"

And she stabbed him in the corner of his eye with the corkscrew.

He screamed and fell away. Beth heard rocks breaking off and tumbling free, heard another scream, and then only the sounds of the receding storm.

BANTAM BOOKS BY KRISTOPHER FRANKLIN

SILVERCAT
THE HIGH SAN JUAN

THE HIGH SAN JUAN

KRISTOPHER FRANKLIN

BANTAM BOOKS
NEW YORK · TORONTO · LONDON · SYDNEY · AUCKLAND

THE HIGH SAN JUAN

A Bantam Book / September 1990

Grateful acknowledgment is made to reprint an excerpt from "The Wide Land" from *The Selected Poems, Expanded Edition*, by A.R. Ammons. Used by permission of W.W. Norton & Company, Inc. Copyright © 1986, 1977, 1975, 1974, 1972, 1971, 1970, 1966, 1965, 1964, 1955 by A.R. Ammons.

ISBN 0-553-28623-4

Published simultaneously in the United States and Canada

*Bantam Books are published by Bantam Books, a division of
Bantam Doubleday Dell Publishing Group, Inc. Its trademark,
consisting of the words "Bantam Books" and the portrayal of
a rooster, is Registered in U.S. Patent and Trademark Office
and in other countries. Marca Registrada. Bantam Books,
666 Fifth Avenue, New York, New York 10103*

PRINTED IN THE UNITED STATES OF AMERICA

OPM   0 9 8 7 6 5 4 3 2 1

Dedication

This book is dedicated to my wife, Kathy —to me the spiritual embodiment of the qualities I came to love in the character of Katherine Elizabeth Davidson. Without Kathy, I'd probably still be a discontented English teacher, dreaming vague dreams, but . . .

She told the pond frog about the ocean.

Author's Note

This is a story of two cultures, and of two languages which may occasionally overlap. For purposes of clarity, within the flashback segments in Texas and Mexico all character dialogue should be assumed as being in Spanish, except where specifically stated otherwise.

OBSESSION:
An overwhelming fixation, an all-encompass-
ing desire, a ruling passion. A form of mono-
mania not unlike maniacal possession. . . .
—Roget's, Webster's, et al.

PROLOGUE

–September, 1914–

It was sunset when the four men crossed into a high basin of Colorado's San Juan Mountains. The peaks surrounding them were already snow-laden in early autumn, gleaming ivory in the fading light.

They'd been singing, more from habit than enthusiasm after four hundred miles, a song of their childhood . . .

> *"La Araña se sale a pasear*
> *Viene el Ratón y se trina,*
> *El Ratón, la Araña, el Ratón, la Araña*
> *Cantando al lado del agua verde. . . ."*

. . . but then the old canticle of the Spider and the Rat died on their lips, silenced by what they saw from the top of the pass.

"Dios mi," whispered their tall young leader, stunned by the unearthly beauty of the place. And with the others, men of the desert and dry brown hills, he dropped to his knees next to the mules.

The basin was roughly oval in shape. High in glacial pockets at its northern end, they saw a series of lakes that fed a silvery waterfall and then a stream. The stream became a river as it passed meadows and stands of aspen and evergreens, then flowed between two hills on the basin's floor. One hill was small and rounded. The other, a half dome, was considerably higher with a sheer face on its south side. Finally the river disappeared as roaring whitewater through a narrow canyon and left the basin behind.

"Aquí," The leader nodded and rose to his feet. *"Si Dios quiere, aquí."* This was the place, if God was willing. None of the others disagreed.

They mounted their horses, each leading a mule laden

with brown leather sacks, and rode down through dying wildflowers and high grass toward the smaller hill. A herd of elk, cautious but unafraid, retreated from their approach. On the crown of the hill they unloaded their horses among tall trees with leaves of blazing red and gold. And, though it was late and they were tired, they immediately began their task.

"El Gato, el Ratón, el Perro, el Gato . . ." They sang the old song down in rounds as they worked, and then the big man they called Honey Bear altered the last verse.

". . . cantando al lado del Agua Fuerte. . . ."

With the sound of the river roaring in their ears, it seemed appropriate.

That night and then a day and another night passed before they rode away, followed by mules that now carried food and water for their journey into the dust and heat. At the top of the pass they looked back and swore to return to this place where the sharp teeth of La Vigilancia now crouched, guarding their secret. To honor the memory of the man they had loved.

"Viva Madero! Viva Los Centinelos!"

They said it in unison, but it wasn't a shout. It was softer and more enduring. A prayer.

None of them ever saw the basin again.

Saturday Afternoon
May 21

The Cupola

Coincidence exists,
but believing in it will do you no good. . . .
—attributed variously

ONE

Partisan of lost causes, patron of long odds, pilgrim in doubtful dreams—Katherine Beth Davidson led the man and the boy into Cupola Basin, their chosen battlefield. Their weapons were their blind, unswerving faith and the six-inch metal spikes in their backpacks.

Beth was a young woman nearing thirty years of age, her small body almost boyish looking in worn Levi's and hiking boots below a red flannel shirt and a sleeveless down vest. Her hair was an equal blend of light brown and dark blond that normally hung in long curls to the middle of her back, but was currently pulled over one shoulder away from her pack. Her eyes, behind mirrored SP Glacier Glasses, were pale blue and often cynical, the only part of her face that didn't look like a teenager.

The three had crossed Mule Pass, high above and to the east of where the river cut its way through the narrow gorge of Agua Fuerte Canyon and out of the basin, and they'd have to leave the main trail soon and bushwhack down to the trees they were going to spike. Once again, the man was beginning to wheeze.

Beth stopped to give him a breather. The kid Brian, fifteen years old and under her spell, would never complain about his aching legs where she could hear him, but he needed the rest, too.

Beth shrugged off her pack, spikes clanking against the metal frame, and shook out her hair. The day was chilly at ten thousand feet and still bright, but heavy clouds were massing in the west on schedule with the weather forecast. Beneath a Damart insulated undershirt, she felt perspiration trickle between her breasts.

"Over there?" Earl Lowry was playing with his compass again. She'd shown him how to line up magnetic north, but he was still going at it backward, trying to use the needle to indicate direction.

"Close." She smiled. It's all diplomacy *(right, Mother?)*. Just pretend he's another tourist trying his first Stem Christie. "See where the river comes out from behind that hill? Follow it on down to those aspen near the mouth of the canyon."

"God, it's beautiful up here." The man struggled for another breath of thin air, then reached for a pocket inhaler. "Like a picture off a postcard."

"I wanta be there when it happens," said Brian Lowry. He was taller than his father and likewise thin, but without the concave chest and rasping breath of damaged lungs, and he was wearing a maroon and gold Arizona State windbreaker. "I wanta hide where I can see it when one of those damned chain saws hits a spike."

"They won't be in here for several months, Brian." Beth swirled canteen water around in her mouth. "And the idea's for us to be long gone. That's how Ecodefense is supposed to work, remember?"

"Brian and I'll be back in Tempe." Lowry returned the inhaler to his pocket. "Probably with me in an oxygen tent." He smiled to show he was joking. "There's no way . . ." He stopped to take a breath. ". . . I could take this elevation for even a week."

"Are you okay, Earl?" asked Beth. "I told you it was a long hike in here. And we're going to get wet within the next few hours, too. See those clouds?"

Lowry blushed, as he always did when she looked at him directly. "I'll manage," he said. "But you and Brian can have the honor of driving the spikes."

"It's a deal." She reset her pack after glancing at a folded topo map. "We can cross Riqueza Crown, that's the rounded hill this side of the river, and then drop down into the trees before it rains."

"Riqueza?" Brian's laugh came out too high-pitched, like a giggle, and he tried to deepen it. "What a name. Hey, Ricky Riqueza, get it?" He gave an abysmal Desi Arnaz impersonation. "Now, Lucy . . ."

Beth smiled. "It's Spanish, Ricky. Means wealth or prosperity, something like that."

"What about that big mother across the river?" Lowry

pointed toward the towering ridge silhouetted against snowy peaks. "We're not going up there?"

"God, no. That's the Cupola. The half dome. Nobody goes up there anymore."

"Yeah?" Brian studied it through K-Mart binoculars. "What's it, haunted or something?" He began whistling the "Twilight Zone" theme.

"Maybe, in a way." When she failed to return his grin, it faded. "Remember seeing the south side from up in the boulder field? It's a sheer wall over five hundred feet high. Cupola Face is the name on this topo map, but the rockheads call it La Brujería."

"Which means . . . ?" asked Lowry.

"Witchcraft. There've been a lot of climbing accidents on it. Way too many, they say. Things just happen, like stress-tested ropes breaking. Stuff like that. Some very careful climbers have died up there for no good reason. Most of the rockheads I know are a superstitious bunch, anyway, and now everybody just leaves it alone."

"Yeah? Doesn't scare me much." Brian lowered his binoculars. "Will it be underwater, too? If they build the dam, I mean."

"No, but it'll be the only thing in this entire basin that isn't." Beth saw that Earl Lowry had recovered enough, so she led them off the trail and across greening meadow grass down toward Riqueza Crown. "But that's what we're here to prevent, isn't it, guys?"

"Right on!" chimed in Lowry. It sounded odd coming from him, like an echo from another time. "Just like the Monkey Wrench Gang in that book."

"Or the next best thing." She smiled. "Let's take it slow and quiet the rest of the way. I doubt anyone's here this early in the year, but careful never hurts."

"No! *Dejamos!*" The old word exploded out of Stephen without thought. Then, *"Mierda!* Don't go that way!"

He shifted his position automatically after the outburst, hooking the toe of his new Fire Ninja climbing slippers into a vertical crack. With a quick pull he was back onto the flat summit and sliding laterally toward a different

position. Sound always traveled farther than you thought
up here.

There were three of them, and the one in the lead was
a girl. And, unless they hung a quick U-ey, they were
going to walk up right on Riqueza Crown.

"Mierda," he whispered again. Shit.

He put the Ninjas back into their pouch and crept
barefoot to a patch of scrub fir that a gray squirrel abandoned, chattering angrily at him. Then he stood upright,
a freshening west wind at his back, and focused binoculars on the hilltop below and across the river. They were
still down there, of course. El Gavilán and the others.
And Ware.

Stephen James was short, about five feet seven, with a
face hardened beyond his actual age of twenty-nine. He
had olive skin and shoulder-length black hair. Under a
T-shirt bearing a Metolius Mountain Products logo, his
torso was delineated into thick ridges of defined muscle,
matched by the equally extreme development of his
arms and legs. Over the years since El Jornada del Muerto, in countless weight rooms and on nameless rock
faces, he had re-created his body into a duplicate in min-
iature of Joseph Ware.

No flattery was intended.

Stephen watched the newcomers advance through
patches of old snow and up into the trees. There was
nothing he could do for them.

They were tramping through a thicket of newly leafed
oakbrush when they came upon the men digging in the
ground. Beth saw them first, three of them pulling at half-
buried, rotten timbers at the top of the aspen-covered
slope. And another man, somewhat older, standing
nearby.

"Whoa." Her voice was a murmur, but it stopped a
wheezing Earl Lowry. He, in turn, put down a cautionary
hand to Brian. All three froze into stillness below the
curve of the hill.

"What?" whispered the boy, and the sound carried up
to her. "What is it?"

Beth dropped into a crouch, spindly oak branches

scraping the slick surface of her vest. "Four of them." She turned to let Lowry read her lips.

"Forest Service?" he whispered.

She shook her head. She didn't know who the men were, but she was certain they weren't the law.

"Growers, then." Lowry nodded. "Be careful. This whole damned hillside's probably wired."

Beth didn't think so. It was a little early in the year, for one thing. At this altitude, young marijuana plants were best left completely alone for at least another month. But she looked around for booby traps anyway—spiked boards, eye-level fish hooks. Sometimes the growers even trip-wired hand grenades. Good old Viet Cong hi-tech gone American.

When she moved, her pack shifted and one of the spikes clanked against the metal frame again.

Damn. You could hear that clear across the basin. She slid the spike into a side pocket, then motioned the others away, and they began to descend through the scrub. They'd circle below the Crown, she decided. Probably the four men hadn't heard her anyway. They were busy doing . . . whatever the hell they were doing, and their sounds would have covered hers. Which was just fine. If nobody saw them at all, so much the better.

That was when the big man stepped out from behind a tree and into their path.

"First you come and then you go." He smiled. "Like the tide. Are you lost?"

He'd appeared, almost as a conjuring act, from behind a split-based Engelmann spruce, and he was huge. Probably six feet six or more, with a massive, wedge-shaped body that obviously had years of heavy training behind it.

"Lost? This isn't McDonald's?" Brian quipped with a sassy grin. "You mean we missed that off ramp again?"

Still showing off. The damned kid didn't have the sense to be scared.

"Say, that's clever." The big man's grin broadened. He was good-looking if you cared for the type, Beth conceded. Midforties, with a lean, cheerful face creased by smile lines, and short curly brown hair. Good-looking except for his eyes, that is, which the smile wasn't reaching. Not even close.

"You're a real funny kid, aren't you?" the man continued. "What's your name?"

"What's yours?" Earl Lowry took Brian's arm and pulled him away.

"Ware. Joseph Ware." The man looked up the trail at Beth. "And you?"

"Be-Betty . . . Davis." She lied instinctively about her first name, and the second just popped out before she thought.

"Pleased to meet you, Buh-Buh-Bette. I've seen all your movies, by the way. Just backpacking through?"

"That's right." She pretended to miss the man's sarcasm. "Over to the river."

Ware rubbed a finger across his clean-shaven chin, muscles shifting visibly beneath a rust-colored sweater. "You were going the right way, then. Why'd you turn and come back?" There was something in his voice, light and conversational, that chilled Beth. In his eyes, too. Like he knew a joke, and it was funny as hell, but he wasn't telling it.

"We just decided to . . ."

"My friends are up there on the Crown. It almost looked like you were trying to avoid them."

"No, we weren't." Beth felt her midsection go hollow. "We just . . ."

"Let's go back up." Joseph Ware smiled. "I'll introduce you."

Stephen remained behind the scrub fir to avoid skylining himself on the Cupola's ridge. Through binoculars he watched the girl and her two companions top the Crown with Ware close behind them. He saw the others stop their excavation around the old timbers and straighten up, and he saw El Gavilán walk toward them.

The hikers were finished now, and there wasn't a thing he could do to help them without ruining his own plan. It was too early, and he had no contingency for this. It was going to go badly for them.

Apesar de eso. He could only watch.

* * *

The man in the open-necked shirt was Spanish and he was big, though not on the scale of Joseph Ware. He was square in build—wide face, wide shoulders and hips—and only beginning to go to fat in what appeared to be his late fifties. His hair was thick and gray, including the hair that curled on his chest, where a heavy-looking gold coin hung from a chain. His eyes were deeply pouched and worried.

This guy, thought Beth, is familiar as hell. Where have I . . .

"Who are your friends, Joseph?" The man's voice had no trace of an accent. It was a speaker's voice. It projected.

"These bony types"—Ware pointed at the Lowrys—"are Anonymous One and Two. And this young woman is Buh-Buh-Bette Davis of motion-picture fame." He seemed to be enjoying himself enormously.

"Listen to me." Lowry's voice was trembling, and Beth heard the thickness rattle in his chest. "You have no right"—he broke off and lifted the inhaler to his mouth with shaky fingers—"to hold us here against our will! We—"

"Who's holding you against your will?" The man's voice was rich and reassuring. "I don't know you from Adam, sir, so why should I wish to detain you? You've come walking up this hill. I imagine you can just as easily walk back down it."

Out of the corner of her eye, Beth saw one of the other men move casually toward the oakbrush thicket behind them. Thunder rumbled down from the high peaks.

Not back then, in spite of the man's words, nor forward. And certainly not to her left where Joseph Ware stood watching her, the same look of amused curiosity on his face.

"Maybe . . . maybe I misunderstood," Lowry was saying. "If so, I apologize. Bette, why don't we go along and let these people—"

"Hey, I know you!" Brian pushed past his father. "I remember now. I've seen you on TV."

The man's face paled beneath dark skin. His eyes

darted from father to son. Then he shrugged and smiled, and Beth saw him relax. As if a difficult decision had just been made for him.

"Really?" he asked.

"Yeah . . . yeah, I was trying to remember before." It was all a game to the boy. He was oblivious of Lowry or Beth. "On the motel TV in Durango. Reporters were asking you about the dam project, and you were against it. Hey, you're on our side, man! Raymond . . . something"

Beth's eyes widened. Jesus Christ, the man was Raymond Cuellar!

"Very good," murmured Cuellar. "Excellent! The best minds are always the young minds." And he nodded slowly.

Beth heard the hard *snick* of a bolt action being cocked. The man behind them had an automatic pistol, its clip descending from the short handle beneath his hand.

"What the hell . . ." Lowry spun around and saw the weapon. The other two men had moved up in a loose half circle. They were similarly armed, and Beth felt a wave of revulsion almost stronger than her fear. God, she hated guns!

"Remove your packs, please." Cuellar's voice had become positively jovial. "I'd be interested to know why you clank when you walk."

Beth reached around to shrug out of her backpack. As she lowered it to the ground, her hands were momentarily hidden from view. She pulled the extra spike from her side pocket and slid it up the left sleeve of her flannel shirt. She stepped away from the pack and glanced at Ware. He was still watching her, and he suddenly winked.

One of the men unfastened her pack. He was very young, probably still a teenager, with his head shaved in a ragged, erratic crewcut. He grinned, and she saw his teeth were going bad.

"Look." Another of the men, a pale blond with a reddish mustache, pulled the bag of spikes from Brian's pack. "What the hell are these for?"

As he spoke, the boy with bad teeth and the third man, balding and overweight, were finding the same thing.

"It's called Ecodefense." Beth spoke up. Talk, she thought, and keep talking. For some reason she didn't understand, they were in trouble. Bad trouble, because Raymond Cuellar was rapidly becoming a household name in southwestern Colorado, and he wouldn't do something like this unless . . . Talk! "Or Ecotage, if you prefer," she continued.

"I'm familiar with the term." Cuellar nodded. "They're for the trees, then. Down at the canyon."

"That's right." She went on rapidly, eagerly. As long as they let her talk, it was okay. "We can't let them flood Cupola Basin just so some flatlanders downriver can water their lawns! I've heard you say the same thing on television, Mr. Cuellar. It's a political statement. We spike the trees and then weld fence staples into road-rash . . ."

Cuellar stood and watched her. His eyes had glazed with disinterest. He nodded to the balding man.

"Quieter's better," said Ware softly. He sat down on one of the timbers and studied Beth with the same faint smile. "Quieter's always better."

"*Es verdad.* My friend, you're right," said Cuellar. "Gentlemen, quieter *is* better."

The teenager laid his automatic pistol on the ground and pulled a large hunting knife from a sheath at his belt.

His eyes are different colors, thought Beth suddenly. She felt her perceptions shutting down. One's brown and one's green. He stepped toward her.

Sudden movement behind her.

"No! You get away!" Brian's voice shrill, then cut off. A scuffling sound.

The boy came closer. He shifted the knife to an overhand grip.

The sound of Earl Lowry wheezing for air, and the sound of running. She heard someone laugh.

And when the teenager lunged at her, grinning through rotten teeth, knife upraised and shining, his breath foul in her face and his other hand grabbing her vest, she pulled the six-inch spike from her sleeve and drove it point-blank into his throat.

It was pure luck, she knew. She thrust it blindly. He impaled himself.

The boy staggered back, releasing her, and sat down with the spike projecting straight out of his neck. His eyes found hers, bewildered. The knife dropped from his hand.

"This ain't funny," he said, and a thick clot of blood filled his mouth. He spat. "Hey, this ain't so damn funny."

She saw him reach back to steady himself as she spun away down the hill. She saw the blond man crouched over something, twisting and driving his hand deeper into it. She saw Ware still sitting and watching her with a smile on his face. Then she heard Cuellar's voice.

"Get her! Shoot her, goddammit! Oh, you *cabrones!* Shoot her!"

She sprinted through the trees, down from the Crown. She angled sharply to her left as a burst of gunfire shredded a small aspen. Buzzings like enraged wasps flew past her, and she felt a tug at her sleeve. She cut back again and vaulted a patch of dirty snow a second before bits of it flew up behind her.

"Vengan! Vengan acá, goddammit!" Cuellar's voice was behind her. "Get her! Oh, you *cabrones . . ."* It faded into the sounds of footsteps fumbling down the hillside. Only sounds now, hidden from view by the trees as she came onto a faint path and took the line of least resistance.

And ran for her life.

TWO

Stephen's binoculars were Heydreichs, among the finest made at eight hundred dollars a pair. Torie McCallister had bought them for him with her Gold Card, and had probably never missed the money. Each set was individually calibrated in West Germany, and through them he saw El Gavilán's men force the three to remove their packs. He saw the girl gesturing and then El Gavilán giving the signal to commit murder again. He saw Ware sit down and the other men lay aside their Mac-10s and draw knives. He saw Cooper and Leggett attack the two men. One tried to run and the other fought back, but the result was the same. Then he saw the girl thrust out her arm at Freddie Jenkins, who fell to the ground.

And now the girl was running, appearing and disappearing in the trees down the side of Riqueza Crown, toward the river and the log bridge. El Gavilán's men were pursuing, but she was faster than Cooper and Leggett.

Ware wasn't chasing her. He was still on the Crown, standing with El Gavilán and pointing toward the Cupola. Then Stephen understood.

The approachable north side of the half dome was a wooded slope. The path past the log bridge ascended it at an angle to within fifty feet of the top before curving back down toward the Agua Fuerte trail. It was an inverted U, a long half circle once used by rockheads as a back way to the summit.

If the girl stayed on the path, she'd climb to just below the dome cap, then descend back into the basin. Anyone with moderate speed could cross the meadows and forest below the Cupola and wait for her to run right into his arms.

As Stephen watched, Joseph Ware left El Gavilán and raced down from the Crown behind Cooper and Leggett. Freddie Jenkins, completely ignored by his leader, had rolled onto his hands and knees and was crawling toward a lean-to shelter back in the trees.

Ware was as quick and deadly as a tiger. Even with his size, none of them, Stephen included, could match his speed. The girl would have no chance against him.

It was all going wrong. Helping her would ruin everything. He should stay hidden and let the events below take their own course. *Pues nada.* But . . .

He remembered Rodolfo. And Pilar. The faces of the innocents.

He pulled on his low hikers and ran along the top of the dome toward the north rim, where serrated rock overhung the highest point of the trail.

Beth crossed a narrow log bridge in half a dozen strides. It was pitted and slick, and below her the river roared whitewater from the spring snowmelt, but that didn't matter. Better to end up down there than to be caught by them.

On the west side, the path cut through heavy evergreen forest, with new stands of skunk cabbage growing in dappled pools of sunlight. She heard the hollow thump of thunder up ahead.

The trail began to ascend, and she realized it was taking her up the north slope of the Cupola. What if it deadended at the dome? She'd laughed at her friends' horror stories of La Brujería, but she'd never gone past the bridge before.

The Lowrys were dead. She'd better face that sad fact and worry about herself, or she'd be dead, too.

But why? Why would someone like Raymond Cuellar . . .

To hell with why. Worry about it later. Run now.

She was in excellent condition. Summers of 10K competitions and backpacking, and winters spent on the mountain every day as a ski instructor had given her legs and lungs of iron. If she didn't panic, she could skate these bastards off.

Except maybe the big one . . .

To hell with him, too. She reached down for more—more strength, more speed—as the path steepened.

Joseph Ware ran through greening meadows and patches of trees. He ran euphorically, long legs cutting down the distance. He ran thinking of the girl who was climbing the trail to his left, and a tight grin was slashed across his face.

She was something, that one. Buh-Buh-Bette, or whatever her real name was. She had the heart of a samurai.

It was when he saw her hide the spike that he began to develop an interest in the outcome and decided to separate Cuellar's goons from their guns. He wasn't about to allow that developing drama to be spoiled by the blast of a Mac-10. And he'd been right. Poor little Fuck-up Freddie was completely out of his league with that one.

Ware vaulted a deadfall of downed aspen without breaking stride and crossed an open meadow where a mule deer and her newborn fawn bolted away into the trees. As he ran, he watched his faint shadow on the ground.

He'd catch her when she descended the path, long before Cooper or Leggett even got near. And then he'd decide how the game would proceed.

The options expanded in his mind.

The path steepened as Beth climbed, shreds of talus covering its surface. Her breathing began to lose its rhythm and grow ragged.

You can't slip here. You can't slide down, or fall. Keep your footing and you'll gain, because they'll have trouble, too.

Above and to her left, she caught glimpses of the dome's jagged edge. To her right, the slope fell away to pitches of rock shale and stunted trees.

Then the path's angle grew shallow again. After a hundred yards through open light, it leveled off and she was running along a flat trail maybe fifty feet below the rim. Could it be the trail didn't go to the top at all? If it went back down, and *they* knew it went back down . . .

There were narrow rock pinnacles ahead. The path cut through them like a thread between the scabby, upraised fingers of a giant. She instinctively pulled her elbows in. She burst through . . .

And powerful arms grabbed her from the left. Her own arms were pinned to her sides, and she felt her feet leave the ground. The two of them tumbled forward onto granite and loose gravel.

"You . . . son of a bitch!" Her breath came in hoarse grunts as she slashed his face with her nails, drawing blood. She levered her knee toward his groin, but kicked a hard-muscled thigh instead.

"Goddammit, woman!" He wasn't Ware. She'd thought

so at first, but he was much smaller. Long black hair, blood coursing down a dark face . . . An Indian?

"Mierda, mujer!" he snarled. "Hold still, dammit!"

And a piece of cloth, smelling faintly of sweat and something alkaline, was shoved into her open mouth.

Stephen had descended from the dome's summit in a quick traverse down a diagonal cut in the rock. When the girl burst through the opening in the pinnacles, he'd decided against stepping out into her path because she didn't know him. She might have turned and run back the other way.

Jesus, she was tough! She'd raked his forehead above one eye and was set to begin biting when he pushed a scrap from an old chalk bag between her teeth.

"Be still, damn you!" he rasped in a cutting whisper. "Listen to me. Listen! I'm not with them. Do you hear me?"

She grunted a curse through the stiff cloth, and redoubled her efforts. He squeezed her arms into her sides until he expected to hear her ribs crack, and wrapped her flailing legs with his own. Breath was exploding out of her around the cloth. She tried to butt him with her forehead.

"Listen to me." He forced the anger from his voice. "We don't have time for this. There are two of them coming behind you and another waiting ahead. *I'm not with them!*"

He felt her struggling lessen, but her body was still like an iron bar enclosed in his arms and legs.

"I'm going to let you go, 'cause I don't have time to mess with you." His mouth was next to her ear, and he felt blood trickling down his cheek. "When I let you up, you can take off again and get the shit killed out of you, or you can listen to me. You do what you got to do."

He released with both arms and legs and she kicked free, taking a backhand swing at his head that he ducked. She spun onto hands and knees facing him, lips drawn back in a snarl as she spat out the cloth, long hair hanging in her face. Jesus, she was beautiful.

"Who the hell're you?" She reached for a jagged rock.

"Doesn't matter." Stephen jumped to his feet.

"Cooper and Leggett'll be here any minute. Can you climb?"

She'd lost the sunglasses somewhere, and her eyes were blue. She cut them up the sheer slab of rock below the dome, then back toward him. "Better than you," she challenged.

He doubted that, but let it pass. "Okay, good. Then get up to the top as quick as you can. I'm right behind you."

He watched her rise to her feet and edge away from him, and he read her thoughts. She had clear access to the trail again. Then she muttered something he didn't hear and turned to the rock.

She climbed like a novice, all pulling arms, but she was strong and he knew she'd manage. He crossed to the pinnacles and peered out.

There was still time. He heard them laboring below, Cooper probably far in advance of Lead-ass Leggett, but he didn't see them yet. The girl was moving well up in the cut and sloping toward the top. Stephen took another look down the path and turned away.

He vaulted past two granite points and leaned against a vertical crack that fed straight to the rim. He and the girl cleared the face at virtually the same time. Her eyes widened when she saw him.

"Okay, big deal. So maybe I was wrong. . . ."

"Get down!" He cut her off and pushed her shoulder into the rock. There was a rush of sound—running footsteps, first one set and then another a little later—below that echoed and then diminished.

Stephen looked over the edge. There was no one there.

"They've gone past." He reached back and pulled her to her feet as a gust of icy air blew her hair away from her face. "Hurry. We have only a few minutes before they run into Ware. . . .Where are you going?"

She'd hooked a leg over the edge. "Back the other way," she answered. "Where else?"

"Won't work. You'd meet El Gavilán halfway down the path—"

"Who the hell is—"

"—and he'd have your little cream-colored self for dinner. We have to go the other way."

She looked across the flat, rock-shattered surface of the dome. Lightning flashed in the distance. "There's another way down?"

"Yeah . . . yeah, there is. Let's move. Ware'll backtrack with the other two. When he meets El Gavilán, they'll figure you came up top. And there's no place to hide up here."

"Cuellar?" She was still talking, but at least she was following him toward the center of the dome. "This . . . El Who-the-Fuck is Raymond Cuellar?"

He had to grin. "Such language. You eat with that mouth?"

"I get like this when I'm scared," she shot back. "You a fucking priest, or what? Just answer the question."

"Yeah." Stephen gathered his ropes and pack. "El Gavilán means the Sparrow Hawk. Raymond Cuellar's not his real name either, but it's as good as any." He hoped she wasn't noticing the ropes.

"Then you know him." It was a statement, not a question. "How do you know him? Why did he kill Earl and Brian?"

"Not now." Stephen broke into a trot as more lightning knifed from the thickening clouds. "Hurry up."

Dammit, she was going to ruin everything.

Ware pushed up the path, Cooper and Leggett trailing behind him. Leggett was nearly blown and lagged far back. Cooper was in a little better shape, but he clearly didn't want to get too close to Ware, either.

The thunder was a hammer banging iron. Hard wind gusts rolled over the dome's edge and down onto them.

Ware glanced back toward the other two. Where had Cuellar come up with a pair like that? Ugly as a hatful of assholes, and just about as bright. And Lead-ass Leggett, as usual, was deeply involved in nasal excavation—up to the second joint of his index finger, it looked like. Who was it said you truly got what you paid for? He thought of Jaime Agustin and Charlie Pellikern, but only for a moment.

Buh-Buh-Bette had cut off the path somewhere and watched these two rocket scientists dash on past, that much was clear. But where? If she went back, she'd already run into Cuellar. Ware hoped that hadn't happened, because El Gavilán was in no mood for rueful humor. She'd be dead by now.

The trail leveled off and ran beneath the overhang of the rim. Ware stopped to study the rock above him, and especially the loose gravel at its base.

It was possible.

He heard labored breathing up ahead, and although he was certain who it was, he flattened himself against the granite face. His huge left hand instinctively cupped itself into a cutting edge.

Cuellar poked his head through the opening in the pinnacles. He'd heard them, too, or at least Cooper and Leggett.

"Find her?" He walked forward when he saw Ware.

"No. Apparently she cut back." Ware didn't bother to lay the blame on the other two. For one thing, El Gavilán was no fool and would figure it out easily enough. For another, after twenty years together, he'd long since ceased worrying about what Cuellar thought anyway.

"Cut back? She didn't come past me."

Ware nodded, feeling the tiny kernel of anticipation beginning to grow again. "That doesn't surprise me. It leaves two options. Either she went down . . ." He looked off the path at the jumble of trees and scree below them. ". . . or she went up."

Cuellar studied the rock wall. "You've been up there. What's it like?"

"It's no place to hide out. It's a dome, like the name says. Or a half dome, actually. Maybe a hundred feet across, mostly flat with some scrub growing out of the rock. The opposite side from here's La Brujería, that climbing face I told you about. Straight down and slick as camel snot for five hundred feet or more. A solid 5.11 or 5.12."

"Which means?" asked Cuellar. His face tightened at the mention of the cliff.

"Which means unless our Buh-Buh-Bette's a world-class climber, or has ropes hidden on her somewhere, it's completely out of the question. Even if she knew about the caves . . ."

"Caves?" Cuellar's head twisted up so quickly Ware heard his thick neck pop. "What caves?"

Ware shrugged. "Las Cuevas de La Brujería," he said. "In the face, partway down. I guess there's some interior limestone in the Cupola. Doesn't matter. The nearest one's almost a hundred feet down a wall that'd psyche out a housefly."

"And the other walls?"

"Not much better. If she's up there, she's either hiding under a bush or hanging off the edge."

"Cooper, Leggett." Cuellar turned to the two men. "Split up and go down the path both ways. When you reach bottom, work across the base of this ridge toward each other. If she went below the trail, she'll come out down there somewhere."

"What about Freddie?" Leggett's voice had a thick southern accent. "Somebody's gotta—"

"Your little *maricón's* at the camp with gauze stuffed into the hole in his neck. He'll either live or die. You find that girl, and . . ."

The two men had started away in opposite directions. They stopped.

"And don't . . . mess . . . up . . . again."

Cuellar turned back to Joseph Ware as Cooper and Leggett hurried off. "So. Do you think she went down?"

"Probably." Ware grinned. "She seemed to know the area, and she struck me as too smart to crawl out on a rotten limb. Shall I bushwhack down the side here? You could check the dome—"

"Don't toy with me!" snapped Cuellar. "This is all making me quite angry, my friend. *You* check the dome. *Buena caza.*"

He stepped carefully off the path and within a few minutes was gone down the slope, clinging to tree branches and cursing softly to himself.

Ware studied the scattered gravel near the base of the wall. He'd seen Cuellar looking at it, too. After all the years, the man was nothing if not predictable. El Gavilán wanted no part of this particular lady up close after the

way she'd shish-kebabbed Freddie. Especially not above
a five-hundred-foot drop in a thunderstorm. Cuellar was
terrified of heights. Extreme acrophobia, as the late la-
mented Dr. Fleming would've diagnosed it.

Ware went over to the rock face and sighted his best
pattern for the ascent. When he was in a good mood, like
now, he sometimes felt like composing. Old tunes, new
lyrics. He climbed with this one, singing softly to the
melody of "Oh, Susannah."

> "The last time I saw Raymond
> I haven't seen him since,
> He was crawling down the Cupola
> Making fudge bars in his pants."

He loved it out here. Anything could happen. Anything.

THREE

"I have two words for you, pal," said Katherine Beth
Davidson. "And they're not Merry Christmas."

The man didn't answer. He just kept playing out the
multicolored climbing rope. Lightning flashed again, and
she flinched. They were completely exposed on the cliff's
edge.

"Did you hear me?" Her voice was shaking, and she
tried to get control. "I said I won't do it, goddamn you!
I'm not into suicide."

He looked up and smiled faintly. It softened his features and made him almost handsome in a brutal, exotic
way. His black hair was held by a patterned red ban-
danna tied as a headband, and he looked like a movie
Apache from the "Late Show." With the wind molding
his T-shirt around him, he was incredibly muscular,
nearly freakishly so, and that reminded her of Ware

again. Except in reverse, because this one's smile was mostly in his eyes.

"You can do it." His voice was soft. "I'll top-belay, or I can lower you. That's why there's a rappel anchor here." He pointed to a rusty iron bar like a giant staple that had been bent and hammered into the granite.

"No chance. Look, no offense . . ."

"Stephen. Stephen James."

"No offense, Stephen . . ." Where had she heard that name? ". . . but I'm not buying it. Your rope won't even reach the ground, dammit! It's hundreds of feet—"

"Doesn't have to. There's a cave entrance about eighty feet down."

Beth looked off the edge again. The wall was so sheer it actually seemed to curve back in. To overhang. There was a meadow far below, encircled by microscopic evergreens. The inside of her mouth tasted like old coins.

"You . . . think I'm going to hang down that cliff and swing into some cave like freaking Tarzan? I'll be damned if—"

"You will, because you have no choice, and there isn't time to argue about it. I'll swing you to the belay anchor when you get there. Step into this." He thrust a webbed harness toward her.

"No."

"It's a rappel seat. Put your legs through and hold that part with the ring in front of you. Hurry."

"I'm not doing this!"

"Look." His dark eyes held hers, and she saw an edge of anger. Blood from where she'd scratched him had dried on his cheek. "You've got guts, or you'd already be dead. Now use them. Any minute, those *pendejos* are going to pop over that rim back there. You remember their guns? We have no guns up here, girl. What we have is this rope. And we also have about two minutes before the rain hits. So if you have something useful to add, indicate by nodding. Otherwise, shut up and get this on."

Beth angrily jerked the harness up and felt the straps cup her buttocks. Then Stephen James unscrewed the locking carabiner and slipped through a metal Figure

Eight Descender with the rope already looped. She was familiar with the gear.

"Okay." He nudged her toward the edge. The wind was a bludgeon, pushing them back, and she felt the first trace of mist wetting her cheeks. "Your left hand's the guide. Grab onto—"

"I've rappelled before," she snapped. Might as well admit it. The whole damned thing was inevitable now.

"Good." He didn't seem surprised. "There won't be any footing after the first ten feet. Keep your brake hand secure. Now go."

"Oh, God!" She hesitated, her back and shoulders toward the abyss, and dug her right foot into the one patch of shallow earth along the rock edge. Her toe butted granite as he played rope into the anchor.

She'd told him the truth. She had rappelled—on easy pitches where you essentially leaned out and walked down backward—and she did know the basics. But nothing like this. Not ever like this.

Raindrops began to splash against her back.

Sweet Jesus . . .

"What's your name?"

"What . . . ?" She looked up at him. He held the belay through the ring, then around his hips, and he was smiling at her.

"Your name."

"It's Be-Beth." She nearly said Bette Davis again.

"Go now, Beth," he said. "There's no more time."

After several steps, the cliff fell away from her and she dropped. It became clear in that instant as her senses went numb. He was one of them. She'd fall. Another climbing accident on a wall known for accidents, and no one the wiser. . . .

Then she bobbed up, spinning at the end of the rope. She was alive. Stephen James wasn't going to drop her.

He was right about the cliff. The upper area was an overhang, and her feet wouldn't reach the rock. Her spin slowed and stopped, then reversed, and she was hanging straight.

Okay. The right hand's the brake. She let herself slowly descend. Don't look down. Look at the wall. There's an old nest over there in a crack. A hawk's, or maybe a golden eagle . . . The rain was getting harder.

A little faster, even without gloves. He's up there alone. If they find him, they'll shoot him. I'll hear the shots first, then the rope will go slack. Then I'll fall free. . . .

Faster.

"Pull up!" His voice floated down. "See it?"

And she looked a little below her and saw a jagged hole in the rock. It was the upper cave.

He lowered her a few feet from above while she held her brake hand firm. Then she felt herself swing out slightly, then back. Again, with a larger arc this time.

It was the only way that would work. With the overhang, she was at least fifteen feet out from the entrance. There was no ledge, or even a lip. Just a hole in the cliff. The rock was already glistening, slick from the rainfall. When she swung inward, she saw a metal bar that had been driven laterally across a space just inside the entrance.

The belay anchor. It was her flying trapeze. He was going to swing her into that hole like a nine ball in the corner pocket, and it was up to her to grab the bar. But with what? With her guide hand and topple backward? With her brake hand and release too soon?

Bullshit. With *both* hands!

Her outswing got larger. It got huge. She went flying at the hole in the cliff.

Stephen felt slack on the rope and began to pull it up. She was either in the cave or playing Pancake in the Meadow.

The rain had increased, blowing over him in a diagonal spray. He looked back across the dome for any sign of movement.

He'd lied to the girl. He did have a gun, and he pulled his pack closer as he reeled in the rope. It wasn't for this, though. It was a short-barreled .38 Police Special, and he had something entirely different in mind for it.

The clouds rolled across the Cupola as the sky opened

to sheets of rain. The wind howled up over the edge now, but when it got colder, it would go the other direction.

The Figure Eight was still in place, but there was no time to rerig with a prussik knot and he couldn't leave any rope behind anyway. He bent low against the wind gusts and doubled the Maxim kernmantle through the anchor. Then he pulled a doubled length between his legs, up his back, and over his shoulder. He grabbed the pack and cradled it against his chest when he swung out over the cliff.

He went down fast, too fast, with the doubled rope burning his crotch and back. He could no longer see the meadow or the trees below. Only the rock face and the pounding torrent of the rain.

He had to estimate the cave, swinging himself out into the wind. He came in too high the first time and slammed his feet against the rock just above the entrance. Out again, wider, and back, still a little high, but he flew in the entrance with his head scraping the top and grabbed the anchor.

The girl—Beth, she'd said—was huddled partway back when he dropped to the floor. He released one length of rope and pulled on the other. Fast, fast! It had to clear the rappelling ring up top before anyone reached it.

It fell free down the cliff, and he reeled it in.

Dale Cooper shuffled around the edge of an oak thicket and studied some coyote tracks in the mud, his Mac-10 held taut against its canvas shoulder strap. What he wanted was a cigarette.

If she came down from the highest point of the trail above, here's about where she'd come out. He crouched in scratchy brush and watched the hillside. The storm was no help. Because of it, everything up there was moving. Unless he got lucky and spotted her, she could glide right by and he'd think it was the wind.

And that wouldn't do. No, sir. They had to find her, Cuellar had made that clear enough. It would be their asses if she got free.

Where the hell was Leggett?

Cooper dug a crumpled pack of Camels from his jacket

pocket. Filters were for fairies, that's what his Granpaw Jeffries had always said. Anybody can suck smoke through a wad of charcoal, boy, but it takes a real man to face up to ole Boss C and spit in his eye.

He was shielding his body from the wind and trying for a light when he heard someone floundering toward him.

That's not the girl. No chance. That's just Lead-ass Leggett, probably staggering around with one of his headaches. Thunderclappers, he calls them. Cooper stood up slowly so his companion wouldn't start blasting away from sheer fright.

Travis Leggett raised his weapon in a half salute and worked his way over, eyes fixed on the slope. Somewhere along the way he'd fallen and his new safari shirt had ripped, exposing the curve of his pendulous belly. He was trying to look intent.

"Lighten up." Cooper grinned. "Cuellar and Ware aren't here."

At that, Leggett relaxed and ambled over to the thicket, letting his weapon flop from its shoulder strap. He first squatted down by Cooper, who was taking long, grateful drags off the cigarette, then gave it up and spraddled back on the ground with a gasp of relief.

"Seen anything?" Leggett's index finger instinctively probed one of his nostrils. He stopped when Cooper looked at him.

"A coupla deer. And I see you, booger diving like always. Nothing else."

Leggett was working now at keeping his hand away from his nose. "I fell," he said. "Rotten log." He began to rub his left temple with a rotary motion.

"I noticed. Trashed your new Man of the Wilderness outfit, huh?"

"Don't pick on me. This stuff looks—"

"Looks like a mail-order catalog puked all over you," Cooper finished. "That's some fancy garb just to go dig in the ground."

"I said don't pick on me." Leggett grinned a little, beginning to relax. Then his round face clouded. "Freddie. Jesus, I nearly forgot. We gotta go see about the kid, Dale."

"Freddie Fuck-up? Forget him, Leggett. You'll find another honey. Remember that song Ware sings? 'Fish gotta swim, birds gotta fly, Fred's gotta royally fuck up till he die.' " Cooper laughed. "Ware and those damned songs he makes up."

"Yeah? Well, I say Ware"—Leggett looked around carefully—"can go pound sand up his ass. That's what I say." The last part came out in a whisper.

"I'll tell him you said so." Cooper nodded, just to watch Leggett turn fish-belly white. "Meantime, we gotta find that girl. Cuellar's gone totally ballistic over this one."

There was a crackling sound from the slope. Cooper mashed out his cigarette and brought the automatic pistol level with the brush. Out of the corner of his eye, he saw Leggett trying to zip his new bush jacket.

Cuellar stepped from behind a boulder and came down between two trees in a beginning swirl of rain. He stared at Cooper and Leggett for a moment, then lowered his weapon.

"Well?" He crossed a level area near the thicket.

"Nothing," said Leggett, glancing nervously toward Cooper.

"Have you been all along the base of this ridge?"

"Twice," Cooper lied. He wondered how long Cuellar had been there, and what he'd heard. "We passed each other once and then doubled back. I don't think she came down this way, Mr. Cuellar."

"Goddamn! *Chinga el diablo!*" Cuellar glared up through an increasing downpour. Visibility was already gone halfway up the slope. "Then Ware must have found her." He looked back at them. "At least, you'd better hope Ware found her."

Some water slid down Cooper's collar and onto his neck. It was no colder than the ice already forming along his spine.

"I'm going around toward the canyon trail." Cuellar turned away. "You two keep looking. Work along the hillside and over to the river. If she did get off the Cupola, there are only two ways out of the basin this time of year. Mule Pass and the river canyon. Backtrack to the bridge first." He stopped to stare at them. "What are you waiting for? *Hagalo ahora!*"

That means move your ass, Leggett, thought Cooper, and don't make a sound. Don't start whining about the rain or your headache or your sweet Freddie, either. And keep your fat finger out of your nose, 'cause this is as close to dead as we're gonna see till the real thing comes along.

Travis Leggett hurried away behind Cooper, and he didn't make a sound.

Joseph Ware reached the dome's rim as the rain began to fall. He pulled up easily and soundlessly, enjoying the steady flex of lats and biceps, and settled into a slot in the cliff where he could raise only his head over the top.

A freshening wind carried raindrops into his face. The storm was dropping down fast now. Within minutes it would be a downpour.

The dome appeared empty at first inspection, but he was sure she was near. There were several clumps of scrub fir and some depressions in the rock itself.

He wasn't certain he wanted to find her just yet, anyway. The game was nearly over now, except for the Esteban Santiago business, and it had grown boring in the last year. Even the thought of the money no longer excited him.

Twenty years. Figure it that way and it came to a little under a million a year. Not bad, but not as great as it had once seemed. Not when Magic Johnson made two or three million dribbling a basketball.

Of course, there had been some interesting diversions along the way. The different faces, all dead now, and what they knew and didn't know. An intellectual exercise at times.

And now this girl. After the excavation, there'd be loading and moving, mule work, and there'd be listening to an ecstatic Cuellar talk and talk—God, the way the man would talk in an orgy of relief—and there'd be the constraint involved in not killing Cooper and Leggett right away, speaking of mule work. Freddie, too, although the girl may have already taken care of that.

Aside from Esteban Santiago, still a challenge, Ware had already resigned himself to boredom. Get rich and get old. But then Buh-Buh-Bette had come along. . . .

The storm was on him, howling across the dome, raindrops mixed with pellets of sleet. He rose in a crouch, the perfect predator, and moved toward the closest clump of bushes.

Not there. And not in the next, either. Ware was soaked through, water dripping from his curly hair and the sweater plastered to his body. Lightning crackled around him in bright bursts of illumination. He didn't mind.

Cross and countercross. He converted the dome into an imaginary grid. Every low spot, every rise, every bush.

Until he came to the far edge. Someone had hammered a U-shaped bar of metal into the granite, leaving a rusting iron ring. A rappel anchor. He was directly above the caves.

He wondered idly if she'd jumped. No, not that one. She wouldn't quit, he knew that much about her already. Maybe she *had* gone downhill from the path. Maybe the scattered gravel was just clever as hell, and she'd . . .

The footprint was about a size 6. It was in the only spot near the rim where soil still clung to the rock. It was filling with water but, because it was so fresh, the sides hadn't begun to crust. The toe was imprinted harder than the heel, which faced the edge of the cliff, because she'd pushed off against a granite spur.

Come on. It wasn't possible. She had no ropes, and she couldn't free-climb a face like La Brujería, not even on a dry, sunny day. Not unless . . .

The thought tore through his brain—as suddenly and as blindingly as the lightning flashes—and he straightened, whispering the name. A slow smile spread across his face. In that moment he completely forgot the rain and wind tearing at his body.

It was impossible, of course. He'd get back down only to find they'd already located her below the trail. Or that they'd seen her, loose in the basin and trying for the pass. Something.

It wasn't possible because things just didn't work out that way. But . . .

Anything can happen out here. Anything.

"Esteban," he whispered again.

FOUR

She saw him shudder, nearly dropping the coil of rope, and she thought he must be cold. But he was leaning toward the entrance, his head cocked like an animal listening to a sound beyond a human's auditory range.

"What is it?" Beth had to speak loudly to be heard above the increasing roar of the storm. "Did you hear something?"

"Nothing." She saw his lips move more than heard him. "Imagination."

He shivered again.

Outside, rain hammered the face of the cliff. Water ran in the vertical cracks and puddled in the few tiny crevices that could hold it. There weren't many of those. La Brujería, the climbers called it. Witchcraft.

The cave entrance was an outward slope, beginning to coat with sleet freezing to the rock. It slanted downward for about four feet before falling off into open air. Behind that, the floor—covered in a mix of crushed granite, rock dust, and bird droppings—leveled somewhat before tunneling down into the mountain.

Beth sat with her shoulders against one wall, far enough back to stay dry, and watched Stephen James coiling the climbing rope around his elbow and open hand. She was no longer astonished at what he'd been able to do on the cliff because as he swung into the cave, a creature absolutely at home in his own element, she remembered where she'd heard his name.

"Okay," he said, folding the rope atop his rucksack. He rose in a crouch, keeping his head away from the low ceiling, and moved back from the rain. "You made it all right, I see."

"Yeah." She slid slightly away when he sat down beside her. He opened the top flap of a larger backpack that had already been in the cave and removed an insulated undershirt. "It got a little scary when I reached for that bar, but I'm still in one piece," she continued.

She started to look away when he peeled the wet T-shirt over his head, but saw he wasn't watching her anyway. In the faint light, his torso appeared surreal. It spoke of obsession.

(Obsessions are unhealthy, Katie. Remember that great Christian, Joseph Hall? "Moderation is the silken string running through the pearl chain of all virtue. . . .")

Give me a break here, Mother.

"I know who you—" she began.

"This cave's the largest of the four." He pulled down the long-handle top, his hair lying wet along his neck. "It curves . . . Did you say something?"

"Nothing."

"It curves back and down for about thirty feet." His voice had a trace of an accent, and she decided he was Hispanic rather than an Indian. He'd sworn at her earlier in Spanish, just like Cuellar. "Then it narrows into a crack that's way too small—"

"Did you see it?" she interrupted. He was deliberately avoiding what was important with his damned travelogue, and it rekindled her anger. "Did you see what happened?"

"Yes." She barely heard him above the storm.

"Why didn't you do something?" She knew it was unfair as she said it. "At least try . . ."

"I was up here," he answered. "On the dome. I only saw it through the glasses." He nodded toward a binocular case looped around the rucksack.

"Did . . . they kill them?" She found herself wanting a confirmation of what she already knew.

"Yes." When she didn't reply, he continued in a monotone. "I saw you run. They were chasing you, and I saw you coming my way. They had you trapped if you went on down the trail, so . . ." He shrugged.

"Why?" She turned to look directly at him. "Why did they kill them? And don't say you don't know. You know their names. I'll bet you even know what they're doing down there. Raymond Cuellar's a famous man. He's probably going to get elected to the state congress, and he had Earl and Brian murdered just because Brian recognized him. Why?"

Stephen looked away from her, his face a mask. He's trying to decide, thought Beth. He's either going to lie, or he's going to refuse to answer.

"It was bad luck." He finally returned her stare, but his eyes were remote. "Both for you and El Gavilán. You met by accident. It has . . ." His expression hardened, and she knew he'd decided. ". . . nothing to do with you."

"Bullshit! Maybe it didn't before, but it sure as hell does now. Whatever it is you won't tell me, it doesn't change the fact I'm a witness to a double murder, does it?"

He seemed to weigh the question for a moment. "No," he said.

"And Cuellar. Whatever it was before, he *has* to get me now, doesn't he?"

He nodded.

Her anger was winding down, and she was a little ashamed of it. "Look, I'm sorry for yelling," she said. "You saved my life. I guess you could've just . . ." Then her voice trailed off at the expression she saw flit across his face.

Could've just let it go, she thought. And almost did. Whatever he was hiding was important to him. So important he'd considered . . .

A tremor slid through her. Jesus, it could have gone either way, couldn't it?

She was suddenly afraid of the dark man sitting beside her.

Freddie Jenkins coughed up some more blood. He curled on his side in the back of the lean-to and spat coagulated phlegm, cursing weakly. His hoarse breathing was audible above the sound of rain hitting the tarp.

Joseph Ware glanced at him without much interest, then looked out at Cuellar. The man was pacing back and forth, turning the muddy ground to slop and ignoring the water pouring on his head. Ignoring, also, the two sodden forms that lay facedown a few yards away.

Ware sat on the stacked and folded inflatable rafts under the tarp, comfortable again in dry clothes, and placed his feet against one of the rocks surrounding the fire. He'd been in an excellent mood since leaving the Cupola, and when Cooper and Leggett returned empty-handed —as he knew they would—he expected to feel even better. In the time since he'd found the small footprint, he'd gone from skeptic to believer.

It had to be true. Because it was too good not to be.

"Where are they? They've found her, haven't they?" El Gavilán had discovered he was wet. He stomped in out of the rain, spraying water on the fire. "They've found her, and they're hiding her from me."

"I wouldn't think so." Ware smiled. "Those two couldn't find their butts with both hands." He knew Cuellar was convinced these men were plotting against him, too. Same old story.

"They'd better find her. . . ."

"Remember Jaime Agustin?" Ware decided to distract him. "Jaime would've found her."

A tight grin crossed Cuellar's face. "Jaime. Yes, and Charlie Pellikern, too. *De manos a boca.*" The smile drooped. *"Mis hermanos."*

"Yes." It was a barometer. The more frequent his slipping back into Spanish, the more upset Cuellar was. Before long he'd be crying about Engracia Torres again. Ware sighed inwardly. Christ, deliver me from this man's emotional roller coasters.

"Santiago. That little bastard. One day soon I'll—"

"They're coming." Ware stood up.

"Donde?"

"Just listen for a sound like two hippos humping in the underbrush." Ware pointed down the hillside to their right. A few seconds later Cooper and Leggett came out of the trees, both soaked and miserable looking.

"Cabrones!" thundered Cuellar. "Even the dead could hear you approach!" Ware knew he was mostly angry

because he hadn't heard them himself. "Where's the girl?"

Leggett looked green. He was so frightened he was forgetting to pick his nose.

"She's not out there, Mr. Cuellar." Cooper was trying to carry off a brave front. "We were all over. Down to the river and across on this side. Back over to the main Mule Pass trail. I know a little about tracking, Mr. Cuellar, and she'd leave marks in this mud. She can't jump outta this basin from rock to rock. She's gotta still be up there."

"Ware was up there." Cuellar's voice went uncharacteristically soft. "And she's *not*. You two have lost her." He glanced meaningfully at the bodies in the mud.

It was time to break the news. Joseph Ware had heard El Gavilán use that tone before. They needed Cooper and Leggett alive for a while yet.

"Maybe," he said, just to watch Cuellar's reaction, "we should finish up here and leave. A little farther down, and that's the end of it. After twenty years. You can head for the statehouse, and I can buy myself that tropical island."

"She saw me!" snapped Cuellar. "*Tu ves?* She knows me!"

"Everyone around here knows you. That's the idea, isn't it? Who'd believe—"

"No. I can't take the chance. *We* can't take the chance. She knows you, too."

Ware wasn't particularly concerned about that—others had known him, after all—but he didn't say so. "Okay." He nodded and motioned the men past, under the lean-to. Leggett immediately went to Freddie Jenkins, kneeling beside him. Ware took Cuellar's arm and steered him aside.

"Okay, then," he continued softly. "There's another possibility."

"What? What do you mean?"

He turned Cuellar toward the fire's glow. The day was darkening, and he wanted to see the expression on El Gavilán's face.

"When I was on the dome, I saw a fresh footprint." Ware's eyes were intent on Cuellar. "Near the edge of the cliff in a place where there's still some soil. It was very small. Either a child or a woman."

"But you said—"

"I said she wasn't up there, and she wasn't. I expected to find you standing over her body when I got back. But consider, if it was her, where did she go?"

Cuellar's brow furrowed, then he stared up at Ware. "The caves? But you said the cliff was too steep."

"It is." Ware was working hard at keeping a straight face. "She could never have climbed down alone. But suppose . . . someone helped her?"

"Who?" Cuellar nodded toward the bodies. "Clearly not those two."

"True, but what if it was someone else? Someone we didn't see?"

Cuellar was beginning to realize where it was all headed, but Ware took it slow anyway. He watched the corners of the man's mouth begin to twitch.

"It would have to be a climber," he continued. "Someone with the equipment and skill to get down that cliff in the rain."

Cuellar's twitch was getting worse.

"Someone who'd have a reason to be up there, where nobody goes anymore. Maybe because we're at this final point now, after twenty years . . ."

"*Espíritu Santo,*" whispered Cuellar. "It's Esteban Santiago up there, isn't it?"

Ware smiled, watching El Gavilán's eyes. "I wouldn't be surprised," he said.

"I know who you are," said Beth.

It caught him off guard after several minutes of silence. "What?"

"Your name. It rang a bell, but I was kind of distracted before. You're the climber. Stephen James. The free-solo climber, right?"

Stephen let out a burst of pent-up air. That had been stupid. How could she know anything?

"Oh. Yeah, right," he answered.

"I know some rockheads, over in Silvercat where I

work in the winter. I've seen that picture. You know the one where you're swinging by one hand across—"

"Dark Spire, down in Utah. Yeah." This was okay. Let her talk. He could handle this, and it gave him time to think of answers for the questions she'd eventually return to. A few yards away, the storm was getting worse. Turning to hail and sleet.

". . . swears by you," she was saying. "He says you're one of the best."

"Ron Kauk's the best. The rest of us are just hanging around." He'd used that line so often it rolled out. But he sensed she was just talking, too. Marking time the same as he was. She wasn't the groupie type.

Take the initiative. Turn it back onto her. "What were you and those men doing here?" he asked. "It's kind of early in the year for hiking in this basin."

"Or climbing, especially on a jinxed wall," she said pointedly, and was silent for a moment. Then, "Oh, hell, why not? It can't hurt anything now. You know about the Cupola Dam project, of course."

"Yeah." He nodded. He knew about it, all right, though he was certain its significance to him was entirely different than to Beth.

"Then you know congress has approved the dam for Agua Fuerte Canyon. All of this, everything except the Cupola itself's going to be underwater."

He didn't reply. This was good. He'd seen her type before, all soapboxes and lost causes. Let her talk.

"Some of us, Children of the Earth, Zero Hour, and some other groups aren't going to let Cupola Basin become another Hetch Hetchy," she continued. "Do you know what Monkeywrenching is? Ecodefense?"

He did, but wanted to keep her talking. "I just climb rocks, lady," he replied. It was a very calculated answer.

"Yeah?" Her blue eyes flared. She was getting heated up now. "And who keeps the land around those rocks open for everybody? People like—"

"That's why you were in the basin today? To keep the Cupola open?"

Her jaw set. "In a way, yes. It was just a first step. We

came in to spike the trees where the road site will be, at both ends of the canyon."

"Spike?"

"Jesus, don't you know anything? Long spikes. They don't hurt the tree if they're put in right, and when a chain saw hits one . . . it's like July Fourth."

"Really. And what about the guy running the saw?"

She hesitated with a frown, then went on as if he hadn't spoken. "If the saws break, the trees don't get cut. If the trees aren't cut, the road doesn't get laid. And they can't dam the canyon unless they can bring in heavy machinery." She recited it like a litany.

"So, that just stops the whole thing, huh?" He couldn't hide the edge of sarcasm. *Qué sencillo,* yes? Just that simple. There was no question she had great courage, great passion. But she was a child.

She blushed. "No, but it's a start. An irritant to them, and a delay while we fight it in court. Earl had some friends. . . ."

"Earl was one of the men who was with you?"

She swallowed, and he thought she was about to cry, but she surprised him.

"Yes. Brian was his son." Her voice remained steady. "I didn't know them very well, really. They'd come up from Arizona to help. Earl has . . . had some kind of asthma."

She turned toward him, and he saw there were tears in her eyes after all. As he'd done so often with others, he hardened himself against her. After twenty years it had become almost easy. . . .

"They just killed them," she said. "Just snuffed them out like stepping on bugs." A lone tear slid down her tanned cheek, and his resolve had to be iron to keep him from touching it. "And you won't even tell me why. But you know, don't you? It's why you're here, too. You were watching them, not climbing. That's how you saw what happened to us."

He didn't answer. Couldn't. He ached to touch her because she was Allison Brock all over again, only this time with a soul. But he couldn't do that, either.

"Okay." She brushed angrily at the tear. "Then at least tell me this much. What happens now?"

He nodded. It was back on safe ground again. "You were right earlier," he said. "El Gavilán has to find you. I've been thinking what I'd do in his place. When Cooper and Leggett missed you on the path, they'd run into Ware eventually. They're stupid, but El Gavilán's not. And neither is Ware."

"Ware." She shuddered. "He's the one who scares me."

"He should. In my life I've known many bad people, but . . ." Stephen's eyes went somber with memory, then he shook his head. As always, when he thought of the big man, his sense of helplessness returned, like the smell of the baby and old, rancid sweat. . . .

No le hace. He pushed it aside as he usually did. Because it only weakened him, and it no longer served any purpose.

"They'll know you left the trail, either to scramble down the side or climb to the dome," he continued, watching the sleet build up in the cave's entrance. That slope was getting like a skating rink. "So they'd go on top and see you weren't there."

"Do they know about the caves?"

"Probably," he replied. "They knew about the trail curving back down. If so, they know you couldn't get down here, so they'd put everyone searching the other side, below the path and back to the river."

"So what do we do then? Lower down the cliff?"

He shook his head. "Can't. It's what I'd like to do. Rappel to the lower caves and then to the meadow . . ."

"But? What's the problem with that?"

"Like I said earlier, they're smart. If it was me, I wouldn't take the chance you'd somehow made the caves. I'd think to myself, What if she was meeting someone else here in the basin? Someone who's helping her? It only takes one of them to watch the cliff from those trees down by the meadow. We'd be sitting ducks going down a rope if someone's below."

She took it better than he'd expected. "Maybe they're not that smart," she said. "Look out there. You can't see twenty feet—"

"That's up here. They'd be able to see the base of the cliff."

"—and, besides, they only have four people since I . . . I got that one."

"Freddie Jenkins. What did you do to him, anyway?"

She didn't meet his eyes at first. "I stabbed him with a tree spike. I didn't have any choice. He was going to kill me."

"You did the right thing."

"I don't need you to tell me I did the right thing!" she flared, then softened. "But he was just a kid. Like Brian . . ."

"A kid they murdered," countered Stephen. "They've murdered before. Other kids . . ." His throat went tight.

None of that, dammit.

"Look, we need to get further back," he said. "The wind's picking up. Are you hungry?"

"No." She stood carefully and retreated toward a curve in the passage. "I'm more tired than anything. Sleepy, if you can believe it."

"That isn't surprising." He stopped her just past the curve. Ahead, the passageway turned pitch black. "It's probably shock. With what you've been through in the last hour, I'm amazed you can walk."

He pulled his sleeping bag from its stuff sack. "Sit down and get into this. The best thing for shock's to keep warm and dry. Get some sleep if you can. We won't be able to do anything before dark, anyway."

"You won't . . ."

"I'm not going anywhere."

She hesitated, pulling the bag up over her legs. "It's cold in here. I suppose we could both squeeze—"

"No." He saw his reply was too quick, too harsh. Her face paled, then hardened. "I need to check some things." He tried for a lighter tone.

"Suit yourself." She zipped the bag up over her shoulders and leaned against the wall. She didn't look at him.

He walked back toward the entrance and made a pretense of examining his gear. It was better this way. Better to maintain the distance. The hostility between them had waxed and waned, and now it was back. That was okay, because she'd messed up the plan and now he had her to

worry about. He'd have to improvise, to keep her out of
it.

He settled against the wall where he could see her
around the curve. That was another thing, keeping her
away from the back of the cave. He couldn't have
her back there.

It *was* cold. The wind blew in through the entrance
and buffeted him, pushing his wet hair in his face. A fine
spray moistened the parka he'd put on.

She'd fall asleep. She wasn't going anywhere, so he
tugged a wool cap down over his face. It sometimes created a form of sensory deprivation that kept the old
dreams away.

He didn't believe it was going to work this time.

Charlie Pellikern's face was there again in the darkness, twisted in the rictus of its eternal scream. Agustin,
too, and the others. And the colored lights and shiny eyes
of the aquarium. Most of all, the shiny eyes. And the
tropical fish . . .

He molded his body to the undulations of the cave wall,
ignoring the wet and cold, and tried to forget the girl
huddled a few yards away. The curve of her face and the
color of her eyes. Her shape in the sleeping bag. He
willed himself to forget her with the old refrain, constant
in his memory as the drip of endless water on patient
rock.

For Cesar. For Pilar. For my mother and my brother.
For the eleven souls . . .

The icy spray that blew into the cave wasn't so bad.
He'd been cold before. He'd been alone before.

And for my grandfather, Pascual Santiago.

He didn't realize he was singing softly, deep in his
throat behind the wool cap.

> *"La Araña se sale a pasear*
> *Viene el Ratón y se trina. . . ."*

El Jornada del Muerto

I have with me but two gods,
Persuasion and Obsession.
—Themistocles

FIVE

"The Spider goes out for a walk
  Then comes the Rat and he sings with a squawk,
  The Rat and the Spider, the Rat and the Spider
  Are singing beside the Strong Water."

When they came down the slight grade into the southwest edge of Cuidad Juarez, the grandfather stopped with the old song and repeated his warning. In essence: Keep your *ojos* open and your *boca* shut.

Esteban watched the *cholos* of Los Colonias, the tough young men of Juarez's most dangerous barrio, lounging in doorways while he passed. Smoldering cigarettes and dark, hooded eyes as they looked back in contempt.

"Hey, *vato!* Come over here."

But the grandfather, Pascual Santiago, strode along with his proud, old man's walk, carrying the baby Rodolfo in the crook of his arm. Only Cesar returned their stares.

Esteban saw a poster, its edges torn, hanging in the dusty window of an abandoned shop. The young man it featured was gesturing, his head up and his arm raised. Esteban knew he was Kennedy, El Mártir, but he didn't recognize the old man beside him. Sad eyes and long, drooping ears and nose.

Johnson, explained his grandfather. The man who was now *El Presidente de los Estados Unidos.* Esteban studied the face, this ruler of his new homeland.

The three others lagged behind with his mother, Alicia. She didn't want to be there, and neither did they. All the way down the long road from Bavispe to Janos—down from the heights of the Sierra Madre into the heat and dust of a desert autumn—they had cried and complained. Only the strength of Pascual Santiago had drawn them along past the Laguna de Guzman, mostly mud and stinking weeds this time of year, over to the main Chi-

45

huahua highway, and finally into this city. Only the implacable will of the grandfather and the secret of the coin could have pulled them so far.

Juarez. *El lugar malo.* A bad place for the hundreds of thousands who lived there, and worse for those passing through from the south. *Parachiestas*, the Los Colonias toughs called them. Squatters. Esteban moved closer to his grandfather.

The city was huge and dirty. Water fountains sat dry, surrounded by dead flowers, the tiles broken and covered with graffiti. Farther on, the markets had black velvet paintings of Jesus and Kennedy for selling to the yanqui tourists. They hung where swarms of flies covered rotting fruit. The odor filled Esteban's nostrils and it was better to hold Pascual's arm and smell the baby, who needed a change, and his grandfather's rancid sweat. Up ahead an ancient drunk walked carefully, his toes curling inside ragged sandals to keep a firm grip on the planet.

Alicia had gotten scared and had caught up, along with Jorge and Pilar. Only Cesar hung back, determined to show the *cholos* he wasn't afraid. He was seventeen.

This was the worst part of the city, Pascual told them. They must try to walk faster.

A woman crossed the street and spoke to Cesar, and the grandfather stopped. Jorge, who was thirteen, stood watching her with his mouth hanging half open. Esteban thought she was beautiful.

"Whore!" He was astonished at the anger in his grandfather's voice. "Leave the boy alone, woman."

She looked at them, and Esteban saw she wasn't beautiful at all. Only a woman as old as his mother.

"You speak of me thus?" The woman's voice was low and cultured, and she used the formal inflection for the pronoun "you" in addressing Pascual. "He is a man now, and there is no need for you to speak of me thus."

"He is my grandson, and you are a whore," said Pascual, but the heat was gone from his tone. "Both things are what they are."

The woman returned his gaze in silence for a full minute, then nodded faintly and turned away. Esteban imagined he saw tears in her eyes.

"This place," whispered Pascual, watching her leave. "It befouls what it touches."

"How much farther?" asked Alicia. She had taken Rodolfo, also called Rudy, from his grandfather and slipped his head inside her blouse to nurse. Esteban saw the sagging flesh beneath her eyes and how tired she was, and he knew she wanted to rest and change the baby. But she was afraid to stop.

"Not far. We'll rest before the crossing," said Pascual. When they resumed, he walked more slowly to keep pace with his son's widow.

Shadows were stretching across the road by the time they reached the mesquite thicket at the river.

The Coyote was speaking English, and only Esteban could follow much of what he was saying above the continuous crackle of fireworks from town. He was a tall, skeletal outline in the dusk, the glowing tip of his cigarette bobbing up and down as he talked. His name was Jaime Agustin.

He was speaking of money and jobs, mostly money, and of a train to San Antonio. And then of money again. All were to pay before the crossing.

"La mordida." Pascual sneered. Esteban leaned closer, flattered as always when his grandfather spoke to him rather than to Cesar and Jorge, who were older. "Always it's 'the bite.' By the time they pay off these vultures, they have nothing left."

"Then why pay at all, *abuelo?*" asked Esteban. "There's the river, and over there's El Paso. Even a child could go across."

"True." Pascual slipped an arm around Esteban's shoulders. Like all the other *pollos,* they were squatting on their heels in the cooling sand. "But the problem isn't to cross the river. As you say, anyone can do that. The problem's to get out of El Paso and into their country. For that, the Coyote demands his pay."

"To cross the river's not always so easy as you claim," said a man squatting nearby. He was as old as Pascual, but not nearly so tall and strong. He was fat and smelled of garlic. "One spring, the river ran high from Colorado mountain snows . . ."

Esteban's mouth popped open at the word. That's where we're going, he was about to say, but Pascual's fingers tightened on his arm. It was not something to be told.

". . . and the current was swift," the fat man was saying. "My good friend Mateo Archuleta couldn't swim worth shit, so he paid a *curandero* for a charm to protect him from drowning. Partway over, a wave knocked him off his feet and carried him halfway to Laredo. Turned out that charm couldn't swim worth shit, either."

The fat man's mouth popped open in soundless laughter, and Esteban saw he had only his front teeth. He stopped laughing when he saw six-year-old Pilar in tears.

"Don't cry, *hija,*" he said. "This time of year the river's low. And in the town, the festival's loud. No one will notice the poor little *pollos.* In fact, there are strong boys who'll carry you over for an American dime if the water frightens you." And he handed her a coin. Pilar managed a mournful smile.

Firecrackers exploded again to drown out the fat man's voice. It was November 1, *El Día de los Muertos,* the Day of the Dead, and the celebrations would continue until the candlelight procession to the churches the following night. And, on the other side, the Anglos were busy preparing to elect their next president. Pascual had chosen well.

After true dark, the Coyote came by collecting money. He nodded meaningfully as he passed the Santiago family, but he didn't stop or ask for anything. Esteban wondered what his grandfather had told the man, though he didn't worry. Pascual Santiago was as clever as he was brave.

When they crossed, they found the river only knee deep on the adults, but some were paying the *caballos* to carry them over anyway. Pilar rode on Jorge's back and saved her dime. Esteban was surprised to find the atmosphere festive, and many of the *pollos* laughing aloud. Then he remembered his grandfather's words. This was the easy part.

On the American side they climbed a cement incline and pushed through gaping holes in a chain link fence.

"La Migra comes by sometimes," said the fat old man when Pascual pulled him through the fence. "They chase everyone off, and catch a few who get a ride in their air-conditioned trucks. When they drive away, everyone comes back. Nobody gets mad. It's nothing personal."

They crossed a series of railroad tracks, and Esteban watched a group split off and run toward the dark mass of boxcars. Then he and his family followed another group across an unpaved street and to the mouth of an alley by a boarded-up building.

Jaime Agustin, the Coyote, was beside them again. He was still speaking English, and Esteban began to doubt he spoke Spanish at all. He talked very slowly, mouthing his words as if to idiot children.

"Come . . . to . . . the . . . truck," he said. *"Vamanos . . . la . . . coche!"*

Esteban heard Pilar stifle a giggle when the man used feminine gender for the masculine noun. It was true. Here was an Hispano who spoke no Spanish. It was amazing. Who'd heard of such a Coyote?

They hurried down the alley to where an unpainted panel truck sat in the darkness. Esteban had a glimpse of another figure, huge and indistinct, standing by the cab.

"Pascual, Pascual," said the English-speaking Coyote. He draped a bony arm over the grandfather's shoulders. "Come and show my friends, like you promised."

At that, the big man and two others came back from the cab. When they stepped from the shadows, Esteban saw that one was Hispano like Agustin. Another was a small man with light-colored hair below a battered cowboy hat.

Pascual looked carefully at the men, each in turn, then he pulled the old chain out of his shirt. Esteban didn't have to see the heavy coin—it had always hung around his grandfather's neck—but he was surprised. Pascual never showed the coin to strangers. These must be important people.

The dark man, who was broad and thick-chested, leaned forward to look but didn't try to touch the coin.

"You see, El Gavilán?" said Agustin.

"Madero," said the man. His voice was a rich baritone that caused Esteban to instantly like and trust him. "You're quite right, Jaime. *Desde luego.* It *is* Francisco Madero."

Esteban knew the name, of course. He'd heard it all his life. It was the sound dreams were made from.

"And you, *mi hermano.*" The man smiled at Pascual. "There is something you want from me as well." He glanced at the other men, then shifted into Spanish. *"Lo hare con tal que me ayude. Venga."* They walked away toward the cab.

Provided you help him? thought Esteban. Help him how? His grandfather would never tell the coin's secret. Or would he? The rich voice promised friendship, after all. And trust.

They climbed into the back of the truck—eleven of them in all—but the doors were left open at first.

"Where are we going?" whispered one of the *pollos* to the fat old man whose name, it turned out, was Señor Cuyas. "Where are they taking us?"

"We're going with Pascual Santiago," replied Señor Cuyas. His voice was confident. "Those Anglos sought him all the way to Bavispe. Good luck will follow him."

Even in early November, the El Paso night was hot. Esteban sat at the back watching the cowboy and the big man flip coins against the base of the alley wall.

"Some shit, ain't it?" said the cowboy in English. He pronounced the word "shee-it." "Where's Jaime?"

"With them." The big man stepped into the indirect light of a street lamp, and Esteban was entranced. He was a young man, but he already had the muscles of a giant.

"Suckin' up." The cowboy nodded. "When the main man farts, Jaime smells daisies. How many we got?"

"A dozen or so." The big man glanced at the truck, but he didn't appear to see Esteban in the shadows. "Which comes out to about eleven in excess baggage."

"Shee-it. Don't sweat it, Ware. They're easy. Little *pollos.* Ya jus' gotta clobber the pure-dee Jesus outta their asses ever now an' again. Besides, we won't have this bunch for long anyways."

"Better hold it down, Charlie." The man called Ware glanced toward the truck again.

"Wha' for? They cain't none of 'em hablo Eng-lase anyways."

Esteban crawled away from the entrance. He didn't like the little cowboy at all—*qué cosa más malo*—but the man Ware's muscles fascinated him. He flexed his biceps in the dark.

It wasn't until the doors were closed and they bumped away down the alley that he realized Pascual wouldn't be with them. He would be in front with the dark man and the others, Esteban decided. It was a well-deserved honor. As they rode, he occasionally heard the sounds of another vehicle following close behind.

"What were they saying about Madero?" Señor Cuyas's voice came from his left in the darkness. Esteban knew but he wasn't telling, and Señor Cuyas went on as though he hadn't really expected an answer.

"It was in 1911," he said, "when the coalition overthrew that bastard Díaz and sent him running off to France. Francisco Madero, Zapata, the dark Indian Huerta, and the great Villa. I was about your age, Jorge. Maybe a little younger.

"A few years later, Huerta . . . I spit on his father"— the old man ground out the words—"betrayed and murdered the good Madero, and Villa rode with Carranza against his tyranny. Villa's real name was Arango, as you know, and he was a great man—"

"He was horse piss!" snapped another voice from the darkness. "Pancho Villa murdered my uncle's cousin."

"Villa was a patriot, and you couple with goats," responded Señor Cuyas. The other voice fell silent. "In my town near Flores Magón in 1916 it was, April it was, I saw Pancho Villa kill the tyrant's soldiers. He shot one in the belly, a little above his pecker, and then propped him against the schoolhouse wall. He asked the soldier if he wanted anything, meaning to finish him off, I imagine, but the man asked for a drink. So Villa gave him water, and some of it leaked out the hole in his belly. It was pink, with bright little flecks of something in it. I was standing as close as I am to you people, do you doubt it? It took the soldier an hour to die, and Villa gave him as much water as he wanted and they spoke of the flowers in the gardens of Monterrey. I was there, and I saw it all. He was a great man."

This time there was no comment from the other speaker. Esteban could make out shadowy shapes in the truck's darkness, but he couldn't see any faces.

The tale was somewhat like those he'd heard from Pascual, so he supposed it was partly true, though he didn't for a moment believe the business about the pink water. But compared to his grandfather's experiences in the mountains of the American north, it was a tame thing and told to anyone who'd listen. The true stories of the Crown of Colorado were only for the Santiago family, and the dream was theirs alone.

"When will we stop?" It was Pilar's voice, coming from close beside him. It was quavering, near tears again, and Esteban thought he knew why. When the others had relieved themselves in the alley before entering the back of the truck, she'd been too frightened. Now she needed to go, but was embarrassed to say it.

"Not before morning," said Cesar. As always, it seemed, his voice was too loud. It echoed in the stuffy confines and hurt Esteban's ears. Cesar was small like their father had been, and he saw a challenge everywhere he looked. "Don't be such a baby, Pilar. If you have to pee, do it over in the corner."

"Shut up, Cesar." Esteban spoke over the sound of his sister's sudden wailing because he knew Alicia would say nothing. "Leave her alone."

"Coward!" snapped Cesar. "You hide in the dark. Come here."

"Stop it!" Señor Cuyas cut him short. "Both of you shut up. Come here to me, *hija*. I have a small jar. Something to help."

Esteban heard Pilar fumbling her away across as the truck bounced off unpaved road onto asphalt. A little later, the pungent odor of urine rose to his nostrils.

"Muh-Mother?" When Jorge was nervous, he stuttered. And the more frightened he became, the worse it got. "Where's G-Guh-Grandfather? Mother . . . ?"

She didn't answer, of course. Since her husband's death, she hated to be alone, which was why she allowed the persistent widower Rosario to sit by her. And this blackness, stinking with the fear of the *pollos*, was the worst kind of loneliness. They were all afraid, even Cesar, though he'd never admit it. Even Señor Cuyas, telling his lies in the dark.

"Another time, I crossed the river alone. . . ." began the fat old man. Esteban slid over to his mother and laid his head in her lap next to Rudy. Her fingers trembled in his hair. After a while, the stale air made him sleepy. He lay and listened to Señor Cuyas, but his dreams were of Colorado and the Strong Water.

SIX

Fresh air awakened Esteban. That, and the sound of someone vomiting nearby. He uncurled his stiff body and reached for Alicia, but she was gone.

The back doors of the truck were open, and morning light temporarily blinded him. Then he climbed out onto a dirt road already growing warm beneath his thin shoes.

The other *pollos* were squatting in the shade of a mesquite grove. He saw his mother with Rudy squalling fretfully in her arms, and also his other brothers and sister. The man who'd been vomiting rose to one knee and wiped his mouth with a dirty sleeve. Pascual Santiago was nowhere in sight.

Jaime Agustin came back from the cab, the blond cowboy with him. To Esteban, the pair looked even more frightening in morning light. He saw what looked like small, circular red sores covering the backs of the cowboy's hands.

"Where's my grandfather?" he asked in English. He flinched when the Coyote's dull eyes shifted toward him. "Where's Pascual Santiago?"

"He went on ahead for a while," answered Agustin. "There's no need to worry."

"No creo que el diga la verdad," muttered Señor Cuyas, and Agustin glanced toward him without comprehension. Esteban agreed with Señor Cuyas. The Coyote was lying.

"Where are we?" he asked. The panel truck was stopped in the center of a road that twisted through a desert canyon. On either side, high walls of volcanic rock rose from mesquite thickets and sloped upward and away. There was dust and rock and cactus, and the sun was already waves of reflecting heat and light. They could be anywhere at all.

The other vehicle Esteban had heard following them through the night was gone.

"You're as far as ya go, that's where." The cowboy called Charlie answered his question. "At least, as far as ya go with us. You Chilis are on your own now. We got'cha outta El Paso, jus' like we promised."

"Embusteros!" Cesar sprang to his feet, yelling at them in Spanish. "Liars! Where is my grandfather? Dare to tell *him* you're not taking us to—"

"To Colorado?" The big one, Ware, stepped from behind the truck. More than his sheer size, a nearly palpable aura of savagery struck Esteban, and he recoiled from its force. He was, quite suddenly, ice cold in the desert heat, and he didn't feel it alone because, behind him, the squatting *pollos* began to moan. A low sound, almost in unison.

"Colorado's over that hill," Ware continued in passable Spanish, pointing toward a towering redstone cliff. "North a few miles."

He grinned at them.

"No!" shouted Cesar, and took a step forward. Charlie pulled a long-barreled pistol from inside his jacket, and Esteban saw the red sores were actually a network of scabbed-over burns.

"Now you jus' hold still, boy." Charlie looked amused. "Else I'll hafta put one a these where you're real tender."

Cesar stood quivering while the cowboy lowered the

gun with a mocking smile. No, thought Esteban. No, Cesar . . .

But it was the *cholos* from the town all over again, grabbing their crotches and gesturing. And it was also being seventeen.

Hey, vato! Aquí tiene . . .

Cesar lunged at Charlie, throwing a wild right hand the man easily sidestepped. Then Ware grabbed the boy by his ragged shirt and his belt and threw him ten feet through the air, headlong into the side of the truck.

The *pollos'* moans rose to a wail, and Esteban heard his mother scream. Cesar hit so hard that the rear panel crumpled and he rebounded onto the road. He lay facedown, and blood began to trickle from his ear.

"Lordy, lord." Charlie sighed, shaking his head and looking up at the clear sky. "I jus' keep tellin' ya we need some rain, Ware. Flood that fuckin' Rio's what we need. Way too many Meskins crossin' that creek."

In the sudden stillness as the *pollos* fell silent, Rudy began to cry again. Then another baby, and then Pilar. Charlie followed Agustin to the truck's cab, with Ware still standing and looking down at Cesar.

"Where'll we go?" whispered Esteban in English. "What'll happen to us?"

Ware had a half smile on his handsome face. *"Yo no se,"* he finally answered, and walked off.

The *pollos* squatted in the mesquite shade. They watched the truck pull away, and they watched Alicia and Jorge run to Cesar's side. Then they studied the hot, dusty ground at their feet.

Esteban stood in the middle of the road. When he saw Ware's face glancing back in the large side mirror, he raised a stiff middle finger. It was a gesture he knew cut across the barriers of language.

"Me cago en su puta madre!" he shouted.

In the mirror, Ware appeared to study him for a moment, eyes cold and thoughtful, and the expression on the man's face choked off the breath in Esteban's throat. But he didn't lower his hand.

Then El Gigante Malo nodded to him slowly and drove away.

* * *

The afternoon came on with heat, and it took Cesar all day to die.

Two of the other *pollos,* along with Señor Cuyas, carried the boy to a spot in the shade. His head was twisted to one side, and they were afraid to straighten it. A portion of his skull beneath lank black hair was oddly flattened, depressed as though by a powerful push. From time to time, thick clots of blood mixed with saliva slid from his open mouth.

"He never had a life," mourned Alicia. Sobs racked her thin body. "Never a family of his own . . ."

"He goes to the family of God," said Señor Cuyas.

Esteban rose and walked out into the road again, letting the sun beat down on him. Think. Think like Pascual Santiago would. Since his father's death, screaming for all the saints as the cancer ate his body, Esteban had wound his soul like creeping ivy through his grandfather's existence. But the old man was gone. Maybe alive, maybe not, but he couldn't help them right now.

But it's not fair. I'm only ten years old. . . .

"We have to leave here," he told Señor Cuyas when he returned to the shade. "There's no food and no water. We'll die if we stay."

"Cesar will die either way," said Señor Cuyas gently. "His time's nearly done. It can't hurt to wait awhile, for your mother's sake. We'll decide something then. Only a little while."

But it took Cesar all day to die.

"I remember when my father took up his gun to ride with Villa. . . ." Señor Cuyas was talking again. He walked down the center of the road, his shadow long behind him. "The American general, Pershing it was, came down with his horses and his cars. Airplanes, even . . ."

There were six of them, *pollos* walking down the road. Six, and the baby Rodolfo. Four had remained behind at the grave, squatting in the shade with a single canteen of water. They had gone as far as they cared to, they said. They would be fine. La Migra would find them and take them back across the river. La Migra always found them, sooner or later. And maybe later they'd try again. A different Coyote . . .

". . . and then the great Villa told my father, 'Justos Cuyas, your value to me is so great, so immense . . .' "

Among them, they had two canteens and a little food—jerky, corn, salted bread—for six people. According to the pocket watch Señor Cuyas had hidden in his undershorts from the Coyote, they had been walking for about two hours. The road wound and twisted through the canyon and gave no indication of breaking out into open terrain. And, when night came here in this higher country, it would be cold.

In November, it got dark early. The sun, still almost directly ahead of them, dropped behind the cliffs a little past five. When Esteban pointed out a spot where several boulders had fallen to form a mesquite-shrouded hollow, the others looked at him in surprise. He thought then, that if he'd kept quiet, they'd have gone on walking aimlessly through the night.

Andres Rosario and Señor Cuyas were the only strangers who'd come with them. Rosario was a farmer from Los Papalotes whose chunky build and coal black eyes showed his Indian bloodlines. He'd stayed close to Alicia since the crossing, and no one had objected much. She was a widow, still fairly young, and his wife had died during the 1965 diphtheria epidemic. Normally he'd have had both Cesar and Pascual to deal with, but Cesar was dead and Pascual was gone.

Esteban watched Rosario gather bits of mesquite for firewood and place them near Alicia, touching her whenever the excuse presented itself. But he had more important things to consider now. There were only two adult males in the group, and one was sliding away from reality more quickly every hour while the other stood around quivering with lovesickness. They were both virtually useless.

After darkness settled into the canyon, Esteban left the campfire's glare and located the North Star as his grandfather had taught him. Then he used Señor Cuyas's pocket watch, the face visible in the moonlight, as a compass by setting the numeral twelve on the star. The man Ware had told the truth about their direction. They were heading somewhat south of west, indicated by the numeral nine. If they were still in Texas, that meant they could be walking toward El Paso. But if they were in New Mexico . . .

In the night, Esteban heard Rosario crawl next to his mother, and then the fumbling of garments. It was sacrilege, what the man was attempting with Cesar only hours dead, but perhaps Alicia was too tired and sad to object. And too frightened of being alone. Never mind, Esteban decided, and rolled onto his other shoulder, his back to them.

In the cold dawn, six-year-old Pilar awoke needing to relieve herself. She tried to rouse her mother, but Alicia slept as though drugged, the farmer Rosario's squat body wrapped around her and one of his hands still inside her blouse. Rudy was awake, his little brown eyes fascinated by swooping scissortails that took insects on the fly.

Pilar sat up and slipped her feet into her torn sneakers, and the huge scorpion that had crawled into one of them for warmth stung her.

Her screams awoke the others, echoing off the canyon walls and changing to shrieks of terror as she jumped to her feet and crashed wildly around the camp. Jorge was the first to reach her, and then Esteban yanked off her shoe.

The scorpion fell out onto the sand, fully four inches long, its carapace crushed by Pilar's toes. It lay dying, driving its poisonous stinger into its own back until Esteban pounded it with a rock.

Pilar's foot was already swollen to half again its normal size. Alicia, who had pushed Rosario roughly away, knelt wailing next to her daughter. The scorpions of the desert grew to nearly six inches in length. Their sting, though horribly painful, was rarely deadly.

Señor Cuyas roused himself from lethargy long enough to help carry the screaming child back to the campfire. He directed the others as they split the swollen skin with a pocket knife and sucked at the puncture again and again. Then he took a portion of their remaining water and ground up tobacco from his and Rosario's cigarettes into a wet poultice.

"It's okay, hija," he whispered, rocking her on his lap. "It's nothing. Nothing at all." And slowly her wails softened to a whimper.

"She'll be all right," he said confidently to Alicia. "When I was a boy, Mr. Scorpion took a piece out of me, too. For the same reason, because I forgot to shake out my shoes. We'll just keep her quiet and cool. . . ."

But they couldn't keep her cool against the autumn heat in the canyon and, by midafternoon, the water was nearly gone. Pilar's entire leg swelled, the skin turning a dusky purple and beginning to split above her knee. The swelling rose into her groin and she cried herself into dehydration, despite being given the last of the water. She died an hour before sunset.

In another dawn, the *pollos* walked along the road. Esteban tried to calculate through thoughts wrapped in cotton. He believed it was their third morning in the canyon.

There had been no water since the night before, the last of it used trying to save Pilar. His throat felt coated with stone, and it was much better not to swallow.

Rosario was holding Alicia upright and guiding her steps. With the death of her second child in two days, she had become *sonámbulo*—the walking dead. The farmer carried Rudy inside his shirt, and the baby was showing signs of severe dehydration. Alicia's milk had all but dried up.

Señor Cuyas trailed them, still talking to himself. Since Pilar, he'd left them again—this time for good, Esteban thought. The old man's feet followed the dusty, blistering hot road, but his heart and mind rode with his father and the great Villa.

Esteban and Jorge walked ahead. Jorge had never been much for conversation because he was ashamed of his speech problem.

"I wonder where Grandfather is?" Esteban said, just to

be talking. It was painful through a throat dry as ashes. Overhead, the sun tortured them.

"D-dead," responded Jorge. "He's as dead as we'll all be."

"No. No, he's alive, Jorge. And he'll come back—"

"Shit!" Jorge spat out the profanity. "They t-took the coin and thu-they took the map. And then they k-ku-killed him. You know it's true."

But there was no map, because Pascual didn't trust it to paper. Esteban knew that and so did his grandfather, but none of the others. There was only the story of the Crown of Colorado above the Strong Water, in the mountains of the gentle Saint John. Waiting there for over fifty years now, since the summer Los Centinelos rode north for his country and the memory of his friend.

"We'll find them," Esteban whispered, more for himself than for Jorge. "My grandfather and I. And we'll make them pay. . . ."

"Ah . . . ah . . . oh, Holy M-Mother . . ." Jorge had stopped as they rounded a curve. His thin arm quivered as he pointed ahead.

"Ah . . . ah . . ."

Esteban looked in that direction and felt his heart stop.

How odd. How very odd, when you thought you had no more tears to give, when you thought your very soul had gone numb . . .

He ran forward with Jorge to his grandfather's body. The vultures and crows around it took wing.

Pascual was propped in the crook of a mesquite tree. His head had been jammed back at an angle that forced his empty eye sockets to watch the road, and his arms, both broken as were his legs, had been positioned in the parody of welcoming anyone who came around the curve. The fingers of his right hand had all been severed, except for the middle one, which stuck up alone in obscene greeting.

Esteban remembered his gesture toward the panel truck driving away. This last part is for me, he thought. A grown man's joke on a ten-year-old boy.

A plain piece of paper had been impaled over the stiffened fingers of the left hand. *HOLA, NIETO!* had been printed in neat block letters. Hello, Grandson.

Pascual Santiago had been dead for several days. The old chain still hung around the gnawed remnants of his throat, but the coin was gone.

SEVEN

They found shade near where they buried Pascual, digging in the sand as with the others. A section of cliff overhung some mesquite bushes, and the men took off their shirts to drape them across the brush. Jorge and Esteban, too. They were men now, or as close as they were likely to get.

Señor Cuyas lay back on the ground, his once-rounded stomach sagging over his trousers. He mumbled to himself almost constantly.

Alicia slumped in Andres Rosario's arms, Rudy's head inside her blouse. The baby had stopped crying and only moved occasionally, thin legs twitching against her body. Rosario's eyes had retreated into their sockets. What Pascual had once called the thousand-mile stare.

"We'll all die if we stay here," Esteban whispered to Jorge. "We'll follow this road down to hell."

"Wuh-we'll all die anyway." Jorge's eyes were bleak, turning inward like Rosario's. "Let it g-go, brother."

"No!" Esteban tried to push away a growing sense of inevitability. It was too . . . easy. Too comfortable. Try fear. And if that doesn't work, try hatred. Think of Cesar and Pilar. Of the grandfather who hadn't given up. Who had told the pigs nothing, as surely as his grandson's love.

"No," he said again. "Not me. And not you either, Jorge."

". . . the Dead," Señor Cuyas was saying. His voice rose from its murmur.

"What?" asked Esteban.

The old man pushed up on one elbow. His eyes were clearing.

"This is the ending we're told of," he said, his voice firm. A few feet away, Rudy began to cry fitfully. "For all of us it's finally the same. The Journey of the Dead."

"Shut up!" snapped Esteban, and was instantly ashamed. Until his outburst at Ware, he'd never once spoken that way to an adult. "I'm sorry, Señor Cuyas, but the baby . . ."

"I heard what you said before." The old man's eyes were bright for a moment. "And you're right. This road leads down to hell. Find another way. This journey's ours. It's not yours."

"Another way? But how?"

"No! No!" The shouts came from Andres Rosario. "Stop her!"

He was trying to pull Alicia's hands from over Rudy's face. "Stop her! Help me!"

Alicia was smiling, but the sinews in her forearms stood out in cords. The baby kicked feebly, shrunken arms quivering. Rosario had grasped her wrists and was forcing them apart. As he sprang to the man's aid, Esteban saw Rudy's neck diffusing to an ugly purple.

"Little child," Alicia was crooning, her fingers clinging to the baby's face. "Poor Rodolfo. Poor little one . . ."

Esteban pulled his mother's hands loose and heard the baby wheezing for air in Rosario's lap. Alicia smiled, her face vacant and peaceful, and lay back in the farmer's arms. She closed her eyes and slept.

"She did what she could. She'll die now," Rosario whispered, looking at Esteban and Jorge. "So will the old man and the baby. You should leave here. Live if you can."

His words fell with the utter clarity of truth. In that moment, Esteban knew they were true.

"You're right," he answered after a moment. "And you? You're still strong."

"I'll stay with her," said Rosario. "And you're mistaken. Once I was strong. But that was before the diphtheria, and this. Now I'm very tired."

He tightened his arms around Alicia, who smiled in her sleep.

"Little child . . ." she whispered.

For Cesar. For Pilar. For Rodolfo. For my mother. For my grandfather . . .

The words became a chant, the chant a litany inside his brain as they walked. To see the cowboy Charlie. To see the Coyote Agustin. To see the evil giant Ware. To see El Hombre de Sombra, the Shadow Man with the warm voice that said, "Trust me, my friends." To see them all die in torment.

For Cesar. For Pilar . . .

Up ahead, the sun was setting again. The canyon and the road went on forever, down to hell. *El Jornada del Muerto.* The Journey of the Dead.

"We have to climb out." Esteban stopped and waited for Jorge. "Up there." He pointed toward the towering west rim, bathed red on its upper edge by evening sunlight.

"You're crazy," Jorge muttered. He continued to stare at the road, not meeting Esteban's eyes. Beneath one foot, blood seeped into the dirt.

"No, I'm not. It's the only way for us to live. We have to try to live, Jorge. See the cliff? It's no harder than in the Sierra. Easier."

"I'm tired. . . ."

"So am I. We'll climb to that shelf. See it? We'll sleep up there tonight, then reach the top tomorrow."

"Tomorrow?" Jorge's eyes rose to meet his. "The tuh-top?"

"Tomorrow," said Esteban. "I swear it, brother."

He realized all along it was going to be harder than it looked. The rock was soft and crumbling in places, razor-edged and volcanic in others. They ascended through loose talus, working past isolated clumps of mesquite. On two separate occasions they heard a rattlesnake's warning buzz. They'd have to be careful of all hand- and foot-holds in this canyon, even in November.

When they finally reached the vertical wall, Jorge demanded they stop to rest. He was three years older than Esteban and considerably taller—the only one who'd inherited Pascual's height—but he'd always been timid and withdrawn, staying in the house except for school and chores. The climb would be hard for him.

After a few minutes they started up, Jorge following in Esteban's path. There were occasional ledges, usually filled with cactus, and they rested when they could. Esteban's fingers began to swell from the constant pricking of the poisonous thorns that filled nearly every handhold.

He'd always been a climber, from the time he inched up the hard stone wall of the family house at age five. His father had beaten him for frightening Alicia, but then had held him in strong arms until his crying stopped.

"The mountains are in you, *hijo,*" he'd whispered against Esteban's ear. "All the high, secret places. I'll beat you again for this, I'm sure. But you won't stop."

And he never had. Esteban's father was a dreamer, they said in Bavispe. He'd never be a man of commerce, and neither would his third son.

Esteban found a ledge, larger than the others, and pulled Jorge up beside him. The light was fading behind the canyon wall, and it began to get cold.

But it was colder in the Sierra, ten thousand feet high where he'd followed the goats with his dog, and where he'd taught himself to scale the sheer walls of good rock with Eva barking below. This cold was nothing at all.

Jorge sat breathing through his mouth, and Esteban realized how tired his brother was. He was tired, too.

"Cu-cactus." Jorge looked around them. "Always muh-more cactus." He picked spines out of his fingers.

"True," replied Esteban. "But look." With the dull pocketknife he severed a prickly-pear leaf. He held it by one long, ominous-looking thorn and sawed through the tough skin, then peeled open the inner pulp. "Are you thirsty?"

"I knew th-that," said Jorge with a faint grin. "I w-was just so tired I forgot."

Using the knife and some dry pieces of greasewood, they cleared an area against the back wall of the ledge, checking first for snakes. Then they sat and chewed prickly-pear pulp until its cloying sweetness began to make them ill.

"I'm going h-home," Jorge said abruptly, after they'd sat in silence for a while. It was full dark, but the starry sky cast everything into twilight. "Whu-when we get out. Back to Bavispe. To stay."

"What about the Crown?" Esteban was pleased. Jorge was speaking of life again. Of living instead of dying.

"Guh-Grandfather's dead. We're only little b-boys with no father or mother, and the C-Crown's a dream. Bavispe's real."

"What will you do when you get home?" asked Esteban, mostly to keep his brother talking. He knew it was true. Jorge had never wanted to leave. One day soon, they'd part.

"We'll go t-to Uncle Lorenzo." If Jorge noticed Esteban's use of "you" instead of "we," he chose to ignore it. "And we'll get b-back our father's land. Lorenzo's an honest muh-man. Then we'll finish school, like G-Grandfather wanted, and we'll . . ."

He went on, and Esteban made himself listen carefully, although his mind wanted to wander. This was his brother, his only brother now, and it would be one of their last nights together. So he listened while Jorge spoke of the future. Looking back later, he would realize he never knew his shy brother better than he did in that one starry night on the ledge of the desert cliff. And that, next to the grandfather, he would miss Jorge most of all.

Later, when Jorge was lying asleep, curled against the stone wall, Esteban crawled to the edge of the shelf and stared down into the canyon. Unlike the bright starlight above, it was pitch black down there.

He looked back the way they'd come that day, half expecting to see a campfire, but the canyon had many twists and turns. He wondered who was still alive and hoped, in a way, it was all over. Then, alone on the edge of the cliff where no one could see him, he began to cry.

He cried for the eleven souls. For the four *pollos* who would die at Cesar's grave. For Señor Cuyas, who had loved the great Villa, and for Andres Rosario, who had loved Esteban's mother. For Cesar and for little Rodolfo, who would never know life. For Pilar and for Alicia, who had tried to save her baby in the only way she had left. And most of all for Pascual Santiago, that man of courage and honor.

He cried until he fell asleep, lying on the ledge. He was only a little boy, ten years old, and little boys cry, but when he awoke at sunrise his childhood was over forever. And, for nearly twenty years after, he never cried again.

Saturday Night–Sunday Morning
May 21 and 22

Witchcraft

Every man is hunted by
his own daemon, vexed by
his own disease. . . .
—Emerson

EIGHT

Beth awoke from the old dream of a dark-paneled room and a pistol lying on a leather desk cover. And of a hand, fingers curled inward. As always, she awoke just before she saw his face. . . .

She shifted in the warmth of the sleeping bag, her stiffened lower back and hamstrings protesting. But she didn't want to shift too much, because she didn't want to awaken Stephen James.

Outside the entrance, the wind roared like a freight train in the darkness. A mixture of rain and sleet drummed against the wall of La Brujería and into the front area of the cave. Stephen James was a dark silhouette lying a few yards away.

He must have been right. She'd been on the edge of going into shock, which was why she'd slept so readily. She'd dealt with the syndrome before in the EMT training that licensed ski instructors had to take.

Can't imagine why I'd be in shock, she thought. All I've done today is have two friends murdered, stick a six-inch spike through some creep with different-colored eyes, run headlong into goddamn Cochise, then get dropped down a cliff in a monsoon. Piece a cake, right?

The wrong companions, her mother would say, and then make that expression where she looked so sad, but really wasn't. *This is what happens, Katie*—her mother would never call her Beth, too close to Elizabéths—*when you follow the path you've chosen. Your associates get eviscerated by men who use bad grammar. . . .*

Beth stifled a giggle. Damn, maybe her brain was still in the outfield.

What exactly happened to my wrong companions, Mother? And why? Maybe if you'd stop copying Bible verses in that little blue spiral notebook for a second, I could figure this out.

69

Why, you ask? That's simple, Katie. Listen: "Because thou hast mocked me, I would take a sword in my hand, for now would I slay thee." That's from Numbers, the third chapter. . . .

Put a sock in it, Mother. Okay? Let me think.

Raymond Cuellar's running for state congress next year, with a reputation for standing up beside the little man. The champion of public-school reform, of the environment . . .

Who Stephen James calls El Gavilán. The Sparrow Hawk.

Raymond Cuellar's eventually headed for Washington. Everyone says so. His opposition to the Cupola Basin project has energized the environmental movement in this part of the state. . . .

The Sparrow Hawk. Whose talons rend the smallest and weakest of birds.

So, what is Cuellar doing in the basin? Something to stop the dam? But why on top of Riqueza Crown? The men were digging, had been digging awhile. There was a big pile of fresh dirt, and there were those old timbers—rudely cut, not squared off by a machine—that had been in the ground for a long time. A smell of moldy earth . . .

Something on that hilltop's very important to Cuellar. Important enough to murder for. And it's something nobody can be allowed to connect to him. Again, important enough to murder for. If Brian hadn't recognized him, would he really have let us walk away?

Brian. She heard his laugh again. More of a giggle, really. Ricky Riqueza. He'd had a crush and she, flattered, had probably encouraged it. . . .

Probably, Katie? Of course. You've always encouraged it. Remember Leviticus, Katie? "The soul that turneth, to go a-whoring after men, I will even set my face against that soul. . . ."

It's always the Old Testament, isn't it, Mother? The hard, vengeful parts. Leviticus, and Deuteronomy with its entire chapters of curses and blood and threats. Deuteronomy, Chapter 18, Verse 13. "Thou shalt be perfect. . . ."

Or die trying. In a dark-paneled room . . .

She felt tears burning her eyes, and blinked them away. No time for that now. Think harder.

What about Stephen James? Another familiar face. A cult celebrity to the people who climb walls like the one outside. Confrontation junkies, living and dying on the rock, too good—too pure—for pitons and chocks and sensible belays. But he was here because of Cuellar. Not for the climbing, since nobody climbed this particular wall anymore, but because of Cuellar. Stephen James wanted something, too. So badly he'd considered standing aside and letting her die. What was it?

And now she was totally dependent on him. This cold man. She couldn't get up or down without him. She couldn't escape Cuellar without him.

He didn't like her, she could tell that. He preferred crouching in the cold and wet to sharing the sleeping bag with her. And, if she got in the way of whatever it was he wanted, what then? Did he care enough whether she lived or died to continue being inconvenienced?

I'm in some deep shit, Mother.

You'll not talk like that in my presence, Katherine. You'll conduct yourself in a manner—

Shut up, Mother.

Beth unzipped the bag, muffling the sound of the metal teeth by pulling it into her chest. He wouldn't hear it above the storm, anyway. The only sound in their world was the storm.

She had the bag down around her hips. Then she slid one leg out into the air.

God, it was so cold! The cave was a natural funnel for the wind, which blew her heavy hair into her eyes as she climbed to her feet.

A funnel has two ends. Without somewhere to go, the wind wouldn't be so strong in here. What had he said? Something about the cave narrowing, being too narrow to climb through.

Maybe he'd lied, or maybe he hadn't allowed for how slim she was. Occasionally there was something to be said for having practically no boobs. Maybe she could squeeze past and find her way to the lower caves he'd mentioned.

How far down did they go? Far enough to jump from the lowest one?

Her eyes were as acclimated to the dark as they were likely to get. She began to edge along the wall.

The passageway was a natural curve to the left, and soon she had completely lost her line of sight with Stephen James. She was gradually descending, also. She kept her left hand on the wall, fingers relaxed, and her right hand extended in front of her. The wind continued to roar past, blinding what little vision she had by whipping her hair, so she stopped to tie it back with a handkerchief.

She dropped down some more. The cave didn't seem to be narrowing any, though she'd gone a fair distance. He'd lied about that, then. And about what else?

Down was good, so long as it didn't go suddenly vertical. Down led to the lower caves, she felt certain of that. Only now, the air had started blowing back in her face. It was pitch black ahead, and she was walking into a kind of vortex, the wind pummeling her simultaneously from both sides.

"What the hell . . . ?" she murmured, and took a step forward. And fell.

Something caught her boot tip, only for a second, but it was enough. She was unable to muffle a short cry, her hands outstretched, before she hit the rock floor. She felt a bright bolt of pain as a finger jammed back, then her elbows hit, and then her chest.

The floor was covered in rock dust and something else. Something as pungent as ammonia that puffed up into her face.

"Jesus!" She sat up, wiping her eyes with her uninjured hand. "What is this stuff?" She could only see black outlines. "It's all over me."

Then her fingers trailed across something hard. She picked it up and traced its shape with both hands. It felt like a coin, only very heavy and very thick. . . .

"What the hell are you doing here?"

She almost screamed again, pulling away from the dark shape standing over her.

* * *

Travis Leggett was picking his nose and trying to stay dry. It was hard to do both because every time he moved, the branches of the tree dumped water and slivers of ice. He finally put both hands in the pockets of his new safari jacket. His headache was getting worse.

He could see only the bottom of the cliff across the meadow, maybe the first fifty feet before it disappeared into clouds and mist and the darkness. Ware'd said the lowest cave was a small jagged hole about a hundred feet up, and Leggett couldn't begin to see it. The only way to see that high in this weather was to go over and stand right at the base of the rock wall, with absolutely no protection from the storm. Forget that.

Leggett knew he was in Trouble. Capital T. Cooper was, too, but Cooper was trying to be cool. Leggett wasn't as dumb as they thought he was, chickenshit nicknames aside, and he'd figured out a couple of things since they'd entered the basin.

For one, Cuellar looked at him and Cooper and Freddie, and he saw hired meat, nothing more. And hired meat had always been expendable. Leggett had stayed alive through forty years, sixteen of them behind bars, by keeping that in mind.

(Nose down and ass up . . .)

Oh, they talked about shares and stuff like that, but he'd seen how Ware looked at him. The way a green-eyed cat studies a crippled sparrow. Shares be damned, he'd seen that look before.

And, for another thing, they'd killed two people. Cuellar was tied to that as long as the hired meat was alive. . . .

Mister Cuellar. Soon-to-be Congressman Cuellar . . .

You bury your mistakes, Trav. That's what Davey Jefferson once told him on West Bankhead in Atlanta. And if you bury 'em deep enough, you can just act like they never happened. Davey was smart for a spade, or a mulatto or whatever the hell he was. Cuellar was smart, too.

Finally, Cuellar believed they'd lost the girl, and whose fault it was—Ware had suggested the knives—didn't really matter. And if Cooper thought busting their asses to get her back was going to change Cuellar's plans for them in the long run, then *he* was the stupid one.

It was bad Trouble, with a capital T, just sittin' there pickin' and grinnin' and waiting to get worse.

Travis Leggett knew all about Trouble. Hell, he'd known about Trouble all his life.

He shifted to what looked like a drier spot—it wasn't—and hunched up his shoulders against the icy rain. It was May, for God's sake! It was supposed to be warm in May. . . .

The May rain was warm in Garrison, South Carolina, just over the line and fifty miles from Savannah. He'd been standing out in it, soft trickles down through his burr haircut and across his nose, the first time he'd watched his daddy humping Clovis Lee. There was a screened window with a pyracantha bush blooming over it, and he'd been crawling under to stay dry when he happened to look in the window.

It wasn't as though Clovis Lee was a little kid or anything. She was fifteen, six years older than Travis, and she didn't look or sound like she was having a bad time. She already had fat legs like their mama, and she'd wrapped them around Daddy's waist. Her eyes, turned in the general direction of the window, were glazed and her mouth was gaping open. She was making the same kinds of sounds he'd heard Mama make through the thin walls at night. Daddy was, too. The very same sounds.

Travis had moved closer to the screen, which put him just under the eaves, and that was why the warm rain was trickling down over his head. He knew what they were doing, of course. He wasn't stupid, even back then. He felt a heat and a swelling in his groin, and looked down in surprise at his first real erection.

Now that's something you never forget, thought Leggett, the cold and wetness momentarily distant. He could still see his daddy's wide old butt slapping up and down between Clovis Lee's legs.

He'd never known whether Mama was onto them or not. She never acted any different, and he still heard her and Daddy going at it more nights than not. Sometimes he wondered if Clovis Lee listened to them, too, and what she thought. He also wondered if she knew he was watching her and Daddy, every time he could sneak up under the window.

Daddy knew, as it turned out. Because about six years later, he said so.

Clovis Lee was long gone by then, knocked up and married to Jarrod White—Leggett still wondered occasionally whose kid it really was—and Daddy had gotten fatter and balder and older. It was when Travis and his double cousin Wes broke into the mercantile over in Harmony and stole a hundred and thirty-one dollars from the back room. Wes cut his left ring finger nearly half off on some broken glass and they ran to Travis's daddy, who promptly called the county sheriff.

"You're in for some hot times, kiddo," he'd told Travis at their last meeting, waiting for the state-operated reformatory bus. "Instead a hidin' outside the winda watchin' folks fuck, you're gonna be nose down and ass up. They'll be watchin' you, kiddo. And you're gonna learn all about it."

And those, the last words he ever heard from his father, had proved to be true. By the time he'd finished eighteen months as the smallest, weakest boy in his dormitory, he'd learned all about it.

It was in the reformatory that he started picking his nose.

When he got home, Daddy was dead from a stroke—a thunderclapper, the doctor'd called it—and Mama was already remarried. The new man didn't warm up much to ex-cons, even teenage reformatory ex-cons, so Travis had pushed off for Atlanta. And Trouble had pushed off with him, just pickin' and grinnin' even back then. . . .

Leggett saw movement up high on the wall.

"God!" he whispered, and tried to free up the Mac-10 from inside his safari jacket. His heart was beating hard, pushing into his throat, and the headache tore at his temples. "Oh, God! Oh . . ."

It was a bird. A big one, gliding along the cliff face in the rain. Only a bird.

Leggett leaned against the tree and listened to the thud of his pulse, louder in his ears than the wind. Christ, he had to calm down. Christ, his daddy was about forty when *he* died. A thunderclapper. When he got a headache, he always thought of his daddy.

Just relax. They couldn't get down the wall without him seeing them, the girl and this Santiago character that Cuellar had started raving about. Now, there was a candidate for a thunderclapper. Cuellar. Always going apeshit about something.

They probably weren't even up there. Ware probably knew it and just sent him around here to stand in the rain for the hell of it. Another joke on ole Lead-ass, and a way to keep him from taking care of Freddie. Ware didn't care if Freddie died.

Well, they were wrong if they thought it was going to be that easy. Cooper might not make it, but he and Freddie would. And he just might have a surprise for Mr. Muscles. His fingers brushed the outline of the automatic weapon hanging beneath his jacket. He was deathly afraid of Ware—more than anyone he'd ever known inside prison or out—and he was just a fat little guy waiting for the thunderclapper, but he wasn't as stupid as they thought.

And he knew all about Trouble.

NINE

Stephen put on his flashlight, and the beam impaled the woman on the floor of the cave. When she instinctively raised her hand to shade her eyes, he saw blood dripping from scraped knuckles.

"Take it easy. It's me. Nobody's going to hurt you." He couldn't have her screaming, though there was practically no chance she'd be heard. "Just calm down."

"Then get that goddamned light out of my eyes!" He heard the tremor behind the toughness, and he knew how frightened she was. He angled the light past her, its beam illuminating the leather sacks with a reddish glow.

There was no point in hiding them. She had one of the coins in her hands.

Beth had turned and was staring at the pile, and then down at the old coin. She brushed at the powdery guano that covered the front of her shirt and jeans, and the wind swirled it over her head.

"What is this shit?" she muttered absently.

Even in that moment, Stephen had to grin, because it reminded him of the old Abbott and Costello routine. "Exactly," he answered.

"Huh?"

"It's guano," he said. "You know, bat—"

"Bat shit," she finished. "That's real cute. I can't believe it's so deep in here. . . ." Then she suddenly laughed aloud.

"What?"

"Nothing important. I just remembered something I was thinking to myself earlier, and now it's literally come true. What's in the bags? More of these?" She held up the coin.

It was too much trouble to deny, and useless anyway. "Yeah. A lot more."

"I see that." Her expression was thoughtful in the reflected light. "Wait a minute . . . This is what Cuellar's digging up, isn't it?"

"Yep."

"Only . . . he's not going to find it. Because it's in here."

She was very quick. Several half-truths that had occurred to him could be scrapped. She wasn't going to buy any of them.

"And it's been in here a long time." She was nodding to herself. "Otherwise, the ground down there would've tipped them off. It would've shown signs where you dug it up."

Very quick.

"Less than a year," he said. "It doesn't take as long as you'd think. The aspen leaves fall pretty heavy on the Crown. The snow mulches them, then the melt finishes the job. Over a winter, the ground goes back about like it was."

Like it was, he thought. With La Vigilancia waiting . . .

"This is a strange-looking coin." You had to hand it to her. Her voice was as calm as though discussing the weather report. She turned it over and squinted to read in the flashlight's gleam. "Who's . . . Francisco . . ."

"Madero," Stephen finished. "He was president of Mexico for a while back before World War I."

"There's no date on this coin."

"No, or on any of the others." Stephen squatted down a few feet away from Beth. The constant backlash of wind almost blew him over. "They're called Maderos by the collectors, and you're looking at nearly all that were ever minted."

Her gaze was direct. "So . . . are you going to tell me now?"

"Might as well," he lied. He'd have to tell her part of it, unless he wanted to just drop her out the cave entrance. But only part. "You want to get out of this draft? There are cracks all through here, like I told you. The cliff's honeycombed with them, and the wind finds every one."

She probably thought he didn't see her slip the coin into her pocket when she rose to her feet. He lit a path for her up the passageway and decided he could always get it back later.

"What time is it?" asked Cuellar, who was wearing a gold Rolex.

Joseph Ware glanced down at the watch on his thick wrist. "A little past eleven. You should get some sleep."

"Sleep?" Cuellar's heavy gray eyebrows rose. "Are you serious? That girl's out there exchanging stories with Esteban Santiago, and I'm supposed to get some sleep?"

Ware allowed himself a small smile. "Hey, Ramon. *Qué puta es la vida,* huh? Life's a bitch sometimes. Anyway, we don't know for certain he's around. She may be hiding under a bush somewhere. . . ."

"But you don't believe that."

"And, if he is here, and they're together, it doesn't alter anything. As you said, she has to be found. And, as you've said for a year, *he* has to be found. This only changes it for the better. If he's with her, then we know where they are, and we've got them covered. Trying to keep her alive only weakens him."

"Not him! *Mierda!* You know him. He'd throw her off that cliff to get at me. And at you."

Ware nodded. "Maybe he would." A memory pulled at him. "I knew I should have gone back and finished him that day in Texas, down there in the canyon. He was just a little kid, but I saw in his eyes right then he was no *pollo.*" He shook his head so Cuellar wouldn't realize he was lying when he said, "I should have killed him that day."

"I wish to God you had."

Ware grinned again. "So do Jaime and Charlie, I'd bet. If they allow wishing in hell."

Cuellar swore under his breath and sat down near the back of the lean-to. In his sleeping bag, Freddie Jenkins was gasping for breath, making a clicking sound in his torn throat with each inhalation.

"So," said Cuellar. "What's our next move, my friend?"

"We relax. We get some sleep and wait for morning and hope the rain stops by then. If they're in the caves, Leggett has the bottom of the cliff covered. Even he couldn't miss them with that Mac-10 if they rope down. And, if I'm wrong and the girl's alone, Cooper's over on the Mule Pass trail."

"And what if those *vatos* go to sleep and let her walk on past?"

"In this storm?" Ware chuckled. "Right now they're both huddled up soaking wet, cursing you and me and wishing they could shove those Macs up our asses and squeeze off a clip. But they're not sleeping."

Cuellar lowered his voice. "What about him?" He gestured toward Freddie Jenkins, who had turned on his side, his back to the two men. "He's not going to be much use from here on."

The message was clear enough. Ever the politician, Cuellar rarely spoke of such needs directly, but Ware had always read between the lines.

He nodded, and rose from his seat by the fire.

* * *

". . . and once Díaz was gone, the coalition fought among themselves," Stephen James was saying. "My grandfather was a close friend of Francisco Madero, a comrade-in-arms, he used to say, and after Madero was murdered he came north with the coins in 1914. Even then, they were worth a lot more than their face value." He paused, as if waiting for Beth to ask a question.

She had plenty, but sat silent for the moment, huddled against the wall and out of the howling wind, trying to take it all in. This wild treasure yarn he was spinning. Staring up at the brooding figure standing over her, his long hair blowing around his face, she imagined his eyes burned down fiery in the darkness, but she knew it was imagination.

"It was a time of civil war in Mexico," he continued after the pause. "In fact, every member of the coalition except Villa and Zapata became president sooner or later. I didn't know all that when I was a kid, just what my grandfather told me."

"Why . . ." Her voice sounded rusty, *felt* rusty in her throat. "Why did your grandfather bring the coins all the way up here? To this basin?"

"Ask him." Stephen shrugged. "My father always said it was just something about the north, and the snow. A lot of desert people are like that, I guess. Anyway, Madero was dead. Victoriano Huerta, who'd been his ally in 1911, had taken over. My grandfather believed he was helping keep the gold out of the hands of a dictator. He believed it would eventually be used to topple Huerta from power."

"But it wasn't."

"No. They brought it up here by mule, which is probably where the pass into the basin got its name. And they buried it and swore to use it only for the good of their country. Then they went back to Mexico, and circumstances took over, I guess. That, and the civil war. They got old and died."

"They?"

"Four of them. Nicolas Valdes and a man my grandfather always called Soste Miel, that means Honey Bear, and my great uncle Valentin Portes. And my grandfather. He told us the story when we were little. About the mountains and the snow, and the hilltop with its golden-leafed trees . . ." Beth heard his voice break a little, then harden. "La Corona de Colorado. And how someday we'd come for it, and how we'd be happy . . ." His voice faded to a stop.

"What about those other three men? Wouldn't they . . ."

"They're dead. Nicolas was killed by Pershing's soldiers in 1917, and the others . . . Los Centinelos are dead now."

He wasn't telling her the truth, at least not all of it. Beth was certain of that. When she'd asked earlier how Cuellar knew about the coins, he'd gone on as though he hadn't heard her.

"You said you've known Raymond Cuellar a long time." She tried again. "What did you mean?"

There was a lengthy silence. Then, "Since I was a boy," he replied. "Since I was ten years old."

She waited for him to continue, but he stood silent above her. About twenty years, she estimated. So, why . . .

"Why did you wait so long to come for the coins?" she asked. "If you knew where they were—"

"I didn't. At least, not exactly where." He moved away from her, toward the cave's entrance. "I think it's letting up some," he said. "I'm going to check the meadow."

He was evading her again. Outside, the storm was still pummeling the face of La Brujería. When he wanted to hide something, he either lied or just ignored the question. She watched him crouch carefully on the icy down-slope of the entrance. A flash of lightning silhouetted him there, and she suddenly remembered a display of prehistoric man she'd seen as a child in a Denver museum. Primitive and feral, crouched in a cave entrance, eyes as still and emotionless as death itself . . .

"There's someone down there." He came back to her. "At the edge of the trees."

"How could you tell that? It's pitch black and raining harder than ever."

She had a glimpse of a smile in the darkness. "He jumped when the lightning flashed," Stephen said. "Probably Leggett."

"That's another thing. You still haven't told me how you know those bastards."

"We can't stay here," he said, instead of answering her question, and his words drove it from her mind anyway.

"What? We've got to stay." Her words tumbled out. "You said so yourself. If he's down there with a gun, and we go sliding down the rope . . ."

"Not down. Up."

"Up?" She felt her blood freeze. "Up the cliff? We can't go up!"

"We have to." His voice was soft again. Patient, because he'd steered the conversation back into his comfort zone. "It's like you said, we can't rappel down into the meadow with him there. And we can't wait for morning either. If the storm clears, they'll be able to see everything on the cliff. Right now, this upper area's socked in. If we go up, he can't see us."

"How?" His calm was getting her angry again. "You want to tell me that? You pulled the rope down, remember?"

She saw the thickly developed shoulders shrug. "I'll have to climb it. Then I'll pull you up."

"Climb it?" Her voice got shrill. "Oh, right. How stupid of me. Just climb up a sheer wall coated in ice, then get past that overhang at the top. Without a rope, and in the middle of a goddamned rainstorm." She suddenly wanted to hit him. "Listen, Ace, you may be Stephen James, but you're not the fucking Human Fly."

This time she was sure he smiled. "I'll have a rope," he said. "And you'll be holding a bottom belay for me. You can use the anchor."

"*I'm* going to hold *you?* Listen, I know a little something about this—"

"Good. I was counting on that."

"Shut up! And . . . and I know if you get nearly to the top and then fall, you'll drop eighty feet, plus eighty more before the rope stops you. That's a hundred and sixty feet, Fly. It's too long a belay."

"And I can't risk the noise of working in pitons." His voice was light, almost happy. "That's why I'm expecting you to hold it right. Take it around the anchor, then around your cute little ass—"

"The rope'll break!"

"It's a Maxim kernmantle. I get my money back if it does. Besides"—his voice became sober—"we don't have a choice, Beth. Ware's a smart guy. After the weather clears, he'll look for tracks going out. The pass and the river trail'll both be solid mud, and when he sees you didn't go either way, he'll leave someone full-time to watch the cliff. You like the idea of growing old together in here?"

"What if . . ." The thought sent a chill through her. "What if he's waiting for you on top?"

"Then I'll challenge him to arm-wrestle. What else? We just have to believe there's nobody dumb enough to sit and dodge lightning up there."

She watched him take his climbing harness from the rucksack and step into it. He secured his rope through the front ring, then dug both hands into a brightly colored chalk bag and worked the powder into his skin.

"Don't drop me now," he said. They were near the entrance, rain and sleet blowing in around them, and another flash showed his smile stopping short of his eyes. Eyes that had already gone away somewhere, vacant and cold. "If you do, you'll have to get yourself down from here."

"I'm not going to drop you." She was scared, so it came out angry. She wanted very much to touch him, but she remembered his eyes in the lightning flash, and so she didn't. "You won't fall, anyway." She desperately wished she really believed that.

"Wrap the belay now, and keep it firm. If you don't and I fall, the recoil will take your skull right through the top of this cave. And be alert. If I slip, I can't chance yelling out to you. When I get on top, I'll give two tugs, then two more. Got it?"

"Two, and two more."

"Then you get back into the rappel harness and keep the Descender taut. Don't try to climb. I'll pull you up."

Then, catching her absolutely by surprise, he touched her cheek gently with the back of his hand, and she felt her heart lurch harder than in any of her moments of fear on that terrible day. She reached up to touch him, but he was already slipping down the decline through the blowing rain, and he was gone.

TEN

Out on the wall, the storm welcomed him.

The wind was all downdraft now, cold air plummeting along the sheer face and trying to tear him free. Rain intermixed with rock-hard pellets of sleet pounded the entire back of his body, snapping, stinging, against his scalp. He couldn't see because of the water splashing off the cliff into his face. His hands were a blur a little above his head, the left cradling an outcrop of granite and the right reaching upward for a handhold he remembered from that morning.

He'd climbed the wall twice in the past twenty-four hours, and innumerable times the previous autumn. He'd always been roped in from the top and could have used his jumars, but his ego hadn't allowed it. Now he was grateful for the mental picture he possessed, because it was all he carried into combat with La Brujería and her witchcraft.

He was overmatched.

Could the girl hold him if he fell? He knew she'd try, but . . .

The fingers of his right hand slipped into a diagonal crack, just where he knew it would be. He pulled up, shirt and pants already soaked and heavy, and left the cave entrance behind. The rope played out smoothly below. At least she knew how to feed a belay.

There was ice in the crack. His fingers slipped back an inch or so, and he clung to the face. His left foot, the Fire Ninjas wet through their tops, found the granite outcrop, and he pushed up. He was ten feet above the cave. Seventy feet to go.

With his left hand he dug a three-inch needle of ice out of a depression he was going to need. It sliced his index finger at the cuticle, but the pain was a distant part, blending nearly unnoticed into the whole. He pushed, this time from the chest-level depression, and held himself while his right hand followed the crack. It had widened, so he balled a fist and shoved downward until flesh became a living chock. Then he reached into the chalk bag with his left hand.

The chalk was turning to paste in the wetness. Nearly useless, but still better than his bare hands. He pulled up again, hiking a toe into the depression.

Climb up. Like the boy Esteban Santiago who first scaled a rock wall at age five, then climbed the mountains of his childhood for the joy, the simple ecstasy of ascent. Like the boy who climbed the cactus canyon of the Sierra Diablo in Texas, only that time to live.

He was climbing again to live. There was no ecstasy here, no thrill connected with the concept of topping a legitimate 5.12 at night in a raging downpour. Just survival, like that other time as a boy.

Lightning flashed close behind him, and he fought to keep his concentration in his fingers and toes. He felt the hair at the base of his neck prickle and smelled ozone-charged air before the hollow boom of thunder shook him. His fingers weren't as tough as they should be. Too little rock time lately. He felt the first twinge of old pressure sores that hadn't fully healed.

How far was he up the cliff? It was eighty feet from the cave to the dome, and the top twenty feet of that was the overhang. There'd be no way to maintain four points on the rock up there, or even three. He'd have to find the pitons and their carabiners that had been left by other climbers. He hadn't used them himself, preferring to solo by following an algae-crusted crack that curved up and over the edge. Hands only, five hundred feet above the meadow.

But that was in dry weather.

He estimated he'd covered a third of the distance, close

to thirty feet. The ice was getting worse as he went higher, and his fingertips were bloody from digging it out of the cracks. He felt a bump with his right foot, tested it, and stepped up. When the stickier rubber of the Ninja's midsole came off the left foothold below, he fell.

For an instant his fingers held, and his chest slammed into the cliff. Then they lost traction in the icy cut and he dropped, silent, into the storm.

Beth was playing out rope through the belay anchor in the cave, wishing she could see her watch. Stephen had gone out on the wall at least fifteen minutes ago, she was sure of that. Maybe longer. Maybe twenty. He had to be nearly halfway . . .

The light pull was gone from the rope. It went slack. "Jesus . . ."

She felt it an instant before the dark shape hurtled down past her line of sight.

Later, she saw it all as slow motion in her mind. The shape hurtling by, her hands locking down on the belay, the feel of the rope taut across her buttocks and the kernmantle's loop pulling hard into the anchor above her head . . .

Stephen's weight hit the end of the rope.

Travis Leggett heard a sharp, cracking sound up on the cliff, drowned immediately by the rumble of thunder. He pushed to his feet and ran out from beneath the protection of the trees. The rain instantly drenched him.

There was nothing. Except the wind screaming through the branches and whooping down the cliff face. And the flashes of lightning, getting closer together every minute, followed by thunder. And the impact of rain and sleet on everything—the branches, the ground, the wall, his own clothes and body. It was like standing in the center of a giant's kettledrum.

He was up to his ankles in muddy water. The meadow was nearly flat, with no natural runoff point, and it was filling itself into a pond. When he pulled one foot free, there was a soft, sucking sound. He heard *that*.

But there was nothing else. Only the storm. And he

could see nothing above the base of the cliff. Maybe the bottom twenty or thirty feet, illuminated by the lightning flashes.

"Forget this," he whispered. Only his fear of Ware and Cuellar kept him beneath the wall. Besides, the girl and her greaser could be up there singing the anthem with a five-piece band and he'd never hear them through all this noise. His headache pounded strong and true—in time with the thudding of his pulse—as he tugged his other foot free and retreated beneath the trees again.

Screw this bullshit, he decided. And the fish it swam in on.

The impact yanked Beth cleanly off her feet. If she'd failed to see Stephen's fall and hadn't shut down the belay, his prophecy would have proven true. She'd have gone headfirst into the ceiling.

The anchor creaked, audible above the storm, and she thought it pulled from the rock a little. But before she could consider that possibility, there was slack on the rope and she dropped the few inches back to the floor. He was climbing up.

She brought in rope, having become a top belay now. After a few minutes, Stephen's head appeared in the entrance. A lightning flash showed blood covering his face, and she almost cried out.

"Looks worse than it is." Those were his first words after he crawled back onto the level floor.

She shone the flashlight indirectly past his shoulder and made her own judgment. He was absolutely soaked, sleet standing stiff in his hair and melting off his shoulders. The ends of his fingers were bloody. So was one knee through torn pants. And blood dripped in a steady trickle from both his nostrils and where she'd scratched him that afternoon.

"Looks worse than it is, huh?" Her voice was trembling. "You . . . macho . . . asshole! Looks worse than it is? Don't you know you scared me to death?" She really wanted to hit him, but couldn't see any spot that didn't look injured. She also wanted to grab hold of him, but didn't care to dwell on that thought. "I thought you . . . you . . ."

So, instead she began to cry, which was the very last thing she wanted to do in front of him. But she did it anyway.

And felt his arms go around her and pull her against the wetness of his shirt. She heard his heart.

For a moment her arms went around him, too. Then she remembered everything all at once, and pulled free.

In the reflected light he was watching her, and she was certain she almost caught something in his battered face. But not quite.

"Your nose . . ."

"Is broken. I know." His voice had a muffled, nasal sound. "I hit the rock pretty hard when the rope played out." There was faint amusement in his tone. "Nice belay, by the way."

"Thank you." She was fresh out of snappy replies.

"Can't breathe too well. Listen, I want you to do something . . ."

For a second she froze, certain he was about to send her out on the cliff.

". . . for me. Stick a finger up each nostril, and—"

"What? You want me to . . . to stick my fingers in your nose?"

"If you love me, you'll do it." He grinned. "I've broken it before in the same place. Put a finger in each side, then lift at the same time and pull back. That'll at least clear me to breathe. Come on, my fingers are too thick."

A blush was burning up her neck. "Well, I don't love you, that's for damn sure." She made the retort sharp. "I don't even think I like you."

"*Qué poco amables sois.* Please? I have to get back on the wall again. It'd be nice if I could breathe."

"I'm *not* being unfriendly." She dredged up her high-school Spanish. "I just don't like you." But she did it anyway, and was surprised at the nearly audible click of broken bone as she lifted and pulled.

"Don't forget to wipe your fingers." There it was again, that almost look, and she felt a weakness in her midsection she didn't much care for. Not at all. Then, saying nothing else and hardly looking at her, he pulled up the slack rope and reset his climbing harness. And was gone again, out into the storm.

He climbed carefully, but a little faster for the wall's familiarity this time, until he reached the overhang. In a lightning flash's brief illumination he saw it curve back over him, slick as a punch bowl. Rainwater poured down from it onto his head and shoulders. It was like being under an ice-cold shower.

Sixty feet up from the cave, maybe more. That would be a one-hundred-and-twenty foot fall before the rope went taut, slamming him into the cliff. He couldn't take it. Couldn't survive it.

There was a piton somewhere in the bottom of the curve. It was probably within a few feet of where he clung to the rock. His nose was swelling shut, and he sucked down blood and spat it out.

He saw the piton in another lightning bolt's flash, a little above him and to his left. He grabbed the dangling carabiner as a handhold and pulled up, the piton taking his full weight when he clicked in with the rope.

He rested for a few minutes, holding his own belay by wrapping the rope around one leg. He hung, supported only by the piton, with his toes pushing against the wall and his upper body curled forward. But he couldn't stay there long, soaked by the water and slammed by the full force of the wind sweeping down the overhang. He began to climb.

On dry rock, this was the best part of La Brujería. Pulling upward into the belly of the overhang, feeling gravity take his legs down and away from the cliff, relying on the power he'd built into his arms and back and shoulders. Hand over hand in the algae crack until the wall went back to merely vertical again and he could secure a foothold. He loved it, and to hell with what the other climbers mumbled about there being a Moje on this ascent. He'd never been superstitious.

But in a storm, this was the worst part, not the best. The crack was lined with ice, and his grip became more important than pulling along it. His forearms first pumped, then began to knot up. Each time he shifted a handhold, his fingers nearly slid out.

And then they did, and he fell again.

Only about ten feet this time, because the piton held him. His bruised body smacked the wall then twirled around, back arched and laid out, the height of a fifty-story building above the meadow.

To hell with it. He couldn't make it. He hung in the rope and let the rain pour into his face. What could he do now?

And he remembered a dusty road, hot in November sunshine, and a mocking voice that answered his question.

Yo no se.

So he reached up the rope and pulled himself vertical. It wasn't time to quit yet.

He climbed back to the piton and began again. Hand over hand. Deal with the grip first, then pull along. The lightning was almost constant now, one hammer of thunder nearly indistinguishable from the next. He found the second piton a few feet past where he'd fallen, and clipped into the carabiner. And a little farther on, near the spot where the overhang curved back to form the lip of the cliff, he found a third.

His body was shaking with cold and wetness and spent adrenaline by the time he crawled onto the dome, but he found the rappel anchor and then gave four tugs on the rope. Two, and two more.

ELEVEN

"Pretend you're Freddie when you're not,
  With your head turned to face your twat. . . ."

The melody of the old song was in Joseph Ware's mind. As usual, the lyrics were his own.

Freddie Jenkins's eyes, one green and one brown, were fixed upon a wood tick that scrambled along his bare back, but he wasn't watching the tiny insect. Similarly, the tick had no further interest in Freddie, preferring blood that was warm.

Freddie's torso faced the rear of the lean-to. His head faced the front.

Like Linda Blair, thought Ware, examining his handiwork and recalling the scene from *The Exorcist* where the actress had appeared to turn her head around backward with no ill effects at all. Good old movie magic.

Except it didn't work that way in real life. Maybe for a family of owls, but not for humans. And evidently not for Freddie either.

It made an interesting tableau lying there, and he'd sat for a while exploring its incongruity. It caught and held the eye, this apparent reversal of natural law.

Cuellar sat by the fire a few yards away, still mumbling to himself in Spanish, but Ware ignored him. He'd seen El Gavilán like this often enough—caught in the grip of paranoid delusion, the late Dr. Fleming would have said —and knew the old bastard would eventually shake off his lethargy and rise up nasty as before, like a rattlesnake when the sun warmed its blood after a cold night. That was when Cuellar was his deadliest, as any number of unfortunates had learned. In the meanwhile, though, Ware pretty much had carte blanche.

With faint regret he reached out for Freddie's head. There were others involved, most notably Lead-ass Leggett, and it wouldn't do to leave the body that way. Beneath cooling skin, the boy's neck had the consistency of corn-bread dressing, and Ware felt splintered bone shards grinding as he both literally and figuratively straightened Freddie up for company. He closed the unmatched eyes and shut the jaw, then he zipped the sleeping bag to the top because in his last moment Freddie had fouled himself.

"Don't be embarrassed, Fred." Ware shifted the body into a position of repose. "It'll distract everyone from the smell of your breath."

There. When Lead-ass came dragging in, no doubt

half-drowned by that time, he'd see a sleeping Freddie. Nothing more.

Ware listened to the rain pounding down on the top of the tarp above his head. Leggett would be holed-up by now, back in the trees at the edge of the meadow, but he'd be able to see them if they descended the cliff.

If they descended . . .

Esteban wouldn't do that, he found himself thinking. After all the years, he knew the boy. No, make that man. The frightened little boy in that Texas canyon was gone forever, and so was the young romantic with a heart that could still be broken. The man who remained was a killer several times over.

But still Ware knew him, and Esteban knew Ware. He'd suspect a lookout in the meadow, and he'd know he and the girl were dead if they rappelled down into the gunsight of a Mac-10.

So, what would his adversary do? One of two things, Ware nodded. One was logical, one was lunacy.

Stay in the cave, unreachable and dry. That made sense. Wait the bad guys out, then rope on down when it was safe. He probably had food in there, and the limestone seeps would guarantee abundant water.

The flaw in that plan? Maybe the bad guys would decide to wait *him* out. Once the weather cleared, it'd be hard to hide on the wall of La Brujería. And besides, the operative term where it concerned the mind of Esteban Santiago wasn't safety and never had been. It was revenge.

Which brings us to lunacy.

Climb back *up* the cliff. He'd be invisible from the meadow in this storm, and nobody would be idiot enough to be sitting up top shagging lightning bolts while they waited for him. It would be a terrible ascent under these conditions, but if he made it . . .

Ware opened a rucksack near his feet and removed raingear, a pair of jumars, and a fifty-meter length of eleven-millimeter Edelweiss rope.

"Where are you going?" Cuellar looked up from the fire when he passed. El Gavilán's eyes were muddy and unfocused.

"To the Cupola."

"Por qué? If they're in the caves, it's as you said before. They're trapped as long as Leggett's down below."

"I'm sure you're right," Ware answered, shrugging into a large black slicker, the climbing rope concealed inside. "But you also have to keep in mind that Leggett's dumb as lumber. I'll just take a look. Can't be too careful."

"Or too dead, if *el ralámpago* strikes you." Cuellar made a crackling sound with his mouth. "Boom! *Se termino.*" His laughter was a drunken sound, but Ware knew El Gavilán was sober.

"I'll just have to keep my head low," he answered.

The rain beat down harder than he'd expected when he stepped out from beneath the tarp. Continuous thunder echoed above him as he ran along the path toward the bridge.

Under the tarp, Raymond Cuellar—for that was the name by which El Gavilán now thought of himself— stood up and watched the retreating shape of Ware's huge back until the man disappeared into rainfall and darkness. Cuellar's eyes were no longer as vague.

He went to the back of the lean-to and looked down at Freddie Jenkins. A faint odor of emptied bowels rose from the sleeping bag, but the boy's face was blank and serene. He looked asleep.

So much for this one. *"Cabrón,"* whispered Cuellar, and resisted kicking the body.

And now Ware, *El Maestro de Muerte,* was gone again. Out into the darkness, his natural domain. Cuellar felt the tightness in his chest begin to lighten, as it always did when Ware left him.

Boy and man, he'd constructed this killing machine, polishing and refining what was once only bottomless rage and the total lack of any moral restraint. And, for over twenty years, Ware had operated at his command. Cuellar couldn't remember for certain when he'd first realized he was afraid of his creation.

The key is to handle him carefully. Always remember his intelligence. The key is to make the thing you want him to do the thing *he* wants to do.

And to never forget he's absolutely insane.

Cuellar went back to the fire. Off in the darkness, on the crown of the hill past the soggy bodies of the two Anglos, he could barely see an outline of piled earth gone to mud.

So near. Very soon the twenty-year journey would end. He touched the heavy gold coin hanging on his chest and thought for the first time that night of Pascual Santiago.

La Corona de Colorado, old man. This is what you died for, and it's right over there. What was the *inglés* verse? Journey's end in lovers' meeting?

He didn't know what the old man would have done with the gold. Something sentimental and noble, doubtlessly. But he knew what he was going to do with it. It was his ticket to the high places, the seats of power in this country.

And he'd be free of Ware, the Deathmaster who ruined his sleep and plotted behind his back. That alone would be worth nearly as much as the coins.

They were nearly all gone, all the ones who knew him by another name in those days along the Rio. Dark secrets that only Ware remembered now . . .

And Esteban Santiago. The memory of Engracia Torres stabbed at him, and tears filled his eyes. Esteban Santiago, who'd destroyed love and beauty . . .

It would have to wait until he was found, out there in the storm with the girl, with any luck. First the two of them, then Joseph Ware.

"Plugiera a Dios qué fuera ahora," Cuellar whispered, his fingers stroking the automatic pistol that hung at his side. Would to God that it were now.

His eyes were clear and cold again.

Lightning crackled around Stephen James on the rim of the Cupola. He smelled ozone, tasted it, and his long wet hair stirred along his scalp.

The girl was nearly up to the pitons. And those same three pieces of metal that had gotten him through the icy downpour of the overhang alive were going to make it much harder to get her back on the dome.

She'd have to unclip from each carabiner as he brought

her up to it. Otherwise, she'd go no farther. The first one wouldn't be bad—she'd merely swing out from the wall —and the third one, at the lower edge of the lip, would be even easier. It was the middle piton, up in the full underbelly of the overhang, that would be brutal for a novice climber.

It would require strength. She'd have to pull her body weight up for a second to provide slack, and when she unclipped, she'd fall at least ten feet. That was the length of rope to the third piton. Even if he began pulling the instant he felt her go, he couldn't prevent that drop down and out from the overhang into the wind and rain.

She was smart. She'd realize that.

Stephen set his legs again, his feet against the rappel anchor, and took another length on the belay around his waist. Sleet pellets pounded on his head and shoulders as the rope suddenly dug into the ring.

She was way ahead of him. She'd already released the first carabiner. Which meant she was swinging free, away from the cliff, directly below the inverted bowl of the overhang.

He began to bring her up. Flex, and pull back, then stretch forward to pull again. His back was to the center of the dome. And directly across it, a little more than one hundred feet away, a lightning flash illuminated its opposite edge. The edge above the trail.

He pulled Beth up to the second piton.

The log bridge was slick as a sheet of wet glass, but Ware hardly glanced at it when he crossed, or at the churning whitewater rapids of the river fifteen feet below. Rain poured onto the hood of his slicker and, up ahead, the storm had turned the sloping trail into a stream as water followed its line of least resistance down from the half dome. He slogged through it, impervious to it, buoyed by an unflagging good humor that had settled in with the arrival of Buh-Buh-Bette and had refused to dampen since.

Dampen, he thought, and laughed, shaking water off his shoulders.

His moods were like that. With other times and other
stimuli, they could grow quite dark. . . .

He walked on the high side of the ascending trail,
avoiding the worst of the flooding. It must be something
to see on top by now. Thunder boomed down above his
head.

And, if he was right and if his timing was lucky, it might
really be something to see. He grinned, and rainwater
followed the natural contour of smile lines around his
mouth as he pictured meeting them up there.

Really something.

The second 'biner wouldn't release.

Beth grasped the piton and pulled herself up again.
There was an instant of slack on the rope and she
thumbed the gate of the carabiner, but it didn't budge.

She was hanging in the rappel harness, its Descender
locked in place, in the concave center of the overhang.
Icy water poured down over her in a continuous torrent,
and her fingers were going numb. This was the part she'd
dreaded from the moment she realized Stephen had
found pitons in the cliff. Releasing from the carabiner up
in the overhang. Falling . . .

Only now the goddamned thing wouldn't open. And
she certainly wasn't going to slide through it on the rope
unless she suddenly discovered a bottle of Alice's magic
pills. . . .

> (Oh, one pill makes you larger
> And one pill makes you small,
> And the ones that Mother gives you
> Don't do anything at all. . . .)

*I never cared for that song, Katie. For one thing, it's
clearly a song about drugs. For another, it implies the
girl's mother is somehow responsible* . . .

Go to hell, Mother.

Some 'biners had a locking nut, like the one at her waist
attached to the Descender, but nobody would use one of
those here, not in this overhang. This one had a snap-
release gate. She just couldn't open it.

If she cried out, would Stephen hear her above the roar of the wind that was buffeting her body back and forth? And whoever was in the meadow below—invisible in the downpour and the darkness—would he hear her, too?

She tried to pull up again, but her strength was fading and she could no longer feel her fingers. So she hung from the rope above empty air and surrendered to the storm.

Joseph Ware worked his way up the steepest part of the trail. If anything, the weather was worsening as he climbed, rain changing into a mixture of sleet and occasional snowflakes. It was pitch dark, a gray-black darkness, and he operated as much by feel as by sight. But he could sense something looming above his left shoulder and knew the path would begin to level soon.

He was whistling cheerfully, soundlessly, to himself.

Stephen pulled on the rope again, tightening the belay around his waist and straightening his legs against the iron rappel ring. Up six inches, then no more. Just like before.

She had to be catching in the 'biner at the second piton. Which meant one of two possibilities. Either she was afraid to release, or she couldn't get the rope loose.

"Mierda," he whispered, and ran one hand across his forehead to get the water out of his eyes. "Shit, shit, shit!"

Because, either way, his next step was the same.

Shit.

He tied off the rope into the rappel anchor, releasing his own belay when it was secure. Now the ring held the full weight of Beth's body, dangling below the overhang, and it would have to hold his weight as well. He slid to the lip and hooked one leg over, glancing down into the empty blackness of falling rain and sleet.

Might as well get it done, *mano.*

The rope was little help at first. It bore the girl's weight, and it pressed hard into the stone. He might be able to force his fingers under it to climb down. He might be able to lose some of them, too. He'd seen that happen once. Lonnie Dalton had fallen when the rope snapped taut like a rifle shot against the granite, but two of her fingers had stayed behind, pinned to the rock.

Better to avoid the rope now. He could use it when he cleared the lip.

The ice was worse than before, filling all the crevices and stinging the bloody ends of his fingers. It was a pure solo descent above the meadow. No ropes, no nothing.

Halfway down the lip, his toes slid into an opening and encountered something soft. Then a sharp pain, stabbing through the cloth.

"What the hell . . ."

A small bird, a cliff swallow, burst loose past his foot, confused and panicked and flying up into his face. Its claws and beak scraped his swollen nose.

"Get out of here, dammit!"

Then it spun free, down the cliff and away into the darkness.

Stephen held on for a minute while his pulse danced in his throat. Birds always took shelter in a storm like this. Watch your footholds, fool. He descended again.

His slippered foot found the third piton at the drop-off of the lip. Then open rope, stretched almost horizontally back beneath the overhang. Back to where Beth was.

He hooked one leg over the rope, then wrapped the other when he lowered himself beneath the wall of stone. As before, it was wetter here than on the open face. Like crawling under a waterfall.

A flash of lightning showed him the girl. She was hanging a few inches below the second piton in the belly of the curve. Her eyes were closed, and her body hung at a back-bending angle in her harness.

Stephen had both hands on the rope now, and he crossed like the days of his childhood crossing the skinny water pipe over Moscon Creek. Hanging upside down, legs wrapped. Move the hands, slide the feet.

When he reached Beth, she moved in the harness.

"I'm sorry." Her voice was faint. "I . . . couldn't get the damned thing to open. . . ."

"It's okay." His hands felt down past his feet for the carabiner. He pushed on the gate, and it didn't move.

Small wonder, the entire metal length was sheathed in ice.

Stephen released one leg, holding on with the other and both hands. "Close your eyes," he said, and began to kick at the 'biner's gate. The rope snapped with every kick, bouncing Beth back and forth.

Then he heard a faint clipping noise. He rewrapped his legs and reached for the gate. Through splintered ice, it snapped open for his thumb.

But there was no slack on the rope. Beth's weight pulled down on one side of the piton, his on the other. It was going to take a moment of slack to get the rope through the gate. The piton hadn't budged while he was kicking. It wasn't going anywhere.

Now what? Climb back to the lip and let her disconnect on her own? She no longer had the strength. Take her out of the harness? She'd fall.

"Listen to me." He released with his legs and hung above five hundred feet of emptiness by both hands on the icy piton. "Grab around me. When I pull us up, snap the rope free."

"You can't do that. It won't work."

"It better." He tightened his grip. "Otherwise we'll just have to consummate our courtship right here."

"Bullshit," he heard her mutter, and he knew then she'd find the strength. "Not with your wet-goat armpit in my face." She hooked her arms around his neck.

"Now!" He pulled up. Just pretend it's weighted chins. Just pretend she's one hundred pounds of black iron strapped to your waist in the gym. You do it all the time. Pull up!

The instant stretched. Their bodies moved two inches, no more. Beth snapped the gate and yanked the rope free. His grip failed and broke loose. They dropped.

In that moment, Stephen's only hope was the girl. He grabbed her, grabbed the rappel harness and the rope, as they tumbled down and out into the rain.

Their bodies snapped upward when the rope recoiled at its end. The third piton held. The rappel anchor held.

The rope held.

* * *

Ware climbed slowly up the rock wall above the trail. The surface was icy and he had two hundred and sixty pounds of body weight to maneuver. Finally, he looked over the top.

It was almost as he'd imagined. The wind howled across the dome, bending scrub fir before it, and sheets of rain blew into his face. While he watched, lightning struck the tallest bush in a blinding surge of pure heat and light, and he ducked reflexively below ion-charged air filled with the bitter odors of ozone and incinerated wood. Though nearly a hundred feet away, he felt a faint zap through the soles of his boots.

It was a scene from hell. He loved it.

And it was almost as he'd imagined. The only thing missing were the two figures crouched on the rim. He was alone.

He hurried across to the rappel anchor and looked over the edge. Leggett was down there somewhere, or at least he'd better be. They couldn't go down. There was no sign they'd come up. So . . .

Ware attached his jumars and roped into the ring. He lowered himself over the edge.

TWELVE

Stephen and Beth hurried down the curving path that led west, away from the river and away from Riqueza Crown. The rain wasn't letting up, but when they went lower, less of it was sleet. He felt her hand against his back as she followed him blindly. Except for flashes of lightning, the night was a black montage of rainfall and wind-whipped trees.

When he'd finally pulled the girl up over the rim, after first scaling the rope himself and releasing the third carabiner, she'd climbed directly into his arms. And she'd stayed there while he knelt awkwardly, touching her shoulders and back with tentative, stroking movements. The memory of that toyed with his concentration now, making him careless on a downhill path filled with water. Angrily he tried to push it away.

It was getting harder to breathe. Like the previous time his nose had been broken—in the cell in El Pozo—his nostrils were swelling shut. He had to inhale through his mouth.

The path leveled off, back on the basin floor again, and led into the trees. Stephen knew that within a hundred yards it would intersect with the Agua Fuerte trail, which curved around through the meadow below La Brujería. By following it, they could encircle the Cupola and reach the river on the opposite bank from Riqueza Crown. Then, into the canyon itself . . .

Where they'd be cut off.

Stephen stopped short, and Beth bumped into his back.

"What?" Her voice was nearly inaudible above the wind.

"Over here." He motioned toward a huge spruce, and she followed him into its shelter. Despite his rain poncho that she was wearing, she was soaked. Her hair hung down in long wet curls.

"What is it?" she asked again. Her mouth grazed his ear when she spoke, and he flinched as though shocked.

"The canyon trail." He bent close and, for a second, thought he smelled her. Sweat and wetness and warm flesh. Again he tried to fight back a startling, almost painful arousal. "I just realized we can't use it. The river's high anyway with the melt, and now this rain . . ."

"The trail through the canyon'll be underwater," she finished for him. She shifted closer.

Something was happening between them, and he knew she sensed it, too. Right there, under the tree with the storm exploding all around and their lives hanging in the balance, something . . . chemical was trying to take control. It was ridiculous, he thought, but there it was.

"That's right," he finally answered. "The canyon'll be wall-to-wall whitewater. Which means we have to find a way past those *cabrones* and up to Mule Pass. . . ."

Then he remembered what he'd seen before, crouching in the cave's entrance and looking down at the meadow below. Maybe they could improve their odds.

"Come on," he said, and led her toward the Agua Fuerte trail.

Travis Leggett had made a lean-to out of a small piece of canvas he'd snagged when Joseph Ware wasn't looking. He was thirty feet back from the meadow's edge under a thick stand of aspen and had draped the canvas over a couple of low branches. Under its cover and with his back against the trunk, he was fairly dry.

There was no way to see the base of the cliff from there, of course, but Leggett didn't give a low-flying fart about that anyway. Anyone up in those caves was also dry, and was sure as hell going to stay that way.

Not that there was really anyone up there. That Esteban Santiago business was all in Cuellar's head, and the girl couldn't have climbed that cliff alone if she was fucking Wonder Woman. She was probably holed up in the woods on the other side of the Cupola where Cooper would find her, and that was just A-okay with Travis Leggett.

He devoted some more time to staying dry and worrying about Freddie. The neck wound wouldn't kill the kid. Leggett had seen to that before he left camp the last time. Freddie was warm and dry in the sleeping bag, and he'd get by if those assholes left him alone.

Maybe it would all work out. At dawn, Leggett would head on back, getting himself good and wet in the process, and describe a hellacious night crouched at the base of the cliff. Then he'd talk to Freddie. After that, they'd see what happened.

He heard a muffled, snapping sound behind the tree. He considered checking it out, but that would involve leaving his shelter for the downpour. He satisfied himself by twisting sideways and looking around the aspen's thick trunk, and all he got for his trouble was rain in his face. Probably just the wind.

He decided to daydream some more about his share of the money from the coins, even though that did involve a giant leap of faith toward Ware and Cuellar. Together, he and Freddie would get close to a hundred thousand bucks. With that kind of money . . .

Or maybe even more than that. He pushed his dream a bit further, ignoring Daddy's old warning to never tell a pond frog about the ocean. Maybe a lot more than that.

In this particular daydream he was watching nine-millimeter slugs ripping away Cuellar's face, all that expensive bridgework flying around like kernels in a corn popper. And then he was giving it to Ware, only down low so that Mr. Muscles lay there screaming with his guts scattered around like link sausage.

Leggett was so deep into his fantasy, trigger finger twitching and a vacant grin on his face, that when the canvas collapsed on top of him, slamming him open-mouthed into the mud, his mind took *that* as part of the dream, too. Until a vicious blow came down on the back of his head.

Hey! Wait a minute . . .

Then another, worse than his headache.

He didn't even feel the third.

When Joseph Ware was nine years old and by far the largest (as well as the smartest) fourth-grader in Mrs. Wingate's class, he made the long swing across Putnam Creek and the picket fence that backed Old Man Sandifer's property. Teddy Burgess was less fortunate.

The big kids used the rope to swing out from a high limb and drop into the creek on hot, autumn-in-Ohio afternoons. Some of them swung completely across. And the best ones, the high-school jocks, sometimes rode the thing all the way across Mr. S's fence on the far side of the water.

On the day nine-year-old Joseph Ware first committed murder, there were no witnesses around. Teddy Burgess was older, a seventh-grader, though he and Joseph were about the same size.

"You won't do it," Joseph said to the other boy, because he'd learned that was the best way to be sure someone would. "You're too big a pussy."

"Horseshit," replied Teddy, only it came out as "horse-hnit" because of his cleft palate. "Neither will you."

He had him. "Yeah?" Joseph stretched to his full height on the tree branch and grabbed as high on the rope as he could reach. Then he kicked hard and launched himself into the air.

Down in a smooth arc above the water, then back up with the opposite bank beneath him. The fence loomed ahead, then below. He was above it. He twisted in the air like a pole vaulter and pushed away from the rope.

And landed in a tangle of dead grapevines and dirt a good five feet past the fence. Piece of cake.

"You coming?" he called back to Teddy, whose face was clearly turning green even at that distance.

Teddy had the rope in his hand. His bare feet shifted nervously on the branch. "I can hnwing across the creek," he said.

"Hot snot. Swing across the fence, too. I did it."

"I don't have to. . . ."

"And I'm just in fourth. You're in seventh, you pussy!"

Teddy's face was flushed. "Who cares?" he shouted back. "You hnink *you're* hot hnot."

"Hnot?" hooted Joseph. "What's *hnot*, harelip?"

"Dammit, Nyoey!" Teddy's fingers tightened on the rope.

"And who's *Nyoey?* My name's Joseph, harelip. And you're still a pussy!"

Which was when Teddy Burgess came soaring out of the tree on the rope.

Thinking about it later, Joseph Ware was fairly certain he hadn't intended to kill Teddy all along. It was only when he saw the boy wasn't going to drop into the water or onto the bank, that he was trying for the fence and that it would be a near thing, that it popped full-blown into his head.

Really, two things popped in there. The first was to just watch, because Teddy—if he made it—was going to land looking for a fight. That was tempting, but it only took a split second to cast it aside.

The rope reached the top of its arc. Teddy was above the fence, and his eyes were the size of Buick hubcaps when he released the rope.

And Joseph Ware, with exceptional athletic timing

even then, jumped into the air to meet him. He took Teddy's bare feet in his chest without flinching and was slammed back down into the vines.

While Teddy fell directly across the picket fence.

Old Mr. S didn't like kids, and his fence had sharp pickets. One of them tore out Teddy's ribs and punctured his lung. Another passed through his stomach and emerged above his hipbone.

Joseph was impressed by the fact Teddy didn't scream. He just kept trying to pull himself off the fence, without any luck. It took him a minute or two before lapsing into unconsciousness, and just before his eyes rolled back, he stared at Joseph and whispered something that sounded like "Why?"

Joseph had been watching him, his heart pounding loud and fast in his ears. He answered the question with a shrug—because he truly didn't know why, except that for a moment the act had caressed the rage that hid behind his ever-smiling face—and then he vaulted the fence and walked home.

In another time and place, his answer might have been *"Yo no se."*

And now, huge and dark, his shadow filling the entrance, he swung into the upper cave. That other swing, across the creek and the picket fence, flashed through his mind.

Still a thrill, he thought, grabbing the belay anchor with one hand. But he wasn't so carried away that he forgot to drop instantly to one knee and swing the Mac up from its web harness.

There was no one home. At least, not at the moment.

Ware tied off his rope to the belay anchor, then removed a flashlight masked with tape from his pocket and played its faint light along the corridor ahead of him. The silence back there lay heavy, accentuated by the sounds of the storm booming down the cliff outside. He nodded when he saw a backpack lying against the wall.

"Hola, Esteban," he whispered. *"Como le va?"*

And, a little farther back, near where the passage curved and descended, a sleeping bag. He raised it to his face and inhaled her scent.

"And to you, too, Buh-Buh-Bette."

They'd been there, not too long ago, and they'd left before he arrived. That was rude, but it was okay because the cave showed he'd been right all along. He could stand a few bad manners to be right.

Gone. But gone where?

Down the cliff was a maybe, but not likely if Leggett was even semiconscious below. Back up the cliff without a top belay was a distant maybe, and damned impressive if true. Back farther into the cave was a definite maybe. The cave had possibilities. Who could say where it might lead?

Ware squatted down by the sleeping bag and cut off the light to let his eyes reacclimate to darkness, passing the time by inhaling the girl's smell and running his hands along the inside of the bag. After a while he rose into a crouch and moved in silence along the tunnel.

Beth was frozen into momentary immobility by the shock of it. Stephen James was silently and methodically beating the man to death.

"No!" She heard a voice above the howl of the wind and recognized it as her own. "No, Stephen! Stop!"

He didn't look up. He sat astraddle the quivering form under the canvas and raised the butt of his pistol again.

"No!" The feeling returned to her legs and she sprang forward, landing on his back. Both her hands locked around his wrist and still the gun butt came down, slowed only slightly.

She hooked her legs around him and levered back, pulled him past his balance point. They tumbled backward into the mud.

"Please . . ." She grabbed for him. "There's no need. . . ."

And a part of her mind cried, Please. Please don't make me see you like this. Not now . . .

Then he shrugged her off and was back onto his knees. Another burst of lightning shattered the air overhead, and in its glare she saw his face.

And forgot everything they'd found together in that long, terrible day and night.

His eyes were blackening from the effects of his broken nose, which was swollen and blood-crusted with dark rivulets washing down his chin. His lips were pulled back from his teeth in a grimace, and the look he gave her was savage patience, no more. Nothing more.

She fell back, away from what she saw in his eyes.

"Okay." She got wearily to her feet. "Go ahead. Kill him. Kill them all, why don't you? You're just like them, aren't you? Just like Ware . . ."

He stopped then, as if the word itself was a blow. From his knees he looked up at her.

"You don't know anything," he said.

She backed away from him. Behind her the fat man was groaning beneath the canvas, and there was a dark stain in the mud near his head.

"I know you're a goddamned animal!" she snapped, hanging at the edge of hysteria. "I know you even thought about letting me die so you could get them and the gold. I know that."

"You don't know . . . anything." He stood up and pointed his gun butt toward the man on the ground. "Listen to me. I watched that bastard right there put a knife through your friend. And he was enjoying his job, woman. I bet he whistles while he works."

"So you murder him. When all you need is to tie him up . . ."

"Tie him up?" He took a step toward her. "Tie him up, my ass. This isn't some TV show."

"No!" She jumped backward. "You stay away from me. I've had enough of this. I'm getting out of here, and I'm doing it alone. You just get out of my life."

He stopped. "Alone? You're crazy. *Está loco, mujer.* You'll never make it alone."

"Screw you! Don't tell me what I'll make or won't make. I've been taking care of myself since I was sixteen, Mr. Macho. I'll be out of here before you will."

She threw his rain poncho on the ground and spun away.

"Hey."

"Hey, what?" She turned back, her voice brittle with an edge of hope.

He flipped the pistol to her, and she caught it by reflex. "Better take that," he said.

She stared down at the gun and felt her skin crawl, then she shoved it into her pocket and looked up at Stephen James.

He was just going to stand there and let her go. For a moment her resolve wavered, then she remembered his face in the lightning flash.

"And take that poncho, too," he said. "It has a knife in the pouch."

She grabbed it from the ground and ran away, into the trees, quickly before she could begin to cry.

There was an echo inside the frozen, stone face of La Brujería. Up high, where the cave dropped away in a curving, descending tunnel. Back in the flashlight-pierced darkness where the wind created a swirling vortex over the old leather sacks. The echo was muffled by the walls of the passageway and the storm outside and—except for one person below—nobody heard it at all.

The booming echo of Joseph Ware's laughter.

This isn't some TV show. . . .

Beth slogged across the submerged meadow beneath rainfall and the towering cliff. The wind whooped and hollered down its face, and once it sounded faintly like laughter.

Some TV show. Damn him, to imply she was that stupid. That . . . weak.

She'd fought them for her life, and she was still alive. She'd fought them and maybe even killed one of them. He had no right to treat her like she was weak. Especially after she'd begun to . . .

Forget that.

The Agua Fuerte trail crossed this meadow. It was under here somewhere. If she could pick it up in the trees ahead, it would lead her around the Cupola to the river. And maybe he was wrong about it being underwater in the canyon.

She remembered his touch when he'd pulled her to safety from the cliff. His hands had been awkward, clumsy against her back, as though tenderness was some alien landscape beyond their experience. But she'd felt that touch as gentle, and she'd allowed the tough, cynical shell over her wounded soul to soften. . . .

Once burned, twice shy, Katie. . . .

Then she thought of his face illuminated by the lightning. A savage face but, most of all, patient. With the timeless patience of the cold, flat eyes she'd seen in that museum display as a child.

I waited, his face told her in that burst of colorless light. *I waited before you came, woman, and I can wait a little longer. It makes no difference at all. You make no difference at all.*

Beth was barely aware she'd risen out of the flooded meadow and onto muddy ground. Trees closed around her and the rain's impact lessened, and she looked down at her sturdy Timex on its stained-leather band. She waited for another lightning flash and saw it was a little past one. It was Sunday morning.

After a few minutes of bushwhacking along the meadow's perimeter, she found the trail. She followed it into deepening forest, gradually curving to her left. The huge bulk of the Cupola was still there, but it was much less sheer away from the climbing face.

She'd become aware of a steady roaring sound in the darkness ahead and was beginning to quicken her pace toward it when she smelled cigarette smoke.

Beth had never smoked, and her nose for its scent was keen. She stopped in midstride, one foot poised above a thick root growing across her path. She held her breath, and the sound of rain hitting aspen branches overhead merged with the rumble of the river.

In her absolute stillness she heard the swish of a body's movement through the knee-high ferns along the trail. Suddenly faster, and quite loud.

She dove to her left.

THIRTEEN

Joseph Ware released the end of his rope from the belay anchor, then tied it securely around his waist. If worse came to worst, it'd save him a long fall. He didn't have Esteban's technique, but he enjoyed climbing. And, at his level of strength, the jumars and a secured rope were enough.

He balanced in the cave's entrance and looked down through rainswept darkness toward the meadow below. Leggett was down there somewhere and so was Esteban, along with the girl who was beginning to dominate Ware's imagination. Instinctively he knew he'd barely missed them, which meant they'd either regained the dome and fled down the path the opposite of the way he was ascending, or else they'd rappelled La Brujería right under Leggett's nose.

Either way, Leggett was in for some interesting moments. Ware wondered how alert Lead-ass was down there. Probably fretting over Freddie.

His hands on the rope reminded him again of Teddy Burgess. Teddy and Freddie. Freddie and Teddy.

(And I'm ready, ready, Teddy, to rock-'n-roll. . . .)

He'd always enjoyed devising his own lyrics to old songs. It was sometimes necessary . . .

(And *you're* ready, ready, Freddie, to turn to mold. . . .)

. . . because it gave his mind something to do when it started running too fast again, and he could feel his mood beginning to darken.

He swung out into the rain, muscles bunching as the jumars tracked up the rope. Somewhere between here and camp he'd decide whether he wanted to tell Cuellar about the leather sacks in the cave.

Stephen rolled Leggett's body under the cover of a big tree. The man was moaning softly through blood trickling down across his closed eyes. Once he muttered something incoherent about a thunderclap, or something like that. The blood had branched both ways around his fleshy nose and followed deep furrows on either side of his mouth.

I guess you've had a hard life, Lead-ass, thought Stephen. Fat guys aren't supposed to have wrinkles. He recalled Soste Miel's smooth brown face.

For the half-dozenth time since the girl left, he wondered why he hadn't killed Leggett yet. One less to worry about, though admittedly not much of one. He remembered the fat man peeking around the tree when Beth had stepped on a branch, then ducking back to where it was dry.

"Lead-ass, Lead-ass," he whispered in mock exasperation, pulling the muddy Mac-10 from inside the man's torn safari jacket. "Tell me why I don't just go ahead and blow your titties off here and now? *Diga!* Tell me that."

Leggett shifted, and blood trickled into his mouth. He coughed.

"Hurts, doesn't it? But at least you're still alive to feel it. I wonder why."

The hell he did. You're just like the rest of them, she'd said. Like Ware.

He didn't really wonder why at all.

"But it's a mistake." He nodded. And he remembered Pascual's words. The snake you fail to crush is the one that later bites you.

There was an unfired clip in the Mac, and two more in Leggett's jacket. Stephen slipped them into his pocket.

He thought again that he should just let her go. She'd be blundering around in the storm and probably stumble right into their laps, which would provide the diversion he needed. They'd decide she'd been alone all along, and he could go back to the original plan. To Pascual's plan, nearly seventy-five years in reaching its fruition. After he took care of Lead-ass, of course.

It all made sense.

So he wondered why he rose to his feet and took a rough sighting on the direction she'd gone. And why he left Leggett unconscious under the tree, probably dying but not dead yet, to hurry after her.

Only, once again, he didn't really wonder why at all.

Like Leggett, Dale Cooper had been holed up and trying to get dry when the girl came by.

It seemed he'd been wading through an Amazon rain forest for a week. He'd trudged mud over to Mule Pass and then as far back as the north trail leading up to the lakes, and had seen no trace of a human footprint anywhere except his own. By the time he reached a spot just around a bluff from the river, he was filthy and incredibly tired.

"Oh, Jeez," he'd muttered, cutting off his flashlight and trying to get a Camel to fire up in the downpour. "Oh, Jeez, I feel like I been eat by a werewolf and then shit off a cliff."

He'd finally gotten the smoke going and had just squatted beneath some scrub-oak bushes when he heard someone coming up the trail. And this time it wasn't Leggett.

Then he spotted her. She was a small shadow moving through windswept darkness, and it was only her light-colored hair he could see clearly. She appeared to be wearing a rain poncho that flared out around her as she moved.

Thank you, Jesus, my ass is saved.

Just then she stopped on the trail, one foot still in the air. He thought she looked like an Oklahoma whitetail pausing to sniff the wind. He dropped his cigarette and crept through knee-high ferns toward her. When he was less than ten feet away, he launched into a run.

And leaped through empty air onto the wet trail.

"Damnit!" He came up bellowing, with a mouthful of mud. "Dammit to hell . . ."

She was rolling through the ferns and back onto her feet. Something fell from beneath her poncho that looked one helluva lot like a gun, so he dove for it and his head hammered her ribs. She went backward with a grunt of released air but kept her footing, and twisted like a gymnast to bolt away through the trees.

Cooper struggled to his feet and immediately stepped

on the pistol. He pulled it from the mud and slipped it into his pocket as he ran after her.

Where the hell did she get the gun? Maybe Cuellar was right, and there was someone else in the basin. But that didn't matter now, because she was alone and unarmed, and he was going to take her alive. And it might be a somewhat damaged bundle of goods he'd deliver back to the camp later. He deserved a little something for the night he'd put in.

Beth was smaller and quicker than the man, and she reached the brush-filled bluff well before he did. She could hear his heavy breathing behind her.

The bluff was nothing like La Brujería, but it was steep nevertheless. She saw a long diagonal cut running upward at a left-to-right angle and climbed into it. The rock was a tough granite mix with oakbrush growing out its sides, and handholds were plentiful.

"There you are." She heard his voice below her. "Wait for me, darlin'."

She didn't look down, kept climbing. His breathing was labored below her. That's what those cancer sticks'll do for you, asshole, she thought, though she was exhausted, too.

She was halfway up the cut when it turned more vertical. It was also more open to the wind, above most of the basin's trees, and rain blew into her face. Her legs were dead. She was nearly fresh out of running. Then she heard him below, and she pulled herself up again.

Cooper looked up to see the girl's legs in a vertical, three-sided chimney. She was wedging herself along, pushing with her back against one side and her feet against the other. She was moving slowly.

Jeez, he was tired. And the half a Camel he'd had before she came along the path hadn't been nearly enough. Granpaw Jeffries always had the right idea. Load a little nicotine before you load the wagon.

Cooper took less than a minute to light his cigarette. He shifted it to one side of his mouth before crawling into the chimney. He didn't know diddly about rock climbing, so he copied the girl's technique. As slow as she was moving, he'd have her before long.

Beth reached a spot where the chimney's right side dropped away. The rock was still firm against her feet, but there was nothing to brace her back. She saw a small ledge a few feet above.

"What'sa matter, darlin'?" The voice came from right below her. "Run out of room?"

Then she saw a tiny vertical crack, no more than an inch wide, just above her. If she could get her fingers into it . . .

"Better give it up before you get hurt." The voice was closer. "Just slide on down here."

Left hand in. Right hand above the left. She leaned back, fingers sliding upward, her full weight held by her desperately tired arms. Rain pounded on her back.

"Hey, where the hell d'you think you're going?"

The pressure on her fingers rode all the way down into her shoulder sockets. If she slipped, she'd land right in the man's lap. Six inches up, six more . . .

"Hey, dammit! You hold it right there!"

She swung a leg over and locked her toe, then levered herself onto the shelf . . .

. . . just as granite exploded above her, followed by a deafening boom of sound. Chunks of rock sprayed onto her back.

"That's far enough, goddammit!" The voice sounded only a few feet below. "Next one takes a bite out of your skinny little ass."

Beth risked a glance over the edge. As she'd thought, it was the blond man with the mustache. He was wedged into the chimney no more than ten feet beneath her, and he had Stephen James's gun. A mixture of cordite and tobacco smoke drifted past her.

"That's better." She thought she saw the flash of his teeth. "No more tricks now. Climb back down."

"So you can kill me, too?" Beth felt tears welling in her eyes. "No, thanks."

She squeezed in tighter on the tiny ledge and held her

breath, waiting for the bullet. *Was it a searing pain, Daddy, or just a vast numbness? Did you think of me?*

"You're wrong about that," said the man. "If I wanted you dead, I'd have already done it. I couldn't miss from here. Come on down. There's a guy who wants to ask you some questions. . . ."

"Cuellar." She spat out the word.

"The very same. Who knows, if you have the correct answers you might get out of this yet."

Right, she thought. What she'd get out of it was a knife. . . .

"You coming down?"

A knife . . . Stephen's voice was in her head.

(". . . that poncho, too. It has a knife in the pouch.")

A knife. Beth rolled onto her side, back against the rock, and reached for the zippered pouch below the hood.

"No, huh? Okay, but don't start bellyaching if this hurts." There was a scraping sound below. He was climbing up again.

Where is it, dammit? There, the zipper was there. Pull it slowly. He won't hear. He's climbing, and he won't hear because of the noise of the rain.

She reached inside, felt a slight weight at one end. Her fingertips brushed something cold. Below her, the climbing sounds were closer. They sounded right next to her feet. She found what was in the pouch. . . .

Jesus God. In spite of it all, Beth nearly laughed aloud. What she held in her hand was a little Swiss army knife.

Cooper reached a section where one side of the chimney fell away. Above him, maybe another foot or so, he saw the girl's legs.

It'd be great just to shoot her. Forget the plans he'd made for her earlier. He was too damned tired for that, anyway.

Just shoot her. *Bang-o,* then haul her carcass back to the camp slung over his shoulder like a gutted whitetail.

But he couldn't, not unless there was no other choice. Cuellar wanted to talk to her *real* bad. Cuellar wanted to find out if that other character he and Ware were always whispering about was in the basin, and the girl was the one to tell him.

So he couldn't shoot her, not to kill her, anyway. But maybe a nice little flesh wound wouldn't hurt.

That sounded good. If she tried to fight him, he'd plunk her one in the ass, just like he'd warned her earlier.

He gathered himself to lunge upward for the girl's legs.

A Swiss army knife. Shit, maybe Steve the Rockhead has a sense of humor after all.

The blade Beth popped out with her thumbnail was no more than two inches long, and dull and pitted from constant use. What now? Tweak the son of a bitch's nose with the bottle opener? A manic giggle tried to push up through her terror.

Then a hand closed over her boot, dragging her backward and slamming her elbows painfully against the rock. The man's other hand grabbed the ledge and his face appeared, only inches away.

"Okay, that's it." He blew tobacco breath into her face as she frantically jacked up another section of the little knife. "You're coming with me now, or else I'm gonna blow off a chunk of your pink little—"

And she stabbed him in the corner of his right eye with the corkscrew.

He screamed, a high-pitched feminine sound, and grabbed for his face. With her feet suddenly free, Beth pulled up her legs and kicked him in the head.

He screamed again before her heavy hiking boot connected a second time. Then he fell away from her, down and out of her line of sight. She heard rocks breaking away and tumbling free, and then another scream from below that faded into silence.

And then only the sounds of the receding storm.

It was stopping, she realized faintly. The rain was letting up.

Her hand was bloody. So was the knife she still held, its corkscrew blade extending between her index and second fingers. She wiped it on the poncho before she climbed down.

At the bottom of the bluff, the man's body lay doubled

across a smashed oak bush. She made a wide circuit around it.

"I swear to God, Buh-Buh-Bette. Sometimes you astonish even me."

The big dark figure was leaning against a tree along the slope. In that instant, Beth felt the last of her strength disappear. She was so tired . . .

"I said it from the start." Joseph Ware climbed up to get her. "The heart of a samurai."

. . . so tired. She sat down in the mud to await him.

The rain had completely stopped when Stephen found Dale Cooper's body.

He'd heard a pistol shot echoing along the cliff while he was wading the edge of the meadow, patiently crossing and recrossing the brush line for Beth's trail. But then the echo was distorted instantly by the wind and the Cupola's contours. It could be anywhere up ahead.

So, he'd fought back the urge to run blindly after her—and probably into a trap—and continued to move laterally until he finally found her tracks. From there it was only a short distance to where she'd picked up the Agua Fuerte trail.

Not bad at all. She was something, this one. He tried to keep that thought and the sound of the gunshot out of his mind while he moved silently along.

The trail curved left, following the half dome's ragged base, and he'd begun hearing the roar of the river ahead when he came to the spot where she'd been jumped. The underbrush, mostly ferns and skunk cabbage, was beaten down and there was an area of bent aspen branches leading away toward the slope.

A few feet along he smelled tobacco and found a soggy cigarette still smoldering in the wet leaves.

Cooper, he thought, and mashed it out.

The hillside sloped up through oakbrush, with patches of old, dirty snow still unmelted in shaded areas. He climbed carefully, crouching low with the Mac pushed forward, until he reached the base of the bluff and Cooper's body.

The man was propped in a seated position against the

trunk of a tree. His arm, shattered at the elbow, had been twisted with sheer brute force into a triangular shape, the hand upraised in the parody of a greeting. All his fingers were bent down except for the middle one, which stood obscene and erect in a faint flash of receding lightning.

Hola, nieto . . .

The message was clear, and it spanned their relationship, both adversarial and symbiotic, through all the dark and bloody years.

Hola, El Gigante Malo.

A dark figure and its shadow they were, the second always reflecting smaller than the first. Bound together in life and death and time . . .

El Pozo

Men are sometimes free to do
what they wish, but they are
never free in their wishes.
          —Thomas Hobbes

FOURTEEN

The poster still hung in the abandoned shop, in the only window left unbroken. Kennedy and LBJ.

Esteban looked over his shoulder at it as they drove past. Inside the tinted glass of the LTD, the air conditioner hummed quietly.

"Hey, wha'choo looking at, bro?" asked Chuey Delgado in English. "Those little *putas* catch your eye? They're even ugly in the dark, *mano*."

"No." Esteban turned away. "Just the street. I came through here years ago. When I was a kid."

"Shit." Delgado took another hit, and gray smoke caught and swirled in the air conditioner's pull. "We all did, *mano*. Here, or someplace just like it. We all came through here."

Esteban leaned back into the soft cushions and let the conversation go on without him. They'd been up at five and inside the *casas de cambio*—the houses of change— loading the laundered money before six. He was already tired.

Seven years, closer to eight. He tried to remember the little boy who'd asked Pascual Santiago about the poster, but failed. He remembered the grandfather with all the love and reverence he possessed, and he would until the day he died. But he couldn't remember the little boy.

First LBJ, who'd gone on, then Nixon. And now it was Ford, the big man who ran into things with his head.

At seventeen, Esteban Santiago had grown up like his father. He was small and wiry, and he'd kept the agility of his childhood. On his left hand, the nail of that ring finger was dark and oddly convex in shape. It had grown in to replace one he'd lost from infection where cactus thorns had embedded underneath. Embedded during his climb out of a desert canyon at age ten.

With Jorge. It'd be good if he saw Jorge again.

121

Alejandro followed state highway 45 out of Juarez. After a while they turned west and began the slow climb from the Chihuahuan desert toward the Sierra Madre. The big car's engine took the grades with ease.

Easier to drive up than walk down, Esteban thought. Easier to be seventeen than ten.

"No, nothin' is easy, Stephen," Brother Axton Gilbert had been fond of saying in a Texas accent as thick as crankcase sludge. "Nothin'. 'Specially not followin' the will a the Lord."

Brother Axton had called him Stephen from the first day he'd been turned over by Social Services at the age of eleven. Brother Axton had immediately looked up both Esteban and Santiago in a Spanish-English dictionary.

"One means Stephen," he declared. "An' the other means Saint James. The names of two a Christ's apostles. You're in America now, son. Your name's Stephen St. James."

And, for a while after that, Esteban had almost begun to think of himself in those terms. Until Allison Brock.

"Hey, *mano.*" Chuey Delgado studied him through glazed, half-stoned eyes, and Esteban was glad Alejandro was driving. "You're pretty quiet. Anyone ever tell you that?"

"Everyone." Esteban mustered a faint smile. "Just a little tired."

"Tired? Hey, Alito! You hear that?" Delgado poked the back of the driver's seat with his boot. "The *parejo chico's* tired. Shit!"

"So am I. *Tu ves?*" answered Alejandro. "And you should shut up and rest your big *boca* as well, *mano.* It's a long day."

As usual, Gualterio Covarrubias lounged in the front passenger seat and said nothing. His bulk caused the seat to bulge out and back.

"Tired," muttered Delgado, who went back to rubbing his crotch while the combination of marijuana and meth crystal played volleyball with his nerve endings. "Tired, shit. I don't get tired."

No, just wired, thought Esteban. And you don't know

what tired is anyway, *vato.* Try spending a little time with Brother Axton Gilbert.

He was never sure where Brother Axton got the title, though one of the girls told him it came from a mail-order divinity school. Something about not having to pay taxes.

And it brought in the kids, of course, the ultimate in cheap labor, because his house was legally a church. When Esteban got caught in a police sweep along the alleys of Southside and the law could do nothing with him, the social worker immediately thought of the Christ Jesus Eternal Church and School.

He'd become a tough little bastard by then, after a year on the streets of El Paso and Juarez. A chain-smoking, foulmouthed little thief already known as El Mono, the Monkey, for his skill at evading the law by climbing and leaping across rooftops. The police had claimed he was an illegal alien. He claimed he wasn't, and swore he was the child of an Anglo hooker from Big Spring who'd balled one Hispano too many. He was born in an El Paso motel, he said. His English was excellent and the police couldn't prove him a liar, so he ended up with Brother Axton. As Stephen St. James.

You don't know tired from tuna fish, Chuey, he thought again.

Brother Axton was constantly printing sayings with crayon—in English, of course—on lined notebook paper, then hanging them all around the walls for his young acolytes to read if they could. Esteban most vividly recalled one that said, HARD WORK IS THE CALMATIVE OF THE SOUL.

Which was true enough, he'd discovered. On several occasions he got so calm that his legs stopped working. But at least the unending labor had broken his cigarette habit. You needed every ounce of air you could force into your lungs when you were getting calm for Brother Axton.

Outside the LTD the landscape was altering into dry grasses and trees. Up ahead, Esteban saw the faint outline of El Monte Sin Nombre, the Mountain Without a Name. He felt the first stirrings of something that had tried to die.

Jorge would be twenty now. Esteban hadn't seen his brother since a creaking old pickup had dropped them off near the international bridge in El Paso. Jorge had gone home. Esteban had stayed to find the cowboy Charlie, the Coyote Agustin, the giant Ware. And the Shadow Man, who'd put his arm around Pascual Santiago's shoulder and whispered lies into his ear.

But that was a lifetime ago. Maybe Jorge had never made it home.

The car crossed the Continental Divide and, a little later, turned down a hill and onto the main street of Bavispe.

"What a shithole, man," observed Chuey Delgado. "These little mountain villages are all alike, you know? When will we be there?"

"Patience," said Alejandro. "Not long now." Covarrubias said nothing.

Neither did Esteban. As the car crossed Moscon Creek and passed through the village, he leaned back and looked covertly at his old home. It was ridiculous, but he was afraid someone out there would see him. Embarrassed at the idea of being recognized in this company.

The town looked the same, gentle and slow and lovely. Wasn't it supposed to appear smaller now? Shabbier? Wasn't that the way he was supposed to see it?

He'd stop when they came back through, he decided, suddenly angry at the emotions pressing on the closed door of his heart. Or maybe not even then. *Agua pasada no muele molino*, after all. Water that's passed doesn't turn the mill.

A gravel road became dirt, and the trees closed in around the car. They had left Road 2 behind and were climbing again. The LTD began to bottom out in the potholes.

"Chinga!" swore Delgado, who was beginning to tweak as the meth wore off. "Watch the goddamn road, *cabrón!"* Esteban could tell the boy's nerves were in a sorry state.

"Nearly there." Alejandro nursed the car past a long vertical rut, and then they turned into a clearing.

A series of *plantios* lay along the riverbank, shaded by trees. Esteban saw they were all marijuana stands, with no greenhouse in evidence. Apparently the poppies were grown somewhere else.

El Hechicero—called the Wizard in honor of a successful twenty-year avoidance of the law—waited for them beside his Mercedes roadster. "Alejandro!" he called out as they climbed from their car. *"Qué tal, amigo? Queréis echar un trago?"*

"Always," answered Alejandro, switching over into Spanish. "But only if it's cold."

"A beer, then," said El Hechicero. "Carta Blanca?" He was a small man, no more than Esteban's height, with coal black hair and beard. Oddly, his eyes were a clear light green.

Esteban and Chuey Delgado unloaded the suitcases from the trunk. There'd been no problem bringing them into Juarez, and there'd be no problem taking the merchandise back into Texas at Piedra Quemadura Crossing. *La mordida*—the bite—had done its job on both sides.

Later, after some cold beer and an excellent meal of paella that El Hechicero produced from a generator-powered refrigerator, Esteban and Delgado loaded a series of very heavy canvas bags while the adults lay in the shade.

"The young one is strong, yes?" said the Wizard. "Skinny and small, but very strong."

"Maybe. But not like the giant American, Ware." Gualterio Covarrubias spoke for the first time in hours, and flexed a huge arm that was more fat than muscle. "Or like me."

Esteban froze in the middle of transferring a bleach-scented bag, then loaded it and moved closer to the lounging men.

"Like you," Alejandro jeered. "You and Ware? In your grandest dreams, my friend. In your finest, wettest dreams."

El Hechicero laughed at Covarrubias's scowl. "Never mind, Gualito," he said. "What's important now is the mind. It's the age of technology. Of the airplane, and soon the computer."

"Technology!" snorted Alejandro. "My immense testicles, technology. Let me tell you a story. You know Pete Archuleta?"

"Of course," said El Hechicero derisively. "An amateur, but ambitious. He farts higher than his ass."

"A month ago he was flying pot into New Mexico in his new Cessna, okay? Many bails to a spot southwest of Las Cruces. Flying at night, looking for a signal light."

"Of course," said the Wizard again. "I have a plane that—"

"No, no. Listen. So, on the ground some dumb-ass clod farmer heads for his outhouse to take a crap, right? And, because it's dark and his outhouse is full of black widows, he turns on his flashlight."

"Liar!" The bearded man began to laugh.

"No, I swear it. Pete sees the flashlight and thinks it's the drop signal. Bombs away go the bails of pot. Flattened that damn outhouse and the clod farmer inside it. Technology!" He took a sip of his beer.

"No, not technology." El Hechicero laughed. "Pete Archuleta's what that was, and Pete has absolutely nothing to do with technology. Amateurs are like cockroaches, my friend. It's not what they carry off to eat that's so bad, it's what they fall into and fuck up. I tell you right now, in a few years computers will do it all for us."

They went on while Esteban and Delgado finished loading the trunk. Nothing else was said about the man Ware, but Esteban knew what was needed, and soon. A quiet conversation with Gualterio Covarrubias.

First he saw the priest, and then he saw Jorge.

"Stop a minute, please," he said, trying to keep his voice casual.

"Here?" Alejandro looked out at Bavispe's main street. "Why? You have to pee?"

"Someone I know." Esteban opened the door, releasing a flood of cold air.

"I suppose," the driver grumbled, and pulled to the side. "But make it fast. And shut the damned door."

Jorge had grown tall like Pascual, over six feet, and his

thin chest had filled out a little. His eyes widened in astonishment.

"Esteban?"

He started to run toward his brother, then he saw the LTD and stopped. The priest whispered something in his ear, and his expression changed.

"Jorge, what's wrong?" Esteban had also started forward. Then, in the hollow of his back he felt a single, icy drop of sweat that trickled down his spine. He'd seen that look before.

"You're Jorge's brother." The priest was young, which probably meant old Father León was dead. "The one who was lost in the States."

"Yes, Father . . ."

"Brother. Brother Patricio Baca. You've been away from Mother Church a long time, young man." He glanced at the car. "Who are your friends?"

"Jorge . . ." Esteban turned to his brother. "I hoped you were alive, and happy. And home here in Bavispe."

The tears welled up in Jorge's eyes.

"Your friends?" said the priest again. His face was set in grim lines.

"May I s-speak with him, Brother Patricio?" Jorge looked down at the small man. There was meek supplication in his face.

"And then with me," snapped the priest. He stared coldly at Esteban. "You are no longer welcome here," he said. "You, or your friends." Then he stalked away.

"Can you talk awhile?" Jorge glanced nervously at the waiting car.

"Awhile." Esteban stepped near his brother, but didn't touch him. "You've lost your . . . I mean, you speak very well."

"Mostly." Jorge forced a weak smile. He wore a small mustache with waxed ends. "Brother P-Patricio's helping me with that. I thought you wu-were probably dead."

"Sometimes nearly." Esteban groped for common ground. Anything. This was his only family now. "There were a few times. . . ."

"Those men." Jorge looked at the LTD. "In their expensive c-car. They're drug smugglers, aren't they?"

Esteban considered the lie, then dismissed it. "Yes," he said.

"And you also?"

"No. Not really. I . . ."

"What, then?" Jorge's face drooped, and the tears were there again. "If not, then what?"

"I . . . I'm just with them for now. I had some trouble in El Paso. An Anglo girl . . ."

"Trouble." Jorge's smile was bleak. "Trouble, yes. Do you want to know our tu-trouble here, Esteban? People like you. Drug smugglers."

"I told you . . ."

"That you're just *with* them. And what's in the trunk of their big car, brother?"

Esteban was silent.

"Drugs come through here," Jorge continued in a flat monotone. "From the m-mountains to Juarez and Nogales. Marijuana, heroin, even cocaine now. What are you carrying tu-today, Esteban?"

"Jorge . . ."

"They pay off the police in the bigger towns. The Bite, remember? But then the c-customs agents come here, and the American DEA. They spray herbicides on the fields. All the fields. Crops die along with the marijuana. Our crops."

"Jorge, listen." Esteban took his brother's arm. It was rigid beneath the loose shirt sleeve. "I told you, I'm just with them for now. I'm trying to find the ones who killed our family back there in the canyon. I'm going to find them. . . ."

"I thought you were probably du-dead," said Jorge. "Your life and mine are no longer the same."

"I know that."

Jorge looked up at the brown hills surrounding the town. "This place," he said. "This place . . ." He looked back at Esteban. "At first, I pretended you'd come back. Any d-day, I said to myself. Any day. But you never came."

Esteban nodded. "I couldn't," he said. "But my thoughts were always with you, brother. And I hoped the very best for you."

"Brother Patricio helps me, and I hu-help him. I wanted to be a priest, too, but I was too stupid. . . ."

"No! No, you're not."

"Uneducated, then. But I'm a lay brother now, and h-help him help them. The ones your friends have destroyed."

"Jorge, they're not my friends."

The tall young man stepped back from Esteban. A single tear had broken free, and slid down into his waxed mustache.

"Go on, Esteban," he said. "You have to go with them, and I have to get b-back to my work. If you ever find those men . . ."

"I will. I swear to God I will."

". . . I hope it makes you happy." He started to turn away. "Esteban?"

"Yes?"

"I'm gu-glad you're not dead, Esteban."

Then he hurried away up the street, and Esteban could see Pascual Santiago in his brother's long strides.

"Who was that skinny fool?" asked Chuey Delgado, and Esteban took a deathgrip on his emotions. Be still. Be still.

"Just someone I used to know," he answered. "When I was a kid."

"All done, then?" Alejandro's voice had a sarcastic edge. "These reunions are sweet, but we have a job to do."

They drove up the hill toward the Divide and the desert that lay on its eastern side. Esteban sat in the air-conditioned car and thought how difficult it would be to explain to these men if he cried.

But that was no problem, because he never cried.

FIFTEEN

Piedra Quemadura lay southeast of El Paso. Alejandro reached it by returning to state 45, then following a series of gravel roads that roughly paralleled the Rio Grande. The LTD drove into a narrow canyon a little before dusk, and even at that time of day, the July temperature was over one hundred degrees.

Piedra Quemadura—Burning Rocks—was the name given to the towns on both sides of the one-lane bridge. In Mexico it was a group of mud huts and ancient autos sitting up on blocks. Two skinny dogs shuffled down the road, their brains so blasted by the heat they didn't bother to move aside when the car roared past.

At the bridge, on both sides, the stop was quick and perfunctory. Clearly, the bite was in.

Piedra Quemadura, Texas, was a different story from its namesake across the Rio. Just as hot but not so dry, not with water sprinklers and Bermuda-grass lawns everywhere.

Esteban looked around in astonishment. In between two ravaged adobe buildings sat a huge Colonial-style house with towering pink columns along its front. Farther down was a two-story brick with a late-model Cadillac in the driveway. He saw several others that were similar, nearly obscene opulence surrounded by squalor. El Hechicero's Mercedes was in front of one of them, a multilevel chunk of redwood and glass. He'd taken the shortcut through El Paso.

"Surprised, boy?" Alejandro glanced into his rearview mirror. "Hey, this is a special town. There's only one industry in Piedra Quemadura, if you follow my meaning."

They pulled up behind the Mercedes, and Esteban saw the small, bearded man come out of the garage with a huge Anglo. For an instant, his pulse leaped. But the man was old.

"So, Mr. Craddock." Alejandro shifted into English for the first time since the *plantio.* "Think it'll rain?"

"Not unless I shove one a these lawn sprinklers up some buzzard's ass 'n set him flyin'," the big man said in a booming voice that reminded Esteban of Brother Axton. "Who's the new blood?"

"Him?" Chuey Delgado nodded toward Esteban. "His name's Santiago. *Un hombre taciturno.*"

"The silent one," said Craddock.

"Hey, your Spanish progresses, amigo!" said El Hechicero, and the big man beamed at the praise. "This one, he got too close to a little blond *hija* with a big blue-eyed father. You comprende statutory rape, of course."

"Oho!" Craddock laughed. *"La rubia,* huh?" He slapped Esteban hard on the shoulder. "An' now you're runnin' dope, I see. Better be careful. I'll tell ya what dope does, sonny. Dope's what persuades ya to carve up Granny with the butter knife. Jus' move the stuff, don't let it take ya over, like Chuey there."

"Su madre," muttered Delgado under his breath.

"God rest her soul." Craddock fixed the boy with a long cool stare, and Chuey quickly looked away. "Ah, well. That's another story, I guess. Drive into the garage, Alejandro"—he pronounced it "Alley-hand-dro"—"an' we'll let these young bucks get us unloaded."

Melvin Craddock's basement led off the garage. When all the sacks lay on the floor, he cut carefully into one.

"Meskin Brown," he announced, and touched his tongue to the knife. "You gents are a real bargain, y'know? Some a those airplane jocks're gettin' ten, fifteen grand a hop for this stuff. You boys keep beatin' their prices, I'll keep ya in all the work you can handle."

Alejandro shrugged. *"Hay qué trabajar para comer,"* he said.

"Ain't it the truth?" Craddock nodded. "Even me. I gotta work to eat, too. Speakin' of which, you boys have yourselves some beans in the kitchen, then you can bed down by the Rio. It's a mite cooler down there at night. We'll start steppin' on this stuff in the mornin'."

* * *

After dark, it did cool off a little. That was the way of these Texas canyons, Esteban remembered. He lay on a ratty blanket and listened to the Rio Grande gurgle past a few yards away. The night sky was still hazy from the day's heat.

And Jorge's words were there, in his mind.

People like you, his brother had said. Drug smugglers, he'd said.

Where has it all led me? Esteban silently asked Pascual, but there was no answer there. Where had it all gone? From a little boy following his grandfather's dream of *La Corona de Colorado* to a canyon of death. From a workhouse that called itself a church to an Anglo girl without a soul . . .

Steve, she'd called him. Not Esteban, or even Stephen. Steve St. James. Her name was Allison Brock, and he'd fallen in love.

It wasn't hard to do, and he'd certainly had company, because Allison Brock was small and pretty and blond, with breasts that looked too large for her slim figure. Her family had moved in from Lordsburg, New Mexico, and her father bought out Belcher Automotive, a chain of auto-parts stores.

Allison was an instant hit with the local boys and just as instantly despised by the girls, who passed the rumor she was built like that because she'd had a baby over in Lordsburg. But Allison just smiled and did the right things— like not running for cheerleader, which she'd have won in a walk—and the other girls finally accepted her.

She could have taken her pick of the high-school studs, but after a long look at the lean features of Esteban Santiago, a.k.a. Stephen St. James, she shocked Anglo El Pasans to their unliberated cores by going after the boy from Brother Axton's sweatshop. Not that Esteban was a bad kid, understand, but his kind was supposed to date little señoritas, not big-breasted blondes.

She blew his senses away. At fifteen she was two years younger, but her sexual experience far exceeded his, and he discovered realities that made his lonely fantasies

seem tame. He also discovered condoms for the first time.
Allison Brock was nothing if not practical.

So he became Steve St. James, boyfriend of Allison
Brock. For a time he began to forget Charlie and Agustin
and Ware. Even the Smiling Man. Maybe there was more
to life . . .

He went into the headquarters of the Brock Automotive chain on a Saturday morning. Bob Brock, behind the
counter, looked just like his TV ads except for one thing.
He was always smiling on TV.

"Mr. Brock? Hi, I'm Steve St. James. Allison said you
wanted to talk to me."

Brock was a big man, heavy frame just beginning to
overload. He had large hands, meticulously clean, with a
multitude of old scars. Mechanic's hands.

"Yeah, I did. Thanks for coming in . . . Steve." The
man's eyes slid up and down him, then cut away. "The
thing is, you and Allison've been seeing a lot of each other
lately." Brock looked embarrassed, and Esteban felt the
tension in his stomach seize up like a rope pulled taut.

"Yes, sir. I guess we—"

"Might as well get this said," Brock interrupted. "I
don't see any easy way to do it. I want you to stay away
from my daughter."

He finally looked directly at Esteban. His eyes were
china blue.

"Excuse me? I don't . . ."

"You heard me. Look, I've got nothing against you personally, okay? I expect you're a nice kid, but that doesn't
change things. Fact is, your real name's Esteban Santiago.
And there's nothing gonna change that."

Esteban felt a hot flush burn his face. "That's true," he
forced out through a tightening throat. "And what you're
saying is I'm not good enough for Allison. Is that right?"

Brock exhaled deeply. "Well, hell," he finally said. "You
just won't take it the easy way, will you? Okay then, let's
talk plain."

He leaned across the counter and pointed an index
finger the size of an expensive cigar at Esteban's chest.
"You may be one helluva fine boy," he said. "You probably are. But you're not white, and you're not ever gonna

be white no matter what you call yourself. Now, Allison's gonna finish high school and then she's going to college. She's gonna have the very best 'cause I've worked my butt to the bone to give it to her. And that just doesn't leave any room for a Meskin boyfriend. You comprende, amigo?"

The man stopped suddenly, and Esteban saw his big hands were shaking. He put them on the counter to steady them.

"Look, I'm sorry," said Brock. "I don't mean to be unfair. I've got nothing against you people. Never have had. But this is my daughter we're talking about, and that's the way it's gonna be."

Later, Allison was sitting on the front steps of her house when Esteban walked up. She was wearing a tight tank top without a bra, and he felt a familiar heat.

"I'm real sorry, Steve," she said, after he described the meeting with her father. "I just knew he was gonna do that."

"Allison, what happens now?" He touched her bare arm. "I love you."

"Steve . . ."

"Listen, I have some money saved up. We could . . ."

"No." She shook her head mournfully and, for the first time, Esteban recognized the gesture as a tiny bit theatrical. "No, I guess it just wasn't meant to be, Steve. I guess we always knew we come from . . . from two different worlds."

Two different worlds? What was this soap-opera crap? And that was when it hit him with the full impact of prescient knowledge. She was just acting. Had been all along. Playing *Romeo and Juliet*.

"Allison . . ."

"Steve, please don't make it harder." And then she sighed, for God's sake. "It's better if you go now."

And, in that moment, Esteban realized he wasn't really angry, and that he didn't feel sorry for himself. In a flash of unconnected wisdom beyond his seventeen years, he felt sorry for Bob Brock.

A month later, he heard she was pregnant.

The day after that, the police came to Brother Axton's

looking for Esteban Santiago. A fifteen-year-old white
girl was pregnant, and a Mexican boy was wanted for
statutory rape. The fact the boy was only seventeen himself didn't appear to be a consideration.

Two days after that, Esteban found Chuey Delgado
stoned and puking up beer in a doper hangout near the
river. Or rather, they found each other.

Esteban rolled over in the thin blanket and wondered
who was really the father of Allison Brock's aborted baby.
He stretched and looked up at the stars, clearer now as
the night cooled off.

Personally, his money was on Kevin Robbins from the
baseball team. Too bad about the abortion because good
old Kevin was just as fair and blue-eyed as Allison herself.
Not that a blond baby would have kept Esteban out of
gladiator school—the juvenile reformatory—if Papa
Brock caught up with him.

It was better this way. Allison was in the past. Brother
Axton Gilbert's Christ Jesus Eternal Church and School
was in the past. And now, Jorge and the little village of
Bavispe were in the past.

Back to the hunt.

He raised up on one elbow. Chuey Delgado tossed in
his sleep a few yards away, and up the slope toward some
stunted mesquites, he saw Alejandro's blanket. And Gualterio Covarrubias a little farther on.

For all his genial humor, Melvin Craddock didn't allow
Mexicans to sleep in his house. It was understood. They
could have bunked in one of the old buildings that inter-
spersed the fancy homes of the drug lords, but those were
too hot inside. Also full of rattlesnakes.

It was time for a quiet chat with Gualterio Covarrubias.
A talk about a man named Ware. Esteban felt the hard
weight of his knife along his hip.

It would blow him with the others, but that was okay.
He'd already decided to find a phone and call the Border
Patrol on his way out. The smugglers were scum, even
the rich man Craddock, and their touch had stained him.
Jorge would never know about it, but it would make
Esteban feel a little better to bring them down.

He never got the chance.

Blinding lights flashed in his face just as he was crawling to his knees. Then the riverbed was a sea of light and noise . . .

"THIS IS THE BORDER PATROL! BORDER PATROL! YOU'RE UNDER ARREST! LIE FLAT ON YOUR STOMACHS AND PUT YOUR HANDS BEHIND YOUR HEADS!"

. . . and helicopters whirling down from the bluff above the town. Hovering overhead and beating sand up into his face. More lights glaring down on him . . .

"BORDER PATROL! BORDER . . ."

. . . as Chuey Delgado leaped to his feet and fired upward with an old revolver. A spray of gunfire stitched the boy from right to left across his belly, but the Methedrine in his system held him erect long enough to shoot out one of the 'copter's lights before a second burst tore away his throat . . .

"PUT DOWN YOUR WEAPONS! WE WILL KILL YOU WHERE YOU STAND! PUT DOWN YOUR WEAPONS. . . ."

. . . and Alejandro and Gualterio Covarrubias ran for the Rio. The river was only knee deep, but it slowed them enough. Crimson bursts exploded across Covarrubias's broad back and he splashed headfirst, bobbing in muddy water that was spreading a darker stain around him.

No! Esteban started to rise to his feet. *Mierda*, not Covarrubias! Not yet . . .

Then he thought the better of it and flopped forward on the sand, fingers laced behind his head, under the glare of the searchlights. Which was why he only heard them kill Alejandro. He didn't see it.

The others were dead, including the Wizard, found slumped over the wheel of his Mercedes, his magic run out. And Esteban Santiago was left to take the fall.

It was over quickly enough. Two months in the Caliente County jail awaiting trial, and a lawyer who promised only that he'd get to prison alive if he never mentioned Melvin Craddock's name. A prearranged guilty plea in exchange for a shorter sentence, and then the first surprise. He wasn't going to the reformatory, after all. He was going to the federal prison at Bazilak. To El Pozo.

Don't worry about that, said the lawyer. You've done right by a certain party, and that party will take care of things. Ten and ten concurrent's nothing to a tough kid like you. You'll be out in seven or eight, max, with good time. Maybe less. You can do that long standing on your head, right?

Como que no? Why not? Be quiet and stay alive, and out of the long reach of the rich man's killing net. Stay alive and tough it out and wait. And add another name to the list.

Melvin Craddock.

SIXTEEN

The buildings sat at the bottom of a large, bowl-shaped depression in the middle of nowhere, three stories high and radiating out like a starfish from a central core. For a quarter mile in all directions up the dusty slopes, slash and burn was the rule. Nothing but stunted weeds grew out from the base of a ten-foot-high fence, topped by rolls of razor wire, and even those weeds were systematically torched when they reached ankle height. The place was Bazilak Federal Correctional Facility, or just the Baz. But Hispanic prisoners, who made up one third of its population, referred to it as El Pozo. The Hole.

Esteban pushed the olympic bar to arm's length and pulled in a gulp of air. His triceps quivered with the strain.

"Okay, Herculito," said Raul, in English for the benefit of the grinning onlookers. "For your little brown virgin asshole. *Otro más.*"

Esteban flashed his own grin and lowered the weight again. It was too much, three reps past his best, and he'd have to cheat it up. He felt his hamstrings and quadriceps tighten as his butt came off the bench.

"Unnhh . . . No!"

"Yes." Raul didn't take the bar.

It reached the sticking point, hung there a second, then moved. Slowly . . .

"Shittt!"

. . . slowly, and then up. Up to arm's length.

"Otro más." Raul laughed, but he was only kidding this time. He reached for the bar, took it to the rack.

"Pendejo," moaned Esteban, and sat up gasping for air. He felt light-headed, and his pectorals were aflame.

"Hey, little friend." Raul slapped him on a quivering shoulder. "Hey, you listen to the coach now. Have I led you wrong so far?"

Esteban grinned again and glanced toward Odell Granger. "Only when you sent me to shower with the Masai Brotherhood."

"Es mentira!" Raul's big belly bounced with his laughter. "A lie, I swear it! And, even so, have you ever seen such *miembros* in your life?"

"Creo que no. Except perhaps on my grandfather's horses."

Which set Raul off on another journey of laughter as he helped Esteban unload the bar. With two hundred and seventy pounds, more muscle than fat, spread across his six-foot frame, he looked nearly as wide as he was tall.

Raul Galvan was fifty years old, and almost thirty years of hard time showed in his flat, scarred face. His big Pancho Villa mustache was mostly gray, as was his hair, and his right eyebrow was missing entirely from a chain's slash twenty years before. He was a lifer, a twice-convicted murderer who looked like every child's worst nightmare translated into the flesh, and he was Esteban Santiago's savior.

"Nine reps," he said, stepping into the shade to towel his huge chest. "Not so bad."

Esteban joined him. "You do the same with a hundred pounds more," he replied.

"En verdad. But I also outweigh you by that much. Compared to our sizes, you are stronger."

"Oh, yeah." Odell Granger looked back from moving the bar to the incline bench. "He stronger, all right, but odor ain't everthang." He gave a high-pitched giggle.

"Yo mama," Raul replied equably.

"Hey, you hear this fat ole fool?" Granger yelled at two other black men in the weight pen. "Firs' he be talkin' 'bout our me-em-bros, mainly 'cause he jealous, then about somebody's mama."

"Yeah, Odell," said one of the men. "You whup his big ass for us."

"Not me. I need some re-in-forcements."

"Say, we be wit'choo at the end, bro."

"Yeah, but whose end we talkin' 'bout here?"

And they were off, insults and laughter flying back and forth. Esteban sat in the shade with a smile, knowing nothing would come of it. Except when the Aryan Warriors were around, the weight pen was probably the most peaceful place in this violent world.

He'd changed in his five years within El Pozo. Not just physically, with the addition of forty-five pounds of muscle, but inside as well. When he remembered the boy whose love for a faithless Anglo girl had driven him out of El Paso and eventually to this place, he wanted to puke. It was a hardening of the body and the soul. Like Ware, he'd become hard and gleaming in body. And like the Shadow Man, he was relentlessly purging the softness in his soul.

He'd been nervous when they brought him inside, chained at the wrists and ankles and wearing a dirty jumpsuit from the Caliente County jail. He'd been humiliated when they stripped him to search every orifice before dousing him with disinfectant and shaving off his hair to get rid of lice. And he'd been plain scared when the building tender—the trustee for his wing—had shoved him into an empty cell.

"Sweetmeat, I'm gonna say this once." The BT was a tall, sinewy con named Juell Ulibarri. "This here is C Wing. I'm the boss of C Wing. You with me so far?"

Esteban had only managed a nod, which, as it turned out, was the best choice, anyway.

"Not the guards, and not the warden. Just me." Ulibarri had a tattoo of a small blue-edged dagger directly beneath his lower lip, and it moved in the cleft of his chin when he spoke. "Anything happens, you tell me. Anything you think anyone needs to know, it means I need to know. Follow?"

Esteban nodded again.

Ulibarri nodded, too. "Now, understand, I don't give a shit what your thing is. I don't care if it's doin' dope or paintin' butterflies or pumpin' up or beatin' off, as long as it's not children. If you were in for messin' with little kids, I'd already know it, and we'd feed your balls to you. Otherwise, you're on your own. And I might as well tell you, lookin' young and tender as you do, you're probably in for some hard times. I'm sorry about that, but it's your problem to solve. Gettin' yourself an old man might help."

Ulibarri had turned to go, then stopped at the door. "Main thing you need to remember's not to make me look bad. You keep that in mind. As BT's go, I'm a pretty mellow guy, but don't ever make me look bad in front of the men, sweetmeat. I got too much ridin' on it. You're gonna feel about as welcome as a turd in a punch bowl if that ever happens."

Esteban pulled the stained towel over his head and watched Raul Galvan curling a one-hundred-and-eighty-five pound barbell out in the sun. Sweat rolled down the big man's body, pooling and spreading at the waist of his white trousers.

He'd gotten himself an old man, all right, but not in the way the BT had meant it.

The cells in C Wing stood open most of the time, and the men congregated in the corridor except during lockdowns. During those relatively free periods the guards, even with their yard-long black batons, didn't venture in there, and Juell Ulibarri represented the only law. Esteban had been crouched at the back of his cell that first day. His cellmate, a thin old man named Lopez who had the tattoos of chains around his wrists, was down the corridor with some other prisoners.

And then the open cell door had filled with the body of a huge man. Esteban had leaped back in terror against the wall, knocking his new tube of toothpaste into the toilet almost before he realized what he was doing. A wave of blind panic sealed his lungs shut.

"Get away from me, you bastard!" he screamed, his voice cracking into a soprano wail. "You get away from me, you hear? You touch me and I'll bite off your nuts and shove them up your ugly asshole!"

And then he sank down onto one trembling knee.

"*Aiee, vato loco!*" said Raul Galvan. "And, clearly, a most dangerous man."

And then he'd smiled.

"Juell's jugging some new meat," said Philip Espinosa, and the other men fell silent.

There were four of them, Raul and Esteban along with the old man Lopez and Espinosa. Because they'd never joined *Hermanos de la Fuego*—the Brothers of the Fire—and mostly because everyone in the wing was afraid of Raul Galvan, they were left alone. The Hermanos were the largest gang in C Wing, with only a few Masai and Aryan Warriors (who referred to the Hermano as the Lubricanos—meaning grease), so Raul and his friends were usually left in peace.

"White guy?" asked Lopez. Although Ulibarri's accent was pure cracker, he was at least half-Hispanic and it was the Warriors who feared him the most. One of his favorite tune-ups involved a urine-filled toilet and the offender's head. Juell was rangy thin, but he was strong.

"Yeah," answered Espinosa. "Some little shitkicker with a neck as red as the warden's ass. He started giving Juell mouth right away. Called him a spic half-breed. He's paying that off right now."

"A new recruit for the Warriors," observed Esteban.

"For certain. And this is one cowboy who'll need their protection. The word is he ran illegals on the Rio. And that he killed some of them."

Esteban felt a sourness like the taste of old pennies slide up into his mouth. "Did you hear his name?" he asked, and a part of him, a part buried deep and ancient whispered *Please.* . . .

"No," answered Espinosa, a chubby, open-faced young man doing his second turn for forgery. "And after Juell's done touching him up, he may not remember it either. He's just another shitkicker, Esteban. Oh, one funny thing. He has these scabs all over the backs of his hands. Like burn marks, you know?"

Charlie Pellikern didn't have the faintest idea who Esteban was.

He saw the little cowboy the next day, being escorted by Matt Nabors, the main Warriors goon in C Wing. Pellikern was bruised and swollen, but cocky as ever, and the years hadn't changed him much other than to deepen the crow's-feet around his pale little eyes. He looked Esteban up and down when they passed, and no recognition at all flickered on his face.

Which conceived the beginning germ of a plan.

Nabors was a big man, slabby thick but undefined, who used the weight pen only when it was free of those people he called hybrid mud. His tattoos tended toward slogans: KKK, WARRIORS RULE, and PURE ARYAN, along with the inevitable ritual markings such as swastikas and a German iron cross. He walked with a beefy arm around Charlie Pellikern's shoulder, marking his claim, and whispered in the cowboy's ear.

When Esteban saw the small man, he felt a smothering eagerness that nearly took his breath.

To see the cowboy Charlie . . .

"That man," said Raul. "You know him."

Since it wasn't a question, Esteban gave no reply.

He followed Pellikern from a distance for several days. He watched him talking and laughing with the Aryan Warriors, and he saw him when he was alone in the yard. And, on one occasion, he watched the cowboy sitting with a cigarette, occasionally touching its glowing end to the backs of his hands. He saw Pellikern's mouth tighten as he smelled the faint, sweet singe of burning flesh. And, above the cowboy's tight slash of a grin, he saw the man's shrieking, feverish eyes. Whatever his reason for burning himself, it had nothing to do with pleasure.

And the plan expanded in Esteban's mind.

"Always you watch that man," said Raul one day. "The Aryans have noticed you."

"As you said, I know him," answered Esteban. "Do you want to hear it?"

"It's not my business." Raul studied him with dark eyes. "But be careful."

"If I needed a favor." Esteban put his hand on Raul's thick shoulder. "Something very large. And if my reason was good . . ."

"Tell me what you want."

The hoe squad, dressed in all whites, moved along a row of dying cotton, turning up weeds. A thin layer of dust rose around them and settled on sweaty skin. By midmorning all of them, including Odell Granger and the other blacks of C Wing, were a uniform gritty tan. The dust gathered in the creases of their faces, in the folds of their eyelids, in their ears and mouths and noses. Mosquitoes and biting flies hovered and landed and drew blood, and a pause to wipe or scratch without permission was an invitation to the Strikers—trustees assigned to see that everyone kept up.

When they reached the brow of a hill with a grove of scraggly post oaks nearby, Esteban slipped into the spot next to Charlie Pellikern.

"Hey, José, a little breathin' space here," muttered Pellikern, not looking up from his work. "Shee-it, you stink like three hogs in a closet."

"I have something for you," said Esteban in English. He hooked the hoe's edge under a milkweed root and flipped it loose. "I have something for you from your boss."

"Say what?"

Esteban took a chance. *"Un hombre malo,"* he said. "With the coin of Colorado gold."

"Yeah?" Pellikern moved along the row. "El Gavilán's a bad hombre, all right. I noticed you been watchin' me. What is this, the Meskin Mafia Network?"

"Later. *Esta noche.* And alone." Esteban moved away. Beneath the thin white shirt, his arms were trembling with the desire to drive the hoe's sharp corner down into the cowboy's skull. Right then and there. His hatred made him clumsy, and he stumbled when he walked back to his own spot in the line.

"Did you do it?" asked Raul at the lunch break. They sat together in the shade of the trees while armed guards rode past on sleek, grain-fed horses.

"Yes."

The big man's scarred brow furrowed. "This is something you want very badly, my friend. Very badly. I haven't asked you why, and I won't."

"I'll tell you."

"It's not my business. I said that already. I don't want to know. But some will be hurt before it's done, and some could die. And one of them could be you. Do you want it as badly as that?"

Beneath layers of dirt, Esteban's face was a grim mask.

"Worse," he said.

Near sunset the Aryan Warriors always used the weight pen. There were eight of them there with Matt Nabors. Charlie Pellikern would have made nine, but he wasn't there.

"Say, Nabors." Odell Granger stepped into the pen. "You know why rednecks have lips?"

Nabors looked up in astonishment. "What?"

" 'Cause otherwise they couldn't say Bubba," finished Odell with a grin.

"Well, kiss my cock an' call it Nathan!" Nabors let the E-Z Curl bar fall onto the cement floor. "What're you doin' in here, nigger?"

"Say, thass cold, man," said Odell. Behind him, a half-dozen blacks moved along the waist-high rail. "Hey, I'm just checkin' somethin' out. My man Thomas made me a bet."

"Thass right." Thomas was well over six feet tall and thickly muscled. He leaned on the rail.

"Yeah? What kinda bet?" Nabors sneered. "Somethin' about which a you coons I'm gonna open a can a stomp-ass on first?"

"Naw, man. Nothin' like that. My man here bettin' me that you redneck Nazis got dicks the size of a cigarette."

"Winston filter tips." Thomas nodded. "Extra-shawts."

His grin was easy, but he was rolling a loose dumbbell bar back and forth beneath the sole of his sneaker.

"Yeah?" Nabors's wide face creased in a hard, knowing grin, and he reached with one hand inside his sock. "An' how you jungle bunnies figure to find that out? Slip one in your mouth for size?"

"Maybe just take down your pants for a look, *cabrón.*" Raul Galvan stepped into the pen, and Nabors went ashen pale. "Maybe we'll just take a peek at little Nathan for ourselves."

"Okay, José. What's the story . . . ?" Charlie Pellikern stepped into the empty cell and turned just before Esteban hit him between the eyes with a sand-filled sock. His head hit the floor before the rest of him, but he was cowboy tough and not finished yet. He lashed out with one foot as Esteban bent forward. His boot heel, notched for easier tracking if he escaped, slammed into Esteban's nose, breaking it cleanly just before the sand sap caught him again. In the temple and much harder this time. It knocked him cold.

Esteban rocked back on his heels, blood pouring down his shirt. The pain was more than he'd thought possible. He couldn't breathe, his eyes watered shut.

But there wasn't time for it now. It would have to wait. He dragged Pellikern to a bunk and dumped him onto it, then stripped him naked. He used white rags that Lopez had shredded in the laundry to tie the small man's ankles and wrists. He tied them tight, and the cowboy's hands and feet diffused an ugly purple. Then he pressed a clean strip of cloth against his bleeding nose. The pain was like festering shards of glass.

Pellikern began to moan. There was a trickle of blood leaking from his left ear.

"You are one dead greaser," he said, and his tone was almost conversational. "You know that, boy?"

"Esteban. Not boy." Esteban sat on the edge of the bunk. "Not anymore."

"Ess-stay-bun's ass. You're still dead, José."

"Esteban Santiago. Grandson of Pascual Santiago."

Blood dripped from Esteban's nose down onto the cowboy's bare chest.

"Deader'n a taco with shitbugs on it. You better untie—"

"Pascual Santiago." Esteban leaned forward and saw that Pellikern's left eye was beginning to bulge, filling with blood behind the eyeball. "The man you murdered for the coin."

"I don't give a—" Then Pellikern stopped cold. "Wait a minute." The cowboy studied him. "Wait a minute. You're that goddamn little kid, ain'cha? The one in the canyon . . ."

Esteban smiled.

"Holy jumpin' Jesus," Pellikern whispered. "That goddamn little kid. I told Ware . . ." His good eye cut up at Esteban. "What're you gonna do to me? Nabors . . ."

"He's not coming."

"He's . . . not . . . coming." Pellikern nodded slowly. "Well, shee-it. What're you gonna do to me?"

"That's easy enough," said Esteban. "I'm going to ask you some questions, and then I'm going to kill you. But you already knew that."

"So do it then." When the cowboy grinned, there was a savage deadness in his face. "You know what someone told me one time, Ess-stay-bun? He said everthing changes sooner or later. Everthing passes on to somethin' new. Now, that's some pro-found thinkin', ain't it?"

"You know what I want. . . ."

"See, dyin's somethin' new, ain't it? Think about that, Ess-stay-bun. It's brand new ever time, to ever person. Fact is, those were the very words your old granpaw said right before we—"

"Calle la boca!"

Pellikern's grin widened as a trickle of blood slid down his chin. "Hey, I gotcha a good 'un, didn't I? Right in your goddamn greaser nose. Go ahead on, Ess-stay-bun. You think I'm scared to die?"

Esteban fought for the control he felt slipping away. He wanted to smash the tough little man, crush him. But not yet.

"What are those marks on your hands, Charlie?" he asked.

Pellikern's grin faded. "None a your goddamn—"

"You burn yourself. *Carne es quema*, yes? With your cigarette. Tell me, do you enjoy it?"

And then he saw what he'd looked for in the man's face. It was as he suspected.

Charlie Pellikern did it, all right. He did it compulsively and repeatedly. But he didn't enjoy it.

"Mira," he whispered. "Look at what I have, Charlie."

"Oh, Jesus," moaned the cowboy.

"It uses butane, you see?" Esteban flicked the lighter. "A tall, true flame."

"Oh, Jesus . . ."

"There are some things I want to know before you die."

"Jesus Christ . . ." Tears began to trickle down from the man's eyes. The left one was completely blood-engorged, the pupil invisible.

"The one you call El Gavilán. Where is he now? No? Then what if I put this cloth in your mouth so we won't be disturbed? What if this tall, true flame touches you . . . here?"

Pellikern bucked on the bed. His entire body rose into the air.

"It first makes a blister, doesn't it? And the hair around it crackles."

A low moan buffeted the gag in the man's mouth. The flow of blood from his nose and ear increased.

"Now, I'll take out the cloth, and I'll ask you again. Ware and El Gavilán. Where are they now?"

"El . . . Paso."

"Mierda. I lived in El Paso for nearly eight years, and always I searched for them. I looked everywhere. Why would they be in El Paso now?" He lowered the lighter again.

"No! Oh God, no! Please! Listen, they're lookin' for the others. The old men . . ."

"What old men? Why?"

"For the coins, goddammit! The old man . . . your grandfather. He wouldn't tell us where the gold is . . ."

A bursting pride filled Esteban, and for a moment he almost forgot the man tied to the bunk.

". . . an' we found out there were three others. One's been dead for years, but the other two're still alive. Valentin Portes and Soste Miel. They were there, with the coins. El Gavilán's lookin' for 'em."

Esteban felt laughter bubbling up. "You still haven't found it," he said. *"Vatos estupidos!* After all these years."

"Colorado. S'in Colorado . . ."

"Shit, I know that."

". . . someplace northeast a Durango. Someplace in the San Juan Mountains. Those old men know where it is. Your grandfather knew, but the old bastard wouldn't talk. Not even—"

"Not even when you tortured him? When you murdered him?" A thick blackness dropped over Esteban. It was the rage he'd held back, that he couldn't hold any longer.

"Cabrón!" He shoved the gag back into Pellikern's mouth. "You killed him! And you killed my mother . . ."

He saw the cowboy's face bulging in terror and pain, and the sight of it goaded him, took the last of his control.

". . . and my brothers and sister. Goddamn you! You killed my childhood. You killed my soul."

He thrust the bright flame, yellow tipped with blue, against the man's skin again. "And you think I'll just finish you now? Just let you die now? No! Not until you tell me everything . . ."

Pellikern's body thrashed on the bed, back and forth beneath the rising stench of burning flesh, and a high, bubbling squeal rose around the gag. Then he stopped.

"Not until you tell me . . ."

Esteban stopped, too.

"No! Dammit, no!" He yanked away the blood-soaked gag. The man's one good eye was glazing over, fixed on a light in the ceiling. "No, damn you! You don't get to die yet!"

His cry echoed down the empty corridor.

"Nooooo!"

* * *

Before the carnage was cleared in C Wing, four men were dead. Two of them were Aryan Warriors, one with a broken neck and the other with a dumbbell bar embedded two inches into his skull.

One of them was Raul Galvan, stabbed in the heart with a knife made from the metal frame of a bunk bed.

Under the assault of tear gas and high-pressure hoses, the prisoners broke combat and retreated into the wing where they set their mattresses afire. One such burning mattress lay atop the fourth body, that of Charlie Pellikern, until it finally smoldered out hours later. An examination of his corpse revealed only the torso-length burns, heaviest by far in his genital area, and an autopsy declared his death the result of a massive cerebral hemorrhage probably caused by a blow to the head.

The wing was locked down and the men who were damaged, more than a dozen all told, went to the infirmary. Those who could be directly linked to the battle in the weight pen had varying numbers of days deducted from their good time.

A week later there was a fifth fatality. The body of Matt Nabors was found before breakfast in the bathroom, his head wedged into a toilet. Since the wing was in lockdown, and only Juell Ulibarri and the guards had keys, it was a mystery that remained unsolved.

Esteban Santiago served seven years and ten months of his twenty-year sentence. He was paroled partly because of accumulated good time and a record that was spotless except for a broken nose received in a racially motivated attack, and partly because overcrowding through the penal system made his cell necessary for someone more dangerous than an insignificant drug runner. He was two months past his twenty-fifth birthday.

On the day he was released, he walked across a charred, dusty section of ground to the prison cemetery. The bodies buried there were those unclaimed. There were no headstones, only numbered wooden stakes. He went to number 1436 and stood there for a long time, but he didn't cry. Because he never cried.

Behind him, the bus horn honked. He turned, awkward in a too-small suit coat that hugged his muscular torso, and walked away with a new verse for the endless, rhythmless cadence that filled the corridors of his life.

For Cesar. For Pilar. For his mother and little Rodolfo. For his grandfather. For all the eleven souls lost on *El Jornado del Muerto.*

And for Raul.

The Watchful One

> The wind said,
> You know I'm
> The result of
> Forces beyond my control.
> —A. R. Ammons

SEVENTEEN

Because of its mountain barrier, sunrise poured unevenly into the basin. Light found the western walls first, in a jagged pattern mimicking the shapes of the opposite peaks, then slid across the dome of the Cupola, dissolving ice and patches of snow into running water. As the sun advanced, the entire basin began to thaw and flow in layers of movement and sound. From the walls of La Brujería, melting ice poured down in a series of waterfalls. And, in the frigid shadows of heavy forest, three men lay still.

One of them, Dale Cooper, had stiffened into an L-shape against the trunk of a tree. Rigor mortis had drawn his knees up toward his chest, and both his heels were suspended off the muddy ground. Above his head three magpies—large, splendid black-and-white birds—studied him silently and considered the mixed message of the man smell, which was dangerous, and the death smell, which was food. After a while they decided, and dropped down from the tree.

A quarter mile southwest and beyond the meadow below La Brujería, melting ice dripped from overhanging branches into Travis Leggett's face. He groaned and rolled onto his side, and his swollen forehead raked across a protruding root. The resulting stab of pain jolted his eyes open with a memory of something . . . the thunderclapper? Only he'd never dreamed it could hurt so much. Then his fingers touched oozing gashes in his scalp, and he knew it wasn't the thunderclapper at all. He lay there conscious, but only barely.

East of the river and up in the thick aspen growth near the top of Riqueza Crown, Stephen James was watching a small water snake thaw out. A variety called a striper, it lay by a lichen-coated rock a few inches from his left hand. Often in the spring, reptiles able to survive at this

153

altitude came out of hibernation too soon, and the cold nights froze them stiff. The lucky ones found the sun each day and managed a tenuous existence until summer.

Stephen lay flat on his stomach behind a deadfall of branches and rocks. He was less than one hundred feet from the canvas lean-to on the crown of the hill. Leggett's Mac-10 was balanced on the rock above the snake, its blunt nose pointed at the tent.

He'd dozed some, on and off, in the hours of darkness since his arrival at the camp, and his main regret was that he hadn't eaten a bite of food in over eighteen hours. He should have eaten in the cave, whether the girl wanted to or not.

If this was a *Rambo* movie, I'd just eat the snake, he thought. *Con permiso, Señor Culebra. Tengo mucha hambriento.* . . .

Only not quite that hungry yet, he decided.

After a while the sun rose high enough to send dappled light down through the branches, and a thin white mist began to rise from the ground. The striper gradually came to life and crawled away sluggishly across Stephen's hand, and mosquitoes began buzzing around his face. And still he lay and watched the tent.

Beth was pretending to be asleep. She lay motionless on an unzipped sleeping bag near the back of the lean-to. The smell of the dead boy a few feet away—Freddie? Was that his name?—was in her nostrils.

They hadn't bothered to tie her at all, and that contemptuous disregard had seemed almost as bad, at the time, as being caught. But that was stupid. All it really meant was that she was untied, and if they continued to underestimate her, so much the better.

She'd been exhausted, and she'd slept, and she was pretty sure that Cuellar and Ware had, too. Maybe they were asleep right now. She listened carefully.

There were faint, dripping sounds all around that came from the trees. There was the occasional flutter of birds' wings outside the lean-to, and there was the ever-present roar of the river below the hillside. And there was the slow murmur of someone's regular breathing not far away. Someone who was asleep.

She was about to crack one eyelid for a peek when she heard footsteps near the front opening. Then a steady splashing she recognized as the sound of someone urinating nearby and, along with it, Joseph Ware's voice singing quietly.

She heard the splashing stop, and the sound of a zipper. She consciously forced her features to relax. The other sound, the even breathing of a sleeper, continued from somewhere nearby, and Ware was still humming a familiar melody.

"You must remember this . . ." There was a creaking sound, and his voice was nearer. "What you really must remember, Buh-Buh-Bette, is *this*. Sleeping people shift around and get all manner of expressions on their faces. People pretending to sleep, on the other hand, lie very still. Until they're touched . . ."

Her eyes popped open. Ware was sitting on a stack of canvas sacks a few feet away.

"Touched. That must be the magic word," he said with that damned, ever-present smile.

"You son of a bitch!" She scrambled away. "You vile, murdering . . ."

"Now, that's harsh." Ware shook his head in mock sorrow. "After all, like the wind said: 'You know I'm the result of forces beyond my control.' I think that quote's from a guy named Ammons. Him, or maybe Madonna."

Beth slid back into a sharp-edged projection. "You keep your hands off me!"

"But that's not fair, is it?" He grinned. "After all, Freddie's much uglier than I am, and he has one of his hands on you."

The smell washed over her, and she turned to look into the dead boy's face, only inches from her own. His eyelids had shrunk back, exposing a flat, milky gaze, and his stiff fingers pushed through the bag against her shoulder.

She only partially stifled a scream.

"*Chinga!*" Cuellar bolted up into a seated position near the smoldering campfire. "What? What is it?" His thick gray hair was down in his eyes. Haunted eyes, like someone emerging from a bad dream.

"Nothing to get excited about." Ware glanced over at the other man. "Just Buh-Buh-Bette and Fuh-Fuh-Freddie. Together again."

Beth scrambled away from the body. But not too far away, because that would put her next to Ware.

"Mierda," muttered Cuellar, and ran a hand across his face. "What time is it?" Beth noticed he wore an expensive-looking watch.

Ware didn't seem to mind. "Six minutes before eight," he answered, glancing at his own wrist. "Did you have pleasant dreams?"

Cuellar paled beneath sallow skin. "Pleasant enough," he said curtly. "And you?" Beth felt an odd tension below the reply. Something between them, she thought. Something long-standing.

"Someone had to watch," said Ware, and she sensed a point had somehow been scored.

Cuellar didn't answer, but his face was set in a scowl when he walked outside to relieve himself.

"Hungry?" Joseph Ware turned back toward her. If he actually had been up all night, it didn't show. He looked rested and pleased with himself, and depressingly formidable.

Beth was so hungry that sparks of pain shifted in her midsection from stomach acids breakfasting on each other, but the thick smell of the body behind her tickled at the edge of her throat.

"No," she answered. "I'm not."

"That's amazing. What's it been, nearly twenty-four hours since you ate?"

"Maybe not." She tried for a flippant tone. "Maybe I ran into that Euell Gibbons guy. Remember him? Maybe I ate a pine tree."

Then she saw his smile broaden, and she knew she'd made a mistake.

"That gentleman's no longer among us," said Ware. "But it wouldn't surprise me if you ran into someone else who might've fed you. About this gun . . ." He drew Stephen James's pistol from a jacket pocket. "Now, I know what your late squeeze Dále Cooper was carrying, and it wasn't . . ."

Cuellar came back in, and Ware slipped the pistol into his pocket.

"Okay." Cuellar stood over her. He'd washed his face and combed his hair, but the gray stubble on his cheeks made him look old and tired. "Okay, we've wasted enough time, miss. I have some questions for you. Listen to them carefully. And, if you have any hopes for the future, you will answer with the truth."

Not so tired after all, Katie. And not so very polite, either. But these males of the Latin persuasion are known for their fiery temperaments, aren't they?

Jesus, Mother. Not now . . .

Stephen's nearby. He has to be. And he has the fat man's gun. Just stay calm and stall, and don't give anything away.

Beth sat very still and tried to clear her mind.

After he watched El Gavilán relieve himself and then reenter the tent, Stephen began to work his way forward. He could have killed his old enemy with a single shot, just as with Ware a few minutes earlier, and would have done so if they'd come out together. But, each time, one had remained inside with the girl, and her life would have been over in a second.

The mist was waist high around the camp now, feeding upon the wetness of the ferns and the fallen trees rotting on the ground. Stephen kept low, his black hair a shadow within the swirling whiteness. Across the deadfall and into the skunk cabbage on its other side. Closer to the lean-to and the faint sound of El Gavilán's voice. A buzzing swarm of mosquitoes followed, landing on his face and hands. He hardly knew they were there.

He strained to hear. What was being said inside could tell him how much they knew and what his next move should be. And whether or not Beth was still alive.

He listened for her voice. He didn't like admitting it was the girl he was listening for, but it was the truth. If they'd killed her, he'd . . .

He'd what? That was ridiculous. Either way, the end result was going to be the same.

He moved closer, clothes soaked from the humidity and the muddy ground. And he was listening so intently he didn't notice a large gray squirrel behind him break into a chattering run for the safety of a tree. Or what had frightened it.

"When you ran away yesterday," Cuellar was saying. "Where did you go? To the caves?"

"What caves?" Beth kept her expression neutral. "I hid in the woods. I dug under some brush where the cover would keep the rain off. I wish I could've found a cave."

"Oh?" Cuellar studied her. "I doubt that. I believe you were in the caves in the cliff face, and—"

"Cliff?" She put a touch of derision into her reply. But not too much. Try not to make him angry. "How would I climb a cliff? In the middle of a rainstorm? I told you—"

"I went down into the cave last night," Ware said to Cuellar. He smiled at Beth. "I searched it thoroughly. All the way to a small chamber at the back."

Beth felt a breath catch like hot iron in her throat. He knows. Oh, God, he knows. . . .

"And?" Cuellar stared at Ware.

Ware shrugged. "And it was just a cave. A hole in the cliff. And very difficult to reach, even with a rope."

Beth didn't look up at the big man. Why had he lied? What was he up to?

"So." Cuellar looked baffled for a moment, then back at her. "So, then the man who helped you escape has abandoned you. Where is he now?"

"What man?" Beth waited for Ware to expose her lies. He'd seen the gold and he had Stephen's gun. But he remained silent, smiling faintly.

"The only men with me were the men you murdered," she continued, trying to take the offensive and conjuring the image of the two bloated bodies outside the tent. "What are you doing here, anyway? Why would a man like you murder innocent people? My God, I believed in you! I believed—"

"My motivations are my concern." He cut her off easily. "And the questions will be mine as well." He fingered the gold coin hanging around his neck. "So, you'd have me believe you escaped all alone, *ser verdad?* That you ran away from my people, and that you hid all night without a trace. That you killed Cooper just like you killed that boy behind you in the sleeping bag, yes?"

"I didn't kill the boy!" Beth felt tears building behind her eyes. "He was alive—"

"He's not alive now, is he? So don't speak to me of murder." A thick pulse beat in Cuellar's throat. "And don't presume to judge me, either. Just tell me where to find Esteban Santiago."

"Who?" This time her reply was unforced sincerity. "I don't know who you mean."

"I don't think she does." Ware said it quietly. "I don't think she's ever heard of Esteban Santiago. Remember he no longer uses his Spanish name."

Stephen. Beth's mouth fell open, but Cuellar was looking at Ware and didn't see it. The big man nodded to her, amusement in his eyes.

"In English, that name means Stephen St. James," he said.

This time she was ready. "I've heard of Stephen James. The climber. What does he have to do with this?"

Cuellar's dark eyes were like flint. "You know him, then. You admit it."

"No, I don't know him. Don't you understand? He's well-known around here, and I said I'd heard of him. Lots of people around these mountains have heard of him, for God's—"

"Basta!" snapped Cuellar, and turned toward Ware. *"La cosa no va bien,"* he hissed, and Beth's high-school Spanish was good enough to know her time was running out.

Stephen. Jesus, Stephen, where are you?

The voice behind the canvas, El Gavilán's voice, was raised in anger. This thing is not going well, the Sparrow Hawk was saying. Enough is enough. Stephen knew the man was nearly through talking.

He checked the Mac a last time, and then levered up

onto one knee. If not for the girl, he could just open it up, empty the whole damned clip through the side . . .

If. To hell with if's. If it wasn't for the girl, he wouldn't be in this shape to begin with.

He was busy sliding sideways toward the lean-to's open end. He was occupied with the logistics of taking them down without hitting the girl, no mean feat because he was a lousy marksman. He was concentrating, getting centered like before a high-odds ascent, shutting away all outside distractions. All of which were poor excuses for not hearing Travis Leggett, he decided later, but better than none.

Only his reflexes saved his life. As he rose from his crouch a jay on a limb above exploded into squawking flight, and Stephen partially turned in time to glimpse a swollen, distended head and a jack-o'-lantern grin coming out of the white, rising mist. And the thick tree branch hurtling toward his head.

It was too late to duck it. He threw up his left arm to block, and tried to pull the automatic pistol around, but the branch was heavy and swung with raw hatred. It smashed his forearm aside and then slammed into his skull. He felt himself hit the canvas wall and felt it collapsing. He heard a shout from inside and then, in his own head, he heard Pascual's voice . . .

Tu ves, Esteban? The snake you fail to crush is the one that later bites you.

. . . and knew nothing more.

EIGHTEEN

Outside the lean-to, Cuellar paced back and forth in thin mist dissolving beneath sunlight. His voice was non-stop, his exultation limitless.

"Estoy muy borracho!" he shouted, and then began to laugh. "But this time not from liquor, *mi amigo*. Oh, no. I'm drunk with joy. You hear me? Right here I have it all

at last. Both Pascual's treasure and that little *cabrón* as well."

Joseph Ware stood nearby, his eyes flat on El Gavilán's face, hearing but not really listening. He wasn't surprised to feel mildly depressed since he knew the reason well enough. The game was winding down.

Two people sat inside the partly collapsed tent, both indifferent to Cuellar's ravings. Near the back Travis Leggett continued to stare down at the still figure in the sleeping bag. The odor no longer bothered him. He was used to it, and the escalating pain in his battered head made the smell a minor thing anyway. He'd placed a handkerchief over Freddie's face at first, to keep off the flies, but the boy looked so peaceful, so . . . quiet, that he'd removed it. There had been very few quiet things in Leggett's life, so he took some time for it before Trouble with a capital T reclaimed him again.

He rested one hand on Freddie's close-cropped head.

A few feet away, Beth cradled Stephen's body against her breasts. He was a terrible sight. A swiftly purpling lump on his forehead was merging with his other facial bruises. The gash where she'd scratched him was insignificant next to those other injuries, and they were just the ones on his head.

Cuellar had kicked him again and again, cursing in Spanish and wailing some woman's name. The fact that Stephen was unconscious seemed to make no difference at all. Cuellar had kicked him in the chest and the stomach and the groin. And in the ribs.

Beth listened to the hoarse rattle of his breathing. She knew the sound of broken ribs. Even Stephen's thick musculature hadn't been enough to withstand the enraged Cuellar's boots. She watched for the line of bloody froth at his lips that would signal a punctured lung.

And saw how absolutely still he lay.

"I heard recently," she whispered, leaning forward near his ear, "that people pretending to sleep lie very still. Until they're touched, that is . . ."

She saw a faint smile twitch at the corners of his mouth, and her heart contracted painfully as she rested her palm against his cheek.

So this is what it's like, she thought. All the bells and whistles. At this time and in this god-awful place, here it is. For all the good it'll do either of us now.

Sorry, Mother, but this is one bit of delicious irony you'll have to do without. We won't be sitting all starched and humble and waiting for you to decide if you ever really loved me or can tolerate him. Not this time.

Her eyes filled with tears.

"Cheer up." His voice was gravelly and low-pitched. "Christ, you have only two expressions, woman. Pissed off and mournful. You know that?"

Beth glanced over at Leggett, but the fat man never looked their way. He was rocking slowly back and forth, eyes glazed. He was gone somewhere else.

"I'm sorry I ran away last night," she whispered, blinking back tears. "I really messed things up for both of us, didn't I?"

He grinned a little. "I wasn't going to mention that," he said.

"You didn't have to come after me."

"Of course I did."

"But I prayed you would. Only, not for it to end up like this."

"We're not gone yet." He shifted against her and winced in pain. "Although we're sure as hell circling the drain. El Gavilán wants something more, or else he'd have finished the job on me."

"No." She tried hard for a cheerful tone. "Remember, the villain never kills the hero when he has the chance."

"Oh, so now I'm a hero. . . ."

"Shut up and listen." Her voice broke a little. "You remember how the villain always ties up the hero when it'd be simpler just to shoot him? And you know why? 'Cause if he killed him, the story'd be over, wouldn't it? No more heroes. Just a world full of sorry fuckers like Cuellar."

This time there was a definite smile. "You've still got that mouth, haven't you?"

"So?" she murmured, her fingers tender against his face. "You a fucking priest, or what?"

And then, because she was crying and didn't want him to see it, she bent forward and kissed him.

"When you came up here before," El Gavilán was saying to the girl, "and so rudely interrupted, I had three men digging in this hole. You've killed two of them, my little *brujita rubia*, so it's only fair you two take their place."

He'd been like that, laughing and swaggering, his emotions a roller coaster of anger and exuberance, ever since he'd found Stephen awake in the lean-to. He shifted from English to Spanish and back again, his words tumbling across each other.

He thinks it's over, thought Stephen. Listen to him, this man I've hated most of my life. He's just an old fool now. *Occure con la vejez lo que la muerte.* . . .

Stephen was chest deep in the hole at the top of Riqueza Crown, one arm pressed against his ribs while he shoveled with the other, and thinking of Soste Miel.

Sharp like needles, her teeth . . .

The first time he'd stood in this spot, it had occurred to him this was where Pascual Santiago had once worked and sweated over seventy years before, and the thought had brought a mixture of sadness and pride. But now his thoughts were on other things.

He bumped against Beth, and she stepped a little to one side. She was close by him, digging grimly, and since he'd had no chance to tell her otherwise, she undoubtedly thought of the end of this work as the end of her life.

And she knew the gold was gone.

Beth glanced up at Ware after throwing a shovelful of damp, black earth onto the slope. He was standing near the edge, the automatic pistol cradled against his hip. With the warmth of noon approaching, he'd shed his nylon jacket. He saw her looking, and winked at her. When she thrust a stiff middle finger in his direction, his grin only widened.

Stephen stumbled against her again, and she moved aside. His equilibrium was probably faulty after the blow to his head.

She was pretty sure she'd figured Ware out. He'd found the coins in the cave, all right, and the reason he'd kept quiet—even at the risk of giving Stephen an edge—was to get them all for himself. Sooner or later they'd hit bottom and find nothing but a bunch of dirt, and that's when Ware would cut loose with the gun. And Raymond Cuellar was going to get lit up right along with the rest of them.

What if she told Cuellar that Ware had the gold? Would they turn on each other and create a chance to escape? Not likely. Ware'd kill her before she could get out three words.

Keep digging. Stay alive a little longer. When it happens, Ware'll turn on Cuellar first. Maybe there'll be a chance. . . .

Travis Leggett worked slowly, ignoring the bite of deerflies that swarmed for the salt of his sweat. Each shovelful seemed to get heavier. His head was pounding right out of his skull, throbbing in time with the lurching rhythm of his heart. The more he shoveled the faster his heart beat, and the worse his head hurt.

He kept banging elbows with the girl because the hole was too small for three people to spread out and work, and each touch made him angrier. That seemed to please Cuellar, but his anger wasn't for the reason that Mex bastard thought.

They'd told him how Freddie died, strangling from the wound where the little bitch stabbed him. They weren't doctors, after all. How could they save someone who suffocated in his own blood?

Then Leggett had gone to sit by the body. And sometime, when his hand was on the boy's head, it had touched his neck.

Bastards. Freddie couldn't work. Freddie was in the way. And Freddie was up for a share of the coins. So Cuellar just sent his goddamned grinning Frankenstein Monster back for a quiet visit. Presto, chango. One less share to divide.

And Leggett was pretty sure they didn't plan for him to get out of this hole, either. He and the girl and that

Tonto-face next to her were all going to spend a lot of time together on this hilltop. Under a couple hundred feet of water.

He had to take a chance before it was too late. He began to work his way across the hole. Maybe a shovelful of dirt in Ware's eyes . . .

"Here it is, *cabrón*." Tonto-face straightened up and stared at Cuellar. "Here's what you spent twenty years looking for."

Leggett saw a leather sack partly unearthed beneath the man's feet.

"*Dios mi!*" He saw Cuellar step onto the mound of loose earth. "Hand it up to me!"

"Come get it yourself, asshole. This was my grandfather's."

"*Me cago en tu abuelo!*" snapped Cuellar, starting down the side. "*Largo de aquí!*"

This was the chance. A bolt of bright pain pounded Leggett's temples, but he lunged forward with the shovel, knocking the girl aside. This was for Freddie. . . .

Just as a harsh cracking sound came from beneath his feet. Everything collapsed below him and he fell, and then razor-edged agony ripped up through his legs and groin and stomach. Good ole Trouble with a capital T had found him again, for the last time.

And Trouble had sharp teeth.

Joseph Ware saw it all in a series of frozen vignettes:

Cuellar starting down into the hole. Leggett lunging forward with his shovel upraised, knocking the girl aside just as Esteban grabbed her and dove toward the slope.

And the earth breaking open beneath them.

Leggett fell screaming into darkness as Cuellar's feet went out from under him. El Gavilán slid toward the edge.

By reflex, Ware grabbed the man's collar, and the sudden pull of two hundred pounds yanked him forward where he could see into a new pit yawning open beneath the center of the hole. Down to where Travis Leggett hung, twisting on a bed of wooden stakes.

Ware began to laugh. He couldn't help it.

That old bastard. That clever, clever old bastard . . .

"Pascual!" he yelled, and the sound burst out into the clear air. "Pascual, you sly old son of a bitch! *I love it!*"

Esteban and the girl were out of the hole and trying for the lean-to where the extra weapons were stored. Ware watched them go, shaking with laughter.

He considered dropping Cuellar. The man was hanging over the edge, grabbing for Ware's sleeve. His legs flailed at empty air above another row of spikes five feet below him.

"Socorro! Socorro!" he was shrieking, clawing at Ware's arm. *"Socio mi . . . !"*

It would be easy. Release his collar and Cuellar would fall forward and down. The sharpened stakes would slice his body like a toothpick through soft cheese. Ware saw it all, clear and focused in his mind's eye. Except that El Gavilán had become Teddy Burgess, bleeding on an unpainted picket fence.

(. . . and I'm ready, ready ready, Teddy . . .)

He reached for the screaming man's belt and pulled him to safety. He wasn't sure why. Probably because the game wasn't over after all.

Stephen shoved Beth behind a stack of canvas sacks and fumbled for the Mac-10 he'd noticed earlier. Back on the crown of the hill Ware was pulling El Gavilán out of the hole. Stephen slapped a clip into place and sighted in, but the two men had already dropped behind a wall of dirt. He sent a short burst their way anyhow, as a reminder of the change in circumstances. Nine-millimeter slugs tore off a top level of muddy earth.

It hadn't worked the way he'd hoped. In his plan it was always El Gavilán screaming down into Pascual's snare.

"My God, what was that?" Beth crawled over next to him. She'd found another of the automatic pistols and was holding it away from her like a live snake. "What happened out there?"

"La Vigilancia," said Stephen, loading a sixteen-round clip for her. "The Watchful One. A little surprise left many years ago by my grandfather. For unbelievers."

"You . . . knew it was there? With those spikes? Of course you did. You had to. What if . . ."

"The timing had to be right." Stephen watched for movement behind the mound. "That false bottom was shaved to hold weight except in the center. That's why I kept nudging you to one side. Only it wasn't supposed to be Leggett who broke through."

"Jesus Christ! Did you know about it the first time? When you found the coins?"

He smiled thinly. "Maybe I'll tell you about that sometime. But right now, line up your barrel with the edge of the mound. If you see anyone—"

"You don't understand. I hate guns! I swore I'd never—"

He pulled back the cocking bolt for her, then thumbed the selector to semi-auto. "It's been converted, so it's likely to still fire in bursts. Be ready for . . . Look out!"

He pushed her head down as bullets stitched across the top of the canvas.

"Oh, shit!" Beth brought the weapon up. "Oh, shit, I hate guns!"

"Chinga su madre!" Cuellar ripped off another burst at the lean-to. "That little bastard! Kill him! Kill them both! Blow that goddamned tent to the ground!"

"Bad idea," said Ware, who was lying near the other end of the mound. From time to time he saw the girl's blond head moving. He could have already nailed her at least twice if he'd wanted to.

"What do you mean?" Cuellar lay back behind the cover of damp earth. "He's not going to escape again. I swear . . ."

"No, but use your head. The coins aren't in the hole, are they? And Esteban knew about the trap. Which means he knows where the gold is."

He saw El Gavilán's face change, saw thoughtfulness replace rage. Then the look he knew so well. The look that crossed Cuellar's face whenever he spoke or thought of the treasure.

Obsession, thought Ware, not for the first time. Pure and simple.

"You're right," Cuellar said after a long pause. "My revenge can wait a little longer."

Obsession and revenge. The fuel that had transported both Cuellar and Esteban Santiago through the years. Oh, well. Ware smiled and thought of the girl in the tent. We all develop obsessions.

"So, what do you suggest?" Cuellar asked.

Ware shrugged. "They're in there with their Macs. We're out here with ours. If we keep plunking away at each other, someone's going to get hit sooner or later. It's bad if that someone's you, worse if it's me . . ." He grinned at Cuellar's sudden scowl. ". . . and worst of all if it's Esteban, because the secret would die with him."

"So?"

"So, why don't you stay here and draw a little fire from time to time. I'll work around one side. Maybe I'll get a disabling shot at Esteban, or maybe put the girl in jeopardy somehow. He seems to care about her."

"Him? He cares only for his hatred."

"You think so? He could've killed us both before Leggett got him. Just sprayed the tent with bullets. Why do you suppose he didn't? It was because the girl was in there."

Ware began to inch backward, keeping the mound between him and the lean-to. "Watch your ass," he whispered, then turned and ducked into low brush.

"You too, *hermano*," said Cuellar, but his voice was cold.

"There's one thing I don't understand," said Beth. She leaned her head against the canvas sacks while Stephen kept watch.

"Only one?" He grinned, and then winced. She saw it hurt him to even smile. His face was a mottled, swollen mask.

"Ware. I don't understand—"

"Don't try." His smile faded. "Just believe me when I say he's beyond your understanding."

"But the coins . . ." When she'd told Stephen about Ware's descent into the cave, he'd looked surprised for a moment, then he'd slowly nodded. "If he knew where the gold was, why the charade of digging it up? At first I thought it was to double-cross Cuellar, but then he pulled him out of the trap. And why keep us alive? You say he's beyond my understanding. Do *you* understand him?"

"A little, maybe." Stephen sighted in on a movement at the mound, but didn't fire. "To Ware, it's all a game."

"A game . . ."

"Like with chess pieces. I think he gets bored sometimes because the game's so easy for him. So he gives us a few extra moves for free."

"But, with all that gold . . ."

Stephen shrugged. "Maybe he's bored with the gold, too. Maybe right now the game's more important to him."

I'm the result of forces beyond my control. . . .

Beth shuddered. "He's crazy, then," she said aloud.

"Probably." Stephen glanced at her. "But not in the way you . . . Dammit!"

"What?" She raised up to look.

"I just realized El Gavilán's alone out there, trying to look like both of them. Put those clips and that other stuff I showed you in your pack. We've got to leave before we get trapped."

Beth touched a canvas sack. "I still think a raft . . ."

"Forget it." Stephen pushed her toward the back of the lean-to. "Takes too long to inflate and launch with Ware out there somewhere. Besides, after that rain I'm not sure even an expert rafter could get through the canyon alive. Are you an expert?"

"Not exactly, but I've done some—"

"Neither am I, so why drown? If we can get into the woods toward the pass, I'll have a surprise or two for Ware. He may have given away too many free moves in this game."

They crawled beneath the tarp edge at the back of the tent, then down through heavy oakbrush off the south side of the Crown.

Sitting ten feet off the ground in the crook of a tree near the lean-to, Ware watched them. He reflected on how embarrassing it would be if either of them looked up.

He waited until they were below the slope of the hill, then dropped to the ground. He used a pocket compass to check their exact direction before heading back for Cuellar.

NINETEEN

In the silence of the hilltop, Cuellar climbed over into the hole. He was drawn by the dull gleam of the coins.

The leather bag fell through when the hole collapsed. It had hit one of the stakes and burst open, and the gold lay scattered below.

Cuellar slid across to the pit on his belly, oblivious to the danger from the direction of the lean-to. There were wooden planks beneath the dirt, shaved thinner near the center of the hole, and he crawled to where the wood began to break away at his weight.

He grabbed the edge, ignoring splinters that dug into his soft palms, and lowered himself down. The spikes didn't extend to the far sides of the pit—that would have been wasteful, wouldn't it, Pascual?—so he swung that way and dropped.

The dirt in the bottom was dry and smelled of elderly animal droppings, and there was a network of rodent holes in the walls. Cuellar straightened and began to turn.

Later, he decided he'd been hearing the sound long before he realized it. A faint, irregular scraping . . .

His first thought was the two from the tent. He spun and pulled up the Mac from its web harness. He dropped to one knee.

And saw it was Leggett making the sound. Because Leggett wasn't dead.

The fat man dangled facedownward on the spikes. Two

of them thrust up through his lower back like the spines of a prehistoric beast.

His upper torso hung down at an angle, and blood streamed along his arms into the dirt while his fingers scraped the handle of the shovel that had fallen with him. His head was turned toward Cuellar, and his eyes were clear and lucid with hatred.

He was trying to raise the shovel.

"So," said Cuellar. He reached carefully through the waist-high stakes and lifted the shovel into Leggett's hands. "You want to try again, I see. Let me help you."

Leggett's life was running down the spikes, pooling in the dirt at their base. His face contorted with the effort of raising the shovel.

"You goddamn greaser," he whispered, and more blood trickled out of his mouth. "You killed Freddie. . . ."

"And you." Cuellar nodded and slit the man's throat with his hunting knife.

He stepped back from the twitching body and touched the tip of one of the stakes with a cautious finger. It had been cut to a needle's sharpness. Then he crouched and began to gather the coins. They were heavy and solid, and his fingers caressed the raised likeness of Francisco Madero.

Clever, this. To leave one sack right on top of the weakest spot in the timbers. A trap that had waited in darkness, undisturbed all the years . . .

No, that wasn't true, because Esteban Santiago had disturbed it. Sometime in the past he'd been here. And, because he'd known about the trap, he'd avoided it and taken the sacks away. Then he'd replaced the boards and waited to watch his enemy twisting in agony on the sharp spikes. . . .

Come get it yourself, asshole. That was what he'd said. Even at the edge of his own death, he'd tried to spring the snare. Cuellar's teeth ground together in rage.

Leggett's body was enveloped now in a swarming, living cloud of flies. Cuellar swatted them away from his face.

So, Esteban had taken the gold. But where? The coins

were too bulky to carry far. Which meant they were
probably still in the basin. Someplace only Esteban . . .

The cave, of course. Where better? No one else could
climb that cliff burdened by the weight of the sacks.

Ware could. But Ware had been in the cave, and he'd
said it was empty.

Ware was lying. He'd found the coins in the cave, and
the girl knew it. He remembered the expression on her
face. She and Ware were plotting against him. Maybe
they had been all along.

But how to prove it? And, even if he did, how to get the
coins? He shivered convulsively at the thought of that
sheer wall. He felt the sack of his scrotum contract when
he imagined looking off its edge. For him, the gold might
as well be on the moon.

It was all quite clear now. Ware was plotting to kill him
and keep the coins for himself. Cuellar felt a burning
flood of indignation. The fact he'd planned exactly the
same fate for Ware was beside the point. He seethed at
the man's betrayal.

"Better move your foot."

"Wha . . ." Cuellar jerked as though struck, and one
elbow grazed a sharp spike. He looked up at Ware.
"What?"

The big man was standing at the edge of the hole with
Freddie's body, still in its sleeping bag, slung over one
shoulder. "Your foot," he repeated with obvious amusement. "Those boots are water resistant. That's not the
same as waterproof."

Cuellar looked down at the floor of the pit. He was
standing near Leggett's dangling torso, and one of his
boots was laces deep in thickening blood. Flies clustered
on it like a moving carpet.

"Aagh!" he gasped. His foot came free with a sucking
sound, and he clambered away from the staked area.
"Aagh! Santa Maria!"

"It'll wash off," said Ware from above him. "You should
bring your coins and climb on out. They're gone."

"Gone? What do you mean?"

"I mean they're gone. I circled up on the lean-to from

the side, and it was empty. I found some sign back in the oakbrush. Looks like they're trying for the pass."

"The pass . . ."

Ware tossed the body into the hole, then lowered the end of his climbing rope. "Tie on and I'll pull you out," he said. "If Esteban gets that girl over the pass with her story, you're likely to get some negative sound bites on the ten o'clock news. Plus, we'll never find those coins."

Cuellar tied the rope hesitantly. He'll drop me, he thought. Right on the spikes. He and the girl've planned it together.

"We'll have to split up," Ware was saying. "You head straight for the pass, and I'll track them through the woods."

There was no choice. He had to play along for a while yet. Find Esteban Santiago and the girl. Find out where the coins were. Cuellar felt the rope pulled taut. He climbed, grabbing the edge of the boards and pulling up, then braced one foot on the rim. When he rose, body leaning back helplessly above the spikes and held only by the rope, he saw Ware's grin. He knows what I'm thinking, he realized, and felt his heart lurch as the grin widened.

But Ware didn't drop him.

"What are you doing?" Beth asked. She watched Stephen wrestling a half-rotted log from beneath a thick old spruce.

"Waiting for you to help me," he gasped, and pressed a hand against his ribs. "Unless you'd rather just sit there and supervise. You must've had Mexican servants when you were a kid."

"That's cute." She hurried over to grab onto the wet wood. "How can I help if I don't know what we're doing?"

"Just pull it over here. Very good. Maybe you're more useful than you look." He flinched when the stump of a limb brushed his side. "Okay, now put your foot against that end and brace on something while I push it up."

"I'll ask you again. What the hell are we doing?"

He took a large, dangerous-looking knife from a sheath

inside his jacket. "When I was in junior high, I read this story—"

"Wait a minute. Where'd you get that knife? You had that, and you sent me off with a frigging Swiss army knife?"

"I figured, anyone bothered you, you'd just bite them to death." He grinned. "You also had my pistol, if you recall. Besides, I didn't have this at the time. It's Freddie's. Remember it?"

His eyes were different colors. One was brown and one was green. He stepped toward her. . . .

She shuddered. "I remember it now."

Stephen was chopping a notch into the base of the trunk. "Anyway, I read this story about a guy who fell off a ship and swam to an island. Turns out the owner of the island was this crazy who hunted humans for fun. . . ."

Beth nodded. "The story's called 'The Most Dangerous Game.' I read it, too."

"Then you know what we're doing. Okay, let's slide this over a little more. . . ."

Cuellar hurried along the edge of a creek that flowed past him toward the river. He was gaining elevation and finding it hard to breathe. He knew the creek crossed the Mule Pass trail somewhere up ahead, and then it would be only a matter of turning right. The pass was less than a half mile beyond it.

It would have been easier to take the meadow path, but that was too open. Those two had guns, and there was no way to be sure where they were. Once he held the high ground in the pass, they'd have to come to him.

And, if they did, if Ware didn't catch them in the woods below, who could say what they might be persuaded to tell? If Esteban was really so taken with the little blonde, he might bargain to save her life. Esteban had never cared about the gold, anyway. It was his hatred that had spurred him on all these years. A hatred that had once fed itself upon the object of Cuellar's own love.

He cleared a stand of aspen and stopped to wipe sweat from his face. Up on the hillside he saw a thin horizontal line, lighter in color than the greening meadow. He

wiped his forehead again and continued climbing toward
it.

Joseph Ware placed his foot against the taut bootlace
and pressed it lightly. The bootlace was dark brown and
blended in. Only noticeable if you looked for it.

Not bad. It didn't give, and it wasn't going to unless he
gave it a real push. The kind it would receive if he'd gone
blundering over the deadfall of brush and downed trees
toward those tracks in a patch of dirty snow on the other
side. Not bad at all.

He set himself carefully, balanced on the ball of one
foot. This would make an interesting test for his reflexes.
He shoved hard against the bootlace.

Which released a low limb held under tension. Which
snapped into a notch cut in the base of the rotted log
balanced on one end above his head.

It dropped fast, faster than he'd expected, and
slammed down into the spot he dove away from. A
jagged branch raked the side of his leg.

Whoa. That was too close. Ware sat up and wiped mud
off his sweater. He considered a loud cry of pain but
decided it would be too theatrical. Esteban wouldn't be
fooled.

Maybe he was slowing down a little. Getting old. That
thought sent a jolt of helpless anger into him and his face
contorted, but only for a second. Then it settled back into
its perpetual half smile.

No, that wasn't it at all. He'd just been a little too casual
tripping the snare. If he'd stepped into it blind, he'd have
reacted instantaneously. It never would have touched
him.

He scrambled to his feet with the nonsensical thought
that someone (the girl?) might have seen. Might have
seen him almost fail. He crossed the deadfall and continued to follow their tracks. He moved very carefully now.

"I have to rest," said Stephen.

The admission stunned Beth. "Me too," she said
quickly.

And equally stunning was the dawning realization he was only human, after all.

There had been times she thought it unlikely, because he seemed so driven, so remote. He'd saved her life on the trail that first time, and later on the cliff. And then, moments from death, he'd conjured one last dark bit of alchemy from a pit in the ground to rescue them again. He was tireless, she'd thought, and implacable, pursued by personal demons that left no room for a gentle heart. Or for her.

But now this indestructible man was running down before her eyes, fading into exhaustion and pain. His limitless strength had its limits, after all.

She loved him fiercely.

"Over here." She took his arm, and was shocked to feel it trembling. His breath rattled in his throat when he lay back against a tree trunk, shielded from an open clearing below.

"It's hard to breathe," he said. "On that one side it hurts like hell with every breath." He bent forward to spit. His spittle was flecked with pink.

Oh, God.

Aloud she said, "Do you think the snares'll work?"

He closed his eyes. "I don't know. Ware's smart. If not, maybe they'll at least slow them down."

She put an arm around his shoulder, and he didn't pull away. "How much farther to the pass?" she asked.

"Maybe a mile. A little less. It's going to get steep at the end."

"Can you make it?" It was a question she would never have asked without his earlier admission. It would never have occurred to her.

"There's no choice. We have to, even if you have to carry me." A smile crossed his bruised face. "Rescuing you all the time has put extra miles on my odometer, woman. You know it?"

She tightened her arm around him. "I thought you said you weren't going to mention that."

"I lied. Never pass up an opportunity to . . ." He stopped, and began to cough. Beth pulled him upright and turned her head so he couldn't see her sudden tears.

"Sorry." He leaned forward to spit. "Something in my throat." He spat again, a mixture of red and pink.

"That's blood, isn't it?" he asked.

"It's just from your nose," she lied. "You probably breathed it down."

He started to rise. "We've got to keep moving. . . ."

"No, not for a few minutes." She didn't let go, and he sagged back. "I'm tired and hungry. I'm just a helpless female, remember."

"Tell that to Dale Cooper," he said, but he lay back and closed his eyes.

She held him while sunlight slid across the clearing below, and he quickly fell asleep. So she ate handfuls of trail mix from the pack and tried to stay alert, but the sun was warm where it dappled through the trees across her face. And she was very tired, still hovering at the edge of shock after twenty-four hours of fear and death. . . .

"Beth, can you hear me?"

Of course she could hear him. She couldn't answer, but she heard him just fine, thank you. That drug, Percodan or something like it, was a real blast.

"Beth . . ."

Jesus, Ben. No need to shout. She knew it was her father, because her mother called her only Katie, or Katherine when she was seriously pissed.

Just turn it down a notch, okay, Ben?

Ben and Elizabeth. The original odd couple. He was the dreamer, all idealism and liberal causes. With a heart as soft as newfallen snow, and as easily kicked apart. She was . . . well, she was Elizabeth Davidson, wasn't she?

Her eyelids slid back (that's exactly what they did— they slid), and she had a blurred glimpse of light-colored hair and a pale face.

"There you are. How are you doing?"

His hair was going gray. Give Elizabeth most of the credit for that. Give me the rest. . . .

"Huh?"

"I said, how do you feel?"

"Stoned out of my gourd right now." Her voice was as hazy as his face. "Which is good, 'cause I'll probably feel

like hammered shit by tonight. How did it go? Small scar, or a biggie?"

He laughed. She'd long since lost any desire to shock him. She saved that for her mother.

"No new problems, thank God," he said, and she thought his hand was touching her cheek, but she wasn't sure. "Your mother sends—"

"Forget it, Ben." She wanted to go back to sleep.

"—her love," he finished anyway, but avoided her eyes. He'd always hated to lie.

"Right. So . . . what was it, do they know?"

He shook his head. "After the complications you had, there's no way to tell without tests, and—"

"Do they bury it, or do they just flush it?"

"Beth, don't make it like this. You agreed with the doctor. There was no chance. . . ."

"I'm sorry." And she was. Her vision had cleared enough to see the tears in his eyes. She could never bear to hurt him. "And you're right. I did agree."

He took her fingers below the IV drip in the back of her hand. "Anyway, it's over now," he said. "And I've had a serious talk with your mother. I sat her down, Beth— what's funny?"

Through all the numbness it hurt somewhere when she laughed, but she couldn't help it. She'd flashed on Ben sitting Elizabeth down.

"Nothing," she said, and tried to squeeze his hand. "Go on."

"Well, I just told her the whole thing was none of our business, really. It was between you and that boy . . . man. Rick, isn't that his—"

"He's gone."

"Oh." He studied her face intently. "I'm sorry."

"It doesn't matter, Daddy. You're here."

He blushed with pleasure. "You haven't called me that in a long time," he said. "Listen, Beth, it's going to be different between you and your mother now. You'll come back home for a while. Until you're feeling better. And you and I'll have lots of those long, late-night talks like we used to. . . ."

So she held his hand with her fingers and let his soft

voice wash over her. It wasn't true, of course. None of it was. He hadn't sat her mother down, except maybe in his fantasies, and he hadn't said any of those things to her. But he wished he had, and that was nearly as good.

And she wouldn't be going back to that house, with its dark-paneled rooms and her mother's voice blending into a thick soup of Bible verses and moral superiority. Back to watch her father being slowly crushed out of existence.

So she held his hand and listened to him spin his dreams, and loved him the more for knowing his weakness. And, after a while, the nurse came in to change the drip, and whatever was in the new one began to take her away. The sunlight was warm, dappling through curtains across her face, and she was very tired. . . .

"What . . . ?" Beth sat up with a start. Above her head a magpie flapped off a limb with an alarmed squawk. She looked across the clearing, wondering at her odd feeling of vulnerability at that moment, and felt her skin twitch.

Buh-Buh-Bette . . .

Stephen James shifted uneasily. His head had slipped down into her lap, but now he was pulling himself upright.

"What is it?" His voice sounded thick and muddled, but he did look a little better for the rest. "What time is it?"

"It's . . ." She glanced down and saw her watch had stopped at a few minutes past noon. "Dammit," she muttered.

"It's close to two," he said, looking up through tree branches to locate the sun's trajectory. "You shouldn't have let me sleep."

"You needed it. Anyway, I fell asleep, too. I . . . I had a dream about my father."

Oh?" Stephen climbed to his feet. "The two of you are close?" It was clearly politeness. He wasn't really interested.

"He died," said Beth. "He was crushed to death."

"Pardon?"

"Never mind." One of her legs had gone half-numb, and she rose awkwardly. "Do you feel better?"

"Much." He opened a baggie of trail mix and ate a handful. "I just needed some rest."

He scanned the clearing below them, then studied the trees on its opposite side.

"Anything?" she asked.

"Nope." He picked a raisin from his teeth. "And I'm not sure that's good. It's been too long. We'd better approach the pass carefully."

"You think they went straight there?"

"Maybe. It's lucky I know another way up. If they're there, we'll see them first."

He checked the clip in his weapon, then started up the slope. She watched for a second to be sure of his steadiness, then followed behind. After a few yards, he spat as they passed some low rocks. She glanced at the spittle and saw it was still flecked with red.

TWENTY

Joseph Ware leaned against the aspen's trunk and watched them go. He was thirty feet off the ground, hidden by thick lateral limbs and new spring leaves. Mosquitoes buzzed around his face.

He'd watched the girl through binoculars as she slept. Studied the shape of her face and her golden hair. He'd gotten lost in what he saw there, and the day had shifted into afternoon. When she awoke, for a second she'd appeared to look directly across at him, and he'd seen her shiver.

Esteban Santiago wasn't looking so good. And not feeling so good, either, to judge by the way he'd slept. The Esteban that Ware knew would never have gone to sleep with the enemy on his trail. Not with a bashed-in head or broken ribs or anything else, bless his cold, savage little heart.

Only, maybe not so cold anymore. And maybe that was because of the girl. Maybe she was weakening him.

Maybe she's weakening me, too. He wondered about that. Not sexually, of course, because no one, male or female, had ever affected him sexually in the way he affected himself . . .

(Asexual, that quack—the late Dr. Fleming—had called him. Asexual, just like some goddamned amoeba, the good doctor had once screamed in a rare unprofessional outburst.)

. . . but there was something about her that was affecting him somehow. Her spirit, maybe, as it combined with her beauty. That fierce samurai soul . . .

Whatever it was, he could feel it growing stronger.

Ware waited until they crossed a small knoll before he climbed down from the aspen. He skirted the clearing carefully, half expecting another snare like the one a hundred yards back in the trees, but there was nothing. It looked as if Esteban was fresh out of tricks.

They were climbing, due southeast, which placed them off line for the trail. Either Esteban was in such bad shape he was getting them trapped within the approaching ravine, or else he knew another route up to the pass.

When Ware reached the spot where the girl had slept beneath the tree, he knelt and placed his palm against the ground. It seemed still warm from the touch of her body, but that was probably just the sun.

He squatted for a while with his hand against the ground, then he rose and followed their trail.

Cuellar was thinking of Engracia Torres, and of the murdering butcher who'd taken her from him.

Sometimes the memories caught him unaware, at times when the tears and the catch in his throat were inconvenient, even embarrassing. But the memories never asked permission—*Con perdón, por favor?* They came as they pleased.

He moved into the shade of an overhanging rock. He'd been cold earlier, but now the afternoon light was uncomfortably warm out of the wind. He never grew accustomed to the intensity of the sun at these high altitudes.

He was tired. He'd slept only a little the night before, and it was a ragged sleep, broken by dreams of Engracia and of that damnable aquarium. Bright colors, shining eyes . . .

He wondered if Esteban and the girl were getting near, and how the little *cabrón* was even alive. God, he'd kicked him! And every kick had pushed the dream farther away. Maybe when Esteban was finally dead, the fish-tank dream would die, too.

He was getting too old for this, he decided, and ran one hand along his thick body. It was time to face the fact he'd cut this twenty-year treasure hunt much too close. But he had to be there, because there was no one else he could trust. Not Ware, not any of them.

He rose and looked out past the boulder field. From his location he could see practically the entire basin, from the high lakes at the north down to where the river roared whitewater into Agua Fuerte Canyon. The Strong Water, indeed. A good name. The rafts were useless with the river as it was now. They'd have to get some mules . . .

(Does that amuse you, Pascual? Things haven't changed much in seventy-five years, verdad?)

. . . because the trail was too narrow and rough for motorized vehicles. Also some more stoop labor to replace those three dead *vatos* down below.

It was cold again in the shade. Goddamn these mountains! Goddamn their icy wind and thin air, and goddamn Pascual Santiago for ever coming here!

He found a flat rock that held radiant heat and sat down. He closed his eyes, and when the memories came again, he welcomed them.

"See him?" Stephen leaned against a shattered boulder and tried to get his breath.

"Where?" Beth was pressed against his back, and her nearness—her smell and her touch—was almost enough to cut through his pain and fatigue. He tried to concentrate on it.

"Look at that notch in the cliffs. See it? That's where

the pass goes through. Now look at the boulder field below and to the—"

"I see him. Jesus, he's just sitting out there in plain sight. Why's he doing that? To decoy us?"

"Could be. Maybe Ware's behind one of those rocks." He said it, but he didn't believe it. Ware was somewhere close behind them, ascending through the woods. Stephen wasn't certain why he was so sure of that, but he was. Once or twice along the way, he'd almost *felt* his enemy's nearness. He hadn't mentioned it to the girl, just like he'd hidden the fact he knew exactly what was wrong inside his body.

They had left the trees at the bottom of this long ravine. It had been slow, but it was the only way to reach the pass and still avoid the trail. It narrowed above them to a spot where a grove of stunted evergreens stood beneath a dropoff. Up past there was the boulder field where El Gavilán sat on a rock, in plain view, less than one hundred yards away.

"Too far." He drew a momentary bead on the man. "This gun wasn't designed for distance, and I'm a terrible shot anyway. We'd just scatter them into hiding, and they'd know where we are."

She studied him for a minute. "But we have to do something."

"And we will." He'd been thinking about it since he'd decided Ware was behind them, and seeing El Gavilán confirmed his decision. The problem now was in presenting it.

"We'll have to use the river after all." He watched for her reaction. "On one of their rafts."

"But you said . . ."

"I know what I said, but the situation's changed two ways. For one, they have the pass blocked, and that boulder field's a fortress. They have all the advantages up there."

She looked from El Gavilán back to him. "What's number two?"

"We have a clear shot at the river now that we didn't have earlier. We'd never have gotten a raft launched with them right on us."

"Okay." She nodded, as he expected her to. "So it's Plan B. I tried to tell you before, I've done some whitewater rafting."

"That's good, because I haven't."

"Then it's time for me to hold up my end for a change. Let's go."

"Not yet." He had to handle this part carefully. If she was through it, she wouldn't leave. "We'll have to split up for a little while."

"What?" Her blue eyes narrowed. "No way! I understand now, damn you! It's just a trick to get rid of me while you rush those bastards. You're in no condition—"

"I'm also not that dumb. It's no trick. The river's our best way out of the basin now. All I want you to do is go on ahead for the raft. I've seen you run, remember, and I couldn't keep up with you anyway. I'll follow and cover our tails."

"But . . ."

"Listen to me." He touched her arm and felt her trembling. "I'm just going to buy us some time if we need it. I won't be far behind. When you get there, air up one of the rafts. They probably use a foot pedal—"

"I've inflated rafts before." He saw she was beginning to go for it.

"Okay. Before you air one up, cut holes in the others. Use that little super knife I gave you."

She managed a weak smile. That was good.

"Then haul your raft down by the log bridge. Inflate it down there."

"Stephen . . ."

"Listen. Put the raft by the water and then get someplace where you can see up toward the pass. If you see Ware or El Gavilán, get on the river and go."

"I'm not leaving you."

He took her hands. "Listen to me. It's going to take time for you to reach their camp and get all that done. And, by then, if you see them instead of me, I won't be coming anyway. Do you understand?"

"No . . ."

"Someone has to make it out. Someone has to tell what happened here. Otherwise, those two will win, and more people than you can possibly know will have died for nothing." He squeezed down on her fingers. "Do you understand?"

Tears rose in her eyes. "You're not coming, are you?"

"I'll be right behind you," he lied. "But if something goes wrong, you go alone. Now say it."

She bowed her head, and a single tear fell onto their hands.

"Say it, Beth."

"I go alone," she whispered.

It was easy to send her back in a different direction. If Ware and El Gavilán were in the pass, he told her, it made sense to cut over into the meadow. It was faster that way. He didn't register until later that he hadn't kissed her before pushing her laterally across the ravine. His thoughts had already gone away from her, back to the familiar comfort of that empty place inside him.

Now, thought Stephen. He straightened on shaky legs and ascended toward the evergreens at the base of the ridge above. Now, Ware. Let her go and come along with me. Follow what you see here.

And he spat, pink mixed with flecks of bright red, onto an exposed rock as he passed.

Ware stood staring down at the conflicting messages in the talus.

They'd split up. The girl had crossed to the left and out of the ravine. Esteban had continued on toward that ridge below the pass. Toward where Cuellar sat in the sun like a dozing toad waiting to be stomped.

Where had she gone?

He crouched behind the cover of a rock and considered the possibilities. Maybe she was working her way around to El Gavilán's left. She had a gun; Esteban had a gun. If they believed both he and Cuellar were in the pass, it made sense. Create a cross fire.

Or maybe she'd gone off alone. Where? Back to the camp? Or to the cave for the coins?

Erase that. She couldn't get the coins alone, and she knew he could reach her in the cave.

The camp, then. For more ammunition? They hadn't fired what they had. For . . .

For the rafts?

That was crazy. The canyon was a boiling caldron. It would be suicide.

He decided to follow the girl. Partly because the mental picture of leaving Cuellar sitting up there like a fat Buddha while his very worst nightmare came crawling up from below was an intriguing one, and partly because the girl's grip on his imagination was strong. And growing stronger.

He started laterally across the ravine when something caught his eye. Down low, a reflection of the light. He moved toward it, wary of another snare.

It was a large gob of spittle, like those he'd already seen along their trail. It was drying on the face of a rock. He crouched to touch it and saw clearly what he'd suspected before. It was drying a pinkish gray, except for the thicker patches of red.

Bright red even now, fading in the air. It was bright red because it had been fully oxygenated. Lung blood.

Ah, Esteban. Ware looked upward toward where Cuellar sat unmoving. I was right earlier. You're not doing so well, are you?

So, what is this? Send the girl away and mount a final kamikaze charge up the rocks to tear out El Gavilán's throat with your dying breath?

The idea was irresistible. He'd go after the girl later. She wasn't going anywhere he couldn't follow, and the developing drama in the boulder field wasn't to be missed.

He followed Esteban's trail up the ravine. Partway, before he lost his line of sight, he saw Cuellar stand up and stretch, then scratch his belly before sitting again.

Yes, citizens of Colorado, I give you the future Leader of the People. . . .

When he reached the trees at the base of the small ridge, he stopped. Something was wrong.

The rocks were covered with vines of wild ivy, brilliant green against the stone above a muddy seep in the wall. The vines ran thick and tangled up the rock next to his head, and back in their growth was the shape that had caught his eye.

What's wrong with this picture?

He grinned and stood very still. He'd obviously been mistaken about one thing. Esteban didn't believe he was already up in the pass.

The shape was a vertical line with regular indentations and, generally speaking, nature didn't operate in straight lines. He reached out and gently, very gently, pushed the ivy aside.

The vertical line was a length of thin fir limb, green and limber, its bottom jammed into a hole in the rock. And it was vertical only because its top was held back by the heavy pressure of Esteban's remaining bootlace hooked over its tip. It stood directly in the obvious climbing route like a fully drawn bow, ready to snap forward and out of the ivy at the slightest touch.

The regular indentations he'd seen were the spaces between several of the six-inch spikes from the girl's pack, which Esteban had drilled through the limb. They were coated with drying mud to prevent an accidental reflection off sunlight.

This boy's a fast worker, thought Ware. Give this boy a knife and some wood, and he'll carve us a bust of Speedy Gonzales. A regular boy scout.

He stepped off to one side and studied the snare for a minute, then he reached out with the barrel of his Mac-10. He touched the bootlace.

What's wrong with this picture?

The limb flew forward, metal spikes whistling past him . . .

What's wrong with . . .

. . . and recoiled at the end of its snap as the . . .

What's wrong . . .

. . . two huge rocks it had held in place tumbled down . . .

WHAT?

. . . from overhead onto him. Ware was quick, quick as a cat. But maybe not as quick as he'd once been.

His hoarse cry was cut off when the first rock slammed

onto his shoulder. And the second, sharp-edged and heavy, landed on the back of his neck.

The sound echoed up from below, and El Gavilán leaped to his feet at the same instant Stephen squeezed off on full auto.

And mostly missed, because the man's leap carried him to one side. But not entirely. There was a shrill scream, and El Gavilán dove for cover.

"Mierda!" Stephen rose to his feet looking for a better angle, just in time to see a bloody arm yank an automatic pistol behind the rock. He'd hit him, but apparently not anywhere vital.

"Qué pasa, El Feo?" he called out. *"No gusto usted la sangre?"*

Especially when the blood's your own, he thought.

"Bastardo!" The voice was shrill with rage and fear, slipping entirely into Spanish. "Stand up, coward! Come out from hiding and I'll kill you now! Here and now! Do you hear me?" A burst of gunfire ricocheted off the rocks.

Stephen lay back and let the man scream. If he kept low and yelled out just the right things, El Gavilán might work himself up for a charge. Sometimes that was what very frightened people would do. He'd seen it happen like that once before.

Then he heard another noise from his right, from below the bluff. First the sound of soft, fluent cursing, and then familiar laughter.

Damnit. He closed his eyes for a moment. His trap hadn't worked. Not completely, at any rate.

And, as abruptly at that, everything was changed. Because he'd managed to miss them both. They were on both sides of him, and they were hurt but operable. Probably neither was injured as badly as he was, and they were armed to the teeth.

What was it El Gavilán had said that morning? *La cosa no va bien.* All of a sudden, things were not going that well. He glanced at the sun's angle. By now the girl should be nearly back to the camp. He considered his options.

One was to rush El Gavilán, who obviously wasn't going to jump up in a fit of terrified macho after all. Get him before Ware reached the boulder field.

The idea of rushing anyone was pretty funny. The best he had left in him was a rapid shuffle.

Another was to dig in and wait. He might get lucky.

But if he didn't, Beth would have to take on the river alone.

Which left Plan B. He'd never intended for either of them to use the raft. It was only to get Beth out of the way, and a last-ditch chance for her if things went badly in the pass. And they'd certainly done that. Both his snare and his ambush of El Gavilán had failed through stupid pride. Pride that had refused to recognize his own failing strength.

They had little chance in the canyon, but they had no chance at all if he stayed here.

He heard Ware climbing up from below. He used the cover of the boulder field to get to the trail and then hurried down toward the camp, not running because he couldn't. More like a rapid shuffle.

TWENTY-ONE

The hilltop was like a stinking charnel house.

Beth smelled it before she reached the Crown. The stench hung in still, sunlight-dappled air that was disturbed only by bird sounds and the buzzing of a thousand flies.

She entered the camp cautiously, still not certain Joseph Ware wasn't there somewhere. If he'd stepped out from behind one of the thick old aspen, with his perpetual smile and his damned Buh-Buh-Bette, she wouldn't have been surprised. This was a place of death now. A place where he'd feel right at home.

The flies were everywhere. Big, some of them almost the size of bees, they swarmed and buzzed around her when she approached the dig. They were black and green, with shiny flecks of gold along their backs and wings.

Gold, like the coins in the old leather sacks . . .

She'd never doubted she'd look down into the hole. It was her own rite of passage en route to the rafts. It was the place where she should have died.

A half-dozen magpies and ravens took wing from the pit with startled cries, and the flies billowed up around her in a dense cloud when she stepped onto the dirt mound. The smell came with them and it was alive, too, with its own noxious existence.

Cuellar and Ware had thrown all the bodies into the hole, probably intending to cover them later. Brian Lowry's maroon Arizona State windbreaker wrapped skin-tight, sausage-tight, around a body bloated by internal gasses to half again its normal size. Earl Lowry had slid into the lower pit and hung on the wooden stakes near Leggett. Which had effectively taken care of the bloat. Freddie Jenkins lay faceup near Brian. He was still zipped into his sleeping bag. His eyes, one brown and one green, regarded her without interest.

Oh, God. Oh, Jesus God. They were just boys. The two of them were just boys.

And she'd killed them, she decided. In her own way she'd killed them all, including the fifth body left across the river by Ware for his private joke on Stephen. Killed them all, innocent and guilty, with her idealistic bullshit about saving this pristine basin from the hands of man. Pristine? That was a laugh. The coins had been here, waiting to turn this place used and dirty, for nearly fifty years before she was even born.

"I'm sorry," she whispered. She'd first said it to the Lowrys, then realized she meant it for them all. "I'm sorry. . . ."

Flies swarmed around her and landed on her clothes and her face. In the trees above, the big birds shifted impatiently, waiting for her to leave. This place of death.

And finally she did, dragging her eyes away from a vision she knew she'd carry to her own grave. She went to the lean-to, also alive with flies and the odor of Freddie Jenkins, and began pulling the heavy canvas sacks into the open. There were eight, and she first sawed through each drawstring with the dull little army knife, then brought out the rafts. Some were already torn by bullet holes, but she shoved the blade through their reinforced rubber and neoprene anyway, and cut gaping holes in the bottom. Then she loaded the remaining sack onto one shoulder and started down toward the river, the foot pedal in her other hand.

The first thing Joseph Ware heard, when he topped the ridge onto the boulder field, was a voice swearing in shrill Spanish. And praying, too. The top of Cuellar's head was visible a hundred feet away. It was obvious after a moment the man was alone.

Ware's right shoulder had gone numb, which was helpful because the pain had been paralyzing at first. He figured his collarbone was probably cracked, and the shoulder socket itself was damaged in some deep, fundamental way that bedrest and aspirin weren't going to help. He'd had to laugh, once he realized he wasn't dying. A false snare to set up the real one. Very clever. Like grandfather, like grandson, he supposed.

It could have been much worse. The massive development of his trapezius muscles had probably saved his life because the second rock, which would surely have broken a normal man's neck, had only cut a deep gash. As for the shoulder, he was lucky to be left-handed. He could still use his right arm, if he looked at it and concentrated. He just couldn't feel it.

"Hey, Ramon!" He stepped cautiously forward. "Don't start shooting. It's me."

El Gavilán's head slowly emerged. "Where is he?" he called. "Did I kill him?"

"Doesn't look that way." Ware crossed to a sheltered spot where a discarded weapons clip lay in the sun. "Looks like he left on his own."

"*Chinga!*" Cuellar climbed out into the open. One sleeve of his expensive satin shirt was stained dark and wet. "Dammit, I thought I hit him."

"No blood here." Ware kicked the clip aside. "Except

for what he's spitting up. Looks like you kicked some of
his ribs into a lung."

"Good. I hope he chokes to death. I was just about to
charge him when I heard your voice."

Right, thought Ware. And I was just about to knock off
three or four pliés and then break into *Swan Lake*. Aloud
he said, "You'd have missed him, looks like."

"Coward that he is. But you, you're wounded, like me."
And El Gavilán made a show of cradling his arm.

"Yeah. I guess we'll both live, though."

Cuellar scowled at that. "Where did he go?" he asked.

"Back to the camp, I'd say." Ware stepped up onto a
pointed rock and stretched to his full height to look.
"Probably down the trail and across the meadow."

"Why would he go there?"

"Maybe for the rafts."

Cuellar's mouth fell open. *"Pasar en balsa?* But you
said that was impossible."

"It is. At least, I think it is. But I saw the girl's trail
branch off down below, and now I think Esteban's gone
after her. We'd better hurry."

"I can't," said Cuellar. "You'll have to go alone. My
wound, it's taken my strength."

Ware hid a smile. He knew El Gavilán didn't believe
him about the rafts. Given the man's galloping paranoia,
he probably thought it was a trap.

"Okay," he said. "I'll go, then."

"And I'll keep watch here." Cuellar nodded. "If you're
wrong, someone has to guard the pass."

"Keep your eyes open." Ware turned and crossed the
boulder field toward Mule Pass trail.

"Oh, I'll do that," El Gavilán called after him. "Be
assured I will."

Stephen crossed the meadow toward Riqueza Crown.
He kept near the trees on his left in case someone was
watching from the pass.

How long had it been since Beth left? He'd warned her
not to wait too long, especially if she heard gunfire. It was
possible she was already gone.

He tried to hurry, but without success. Every step now

was accompanied by stabbing pain in his chest, and he stopped often to cough. His entire left side felt heavy.

It would be better if she was already gone, he decided, now that the pass was blocked. She could handle a raft, and he'd only slow her down. He'd continue to his hidden rucksack, and then to the Cupola. Ware couldn't get down to the cave without a rope, and Stephen would get the big man's climbing gear from the tent.

Better if she was gone. The intensity of her emotion drained his strength and demanded a commitment he couldn't make. There was only room for one commitment in his life. He'd been reminded of that—jerked back to its reality—when he'd realized Ware had survived the last snare. His first feeling had been an odd relief, then a scalding sense of shame at that relief.

Because he'd realized, in an instant of bitter epiphany, that they were bound together, he and El Gavilán and Ware. He'd sometimes wondered how he'd feel when his enemies were finally dead, and now, to his shame, he knew. He'd feel lost without the hatred that had carried him so far, and lost without the ones who'd always been there to receive that hate. Lost, and all alone.

He knew now he'd always intended to die with them.

He pushed into oakbrush up the side of the Crown, then found the trail. When he reached the top, he looked back toward the pass.

And saw a tiny figure descending in the distance. He thought he saw an upraised arm.

Beth stared at her watch. It had been thirty-four minutes the last time she looked. Now it was thirty-five.

She'd heard gunfire in the distance while she was descending to the bridge. It was finally happening, up there in the pass, and she'd left Stephen alone to face them. Which was his plan all along, of course, in spite of what he'd said.

You once told me Los Centinelos are dead, she thought. *You were wrong, Stephen, because you're The Sentinel now, and as long as you live, they live.*

She'd have been no good to him, anyway. She looked at the automatic pistol slung over her shoulder. In the lean-to she'd pointed it in the air and fired, but she could never have aimed it at anyone. Not even Ware. When she saw any gun, she'd always see her father's casket.

(Of course it's a closed casket, Katie. It has to be closed. Only so much cosmetics can do, my dear.)

She looked down at the raft, and at the river below it. Even here, the water was as rough as any she'd ever attempted. And in that canyon, with its sheer walls and boulders the size of a bus . . . Maybe it *was* impossible.

She looked for the best place to put in, but there was none. The water boiled over itself, drowning every obstacle that could have created an eddy. She'd just have to dip the nose and jump. Experts sometimes did that for fun, but she'd never tried it.

Thirty-eight minutes.

He'd never intended to come. That's why he'd given her the names before she left him in the ravine. Why he'd made her repeat them, and told her to keep repeating them until they were memorized.

Four people and two places. Two of the names were Spanish, two Anglo. It was a promise, he'd said. A promise he'd never trusted to anyone else. She said the names again.

Thirty-nine minutes. He wasn't coming, which meant *they* were. Oh, Stephen, there's no more time. . . .

She pushed the raft down the slope beneath the bridge. It caught on heavy growths of ferns and springy young aspen and bounced back at her. Spray from the river blew off rocks and drenched her to the skin. Wet hair was in her eyes. She slid down and kicked the raft forward. Its nose touched the cascading water and bounced high into the air.

She pushed it back down and set herself to jump. Forty minutes. There was no more time.

Stephen hurried down the trail toward the log bridge, Ware's climbing gear wrapped around his chest. Ahead, the river's roar obliterated all sound.

She'd done exactly right in the camp. The other rafts were slashed, and she hadn't waited for him. She was tougher than he thought.

When he stepped onto the bridge, he looked down and saw her, fighting the raft's nose onto the surface of the water. She had one leg already in, gathering herself to jump, and didn't see him at all. That was good.

He dropped to his knees, partly to rest and partly to see she made the launch. But mostly to say good-bye.

The pain he felt was confusing, atrophied by time and a hardened heart, and unrelated to his injuries. It welled up and closed off his throat. It hurt like nothing he'd felt, like nothing he'd allowed himself to feel, since that night on the ledge in a Texas canyon. And, when he began to cry, for the first time in nearly twenty years, the sensation was so alien he choked on those tears.

Maybe she heard him, though it was doubtful with the river's roar. Or maybe she looked back one last time because she was afraid to launch the raft, but that probably wasn't it either. When she saw him, her eyes widened, clear and blue, and he saw her mouth form his name.

And then she was climbing the slope to where he sat, slumped down on the bridge, and then her arms were around him and he could hear the astonishing thing she whispered. And his mind flashed for a moment to the last person who'd told him he was loved.

To Soste Miel . . .

El Palacio del Miedo

They must needs go,
whom the devil drives.
—Miguel de Cervantes

TWENTY-TWO

"Hey, *mano,*" said the drunk. "You say another word and I'll cut off your balls."

He hit down sharply with his beer bottle across the bar. When it didn't break, he stared at it stupidly.

"Aiee . . ." He frowned, and tried it again. The bottle rebounded off scarred Naugahyde with a dull thud. It still didn't break.

"Jesus," Esteban muttered, and moved to another stool. Behind him the drunk was still trying to break the bottle and cursing him in a pidgin Spanish Esteban found hard to follow. The man had actually used the word *pelotas* for balls.

Must be from Tijuana, he decided.

"Your health." Someone set a beer on the counter in front of him. A thin spray of ice slid down the bottle's contour.

"And yours . . ." Esteban looked over at a stocky boy no taller than himself. He left the salutation open-ended.

"You don't remember me, do you, Esteban?" The boy had a wispy mustache. He was maybe eighteen.

"You look familiar, but—"

"David. David Delgado. My brother was—"

"Was Chuey Delgado," finished Esteban. "I remember now. You were a little boy."

"More than eight years ago." Delgado nodded. "Eight years since they murdered my brother."

"Hey, I'm sorry, man. . . ."

"And locked you away. In El Pozo. How long have you been out?"

"Awhile. Eight or nine months." Esteban sipped the cold Carta Blanca. "Thanks for the beer."

"My honor. Why is that drunk so mad at you?"

"A remark I made about Reagan. An innocent one, I

199

thought, after he said he used to watch the guy's TV show. He got upset."

Delgado grinned. "If he ever breaks that bottle, we're all in trouble. What are you doing now?"

"Busting horses for an Anglo named Tucker. He calls himself Terry Tucker, the Mean Motherfucker." Esteban said the last part in English.

"What a name. Do you like the work?"

"It's a job," replied Esteban. "Work's not easy to find when you're a Mexican ex-con in Texas."

"Have you considered going home?"

Esteban's jaw muscles tightened. "No," he said softly. "I haven't."

David Delgado pulled at his own beer and studied Esteban carefully. "I know what you mean about jobs," he said. "Especially if you're illegal. In this bar, only last week, federals came and took away all the girls."

"What girls?"

"Hey, didn't you know? This place was topless, *mano*. The girls were all *pollos*. They waded the river like the rest of us, then they came here because they heard there was work. 'Take off your clothes,' said McKettrick. He's the honky bastard who runs this place. 'Show me your tits,' he said. And then he kept the young ones. They didn't even know how to dance to bar music, just stood there looking embarrassed, you know? But McKettrick didn't pay them anyway, just what they got in tips, so he didn't care."

"And La Migra caught them?"

"Every last one. And then threatened McKettrick to fine him a thousand dollars for every *pollo* he hired in the future. That's why there aren't any girls here now. Really pissed the customers. I bet that's what's wrong with that fool with the bottle. I bet he doesn't give a damn about Reagan . . ."

"Ronald Reagan?" The drunk was back. "Ronald Reagan is much of a man. I'll cut the balls off anyone who disputes it." He smacked his bottle down on the edge of the bar

". . . he's just pissed because the girls are gone," Delgado finished. "Let's take our beers outside."

The El Paso night was hot in early spring, but the bar's air conditioner was broken anyway, and eventually that bottle would probably break, too. Esteban followed the boy onto the street.

"So, times are hard and you're busting horses," said Delgado. "A painful occupation. Would you like to do better?"

"Who wouldn't?" Esteban watched a hooker at least forty years old working the corner. "How could I do that?"

"Cross the Rio. Into Juarez." Delgado switched into English. "I know a man over there. He was a friend of Alejandro's. He's a big operator."

Be careful, thought Esteban. It's probably nothing, but . . .

"La Frontera's full of big operators," he said. "What's he pushing, gila monsters?"

The Monday before, a customs official at the bridge had found a perforated box built into the backseat cushions of a car. Expecting drugs, he'd yanked off its top with a flourish to find it divided into compartments containing rattlesnakes, tarantulas, and iguanas. One of the rattlers bounced off the mesh in a game effort for the official's fingers, who promptly emptied both his revolver and his bladder into the backseat.

"Hey, man, those gilas go for two bills apiece in Dallas." Delgado laughed. "But the work I mean's the same as what you did with Chuey, understand? And my friend *is* a big operator. I bet you've heard of him. He's called El Gavilán. The Sparrow Hawk."

To his credit, Esteban's expression never changed.

Of all the chores at Tucker's, Esteban least enjoyed hoof trimming. It was the best opportunity on the ranch to get bitten, or maybe just kicked cross-eyed.

"Hol' still, you swayback sumbitch!" Bubba Lee Barnes pulled the canvas tight. "Hol' his head, Pancho! God-damn you, horse, I'd feed yer nuts to a coyote if ya had any. Hol' his head!"

The piebald gelding lunged up and Barnes was

knocked backward, spraying a mouthful of snuff down his shirt.

"Shee-it, Pancho! Use them goddamn muscles." Barnes waded back in. "Little stud like you oughta be able t' hold down this gluebag all by yourself."

Esteban grinned, and watched the half-lame old cowboy secure the piebald's front legs into their straps. He wasn't offended; Bubba Lee called everyone on the ranch Pancho, including Terry Tucker.

For hoof trimming, the horses were snubbed down on their sides onto a padded veterinary platform framed with angle iron. Straps hooked into the frame held their feet immobile—once they were cinched in, which wasn't always so easy—and two longer straps held their bodies at the shoulder and the girth. The head was another matter.

"Watch his head." Barnes picked up a heavy, two-sided rasp. "Ya think he cain't move it much from there, but he's like a goddamn rattler. Turn yer back 'n he'll bite a whistlin' fart outa yer ass."

Esteban was holding the horse's bridle near the bit, so he moved his hand a little. The next few minutes were the easy part, snubbing the piebald's head while Barnes trimmed off excess hoof and then filed it down.

I'll call you, David Delgado had said. *El Gavilán's always looking for top hands, and he listens to me.* The boy's bragging reminded Esteban of the older brother, Chuey. He wondered if David also shared Chuey's fondness for mixing meth crystal and pot. That combination of dope and too much machismo had left Chuey Delgado facedown beside the Rio.

And the last time Esteban had seen David—before the other night—he'd been a fat little ten-year-old in a Jetsons T-shirt.

Jesus, this place . . . What had Pascual said that time? This evil place, it befouls what it touches.

After meeting Delgado, Esteban had stayed out of the Southside bars because he finally had the contact he'd sought. Now, when he wasn't waiting near the phone at his motel, he revisited some familiar places. Sentimental journeys.

The Christ Jesus Eternal Church and School proved

less eternal than its namesake. The building remained, all creeping sage and cactus, but it was abandoned. Wherever Brother Axton had gone, he took everything with him, including the sign. A family of *pollos* was hiding inside there now, and they refused to leave its sweltering heat, even when he spoke to them in Spanish. La Migra was everywhere, they said. Their luck was bad, *tu ves?* How could they trust him?

Because I was once like you. Hell, I *was* you. And neither of us has had much luck.

Brock Automotive was still around. Esteban had gone in and bought spark plugs for a nonexistent Chevy pickup and was waited on by Bob Brock himself. The big man looked somewhat older, and his face showed no recognition.

So, how's your daughter? Esteban wanted to say, but he didn't. Has she grasped the fundamentals of birth control, or is she still plagued by leaky rubbers? He pictured her at age twenty-three, a shitty-diapered kid on each hip and those world-famous breasts hanging down toward her navel, but he knew that wasn't likely. More probably a sorority pin and a convertible, and a gold-plated future. He left Brock Automotive unaccountably depressed, and crossed the bridge into Juarez in search of the two old men. They were still alive, Charlie Pellikern had said. Valentin Portes and Soste Miel.

"Valentin was your uncle?" asked the neighbor. His Spanish was a hard, flat derivative called Tex-Mex. He sat bare-chested in a tire swing that hung from a tree limb, and rocked back and forth. His eyes were milky and unfocused. "Old Valentin died, nephew. Rotten lungs from the copper mine over at Vado. Coughed his lungs right out."

The man was stoned, probably on heroin judging from the needle tracks inside both arms. A layer of thin, clear snot hung on his upper lip. "Say, nephew," he said. "I was Valentin's friend. Maybe you can help me out."

"Maybe." Esteban forced aside his self-disgust at using the old junkie. "If you help me. I need to find another friend of my uncle's. He's called the Honey Bear."

A startled look crossed the man's face, and he began to

rock faster in the swing. "Honey Bear," he said. "The Honey Bear's gone, nephew. Gone to the Palace, where they don't never come back."

"The Palace? What's that?"

"Gone to the Palace, where they don't *never* come back." The man tried to get out of the swing, but had apparently forgotten how. He pushed backward and fell onto the dusty ground, his legs still caught in the tire.

Esteban reached for a thin arm. "Let me help you."

"No! You go away." The old junkie kicked free and crawled onto his knees. "I have to go pee now. I can't talk anymore."

"But I thought you wanted my help."

"I want you to go away." He made it to his feet. His balance was destroyed by the drugs, and he began lurching sideways toward a discolored adobe house. "Go away and leave me alone."

Esteban watched him miss the door the first time and hit the wall hard. Then he disappeared inside.

Esteban found two bars in Juarez and one in El Paso that were called El Palacio, but no one admitted knowing the name Soste Miel. He'd just have to go there, to a different one each night, until the old man turned up.

What had the junkie meant? he wondered. Gone to the Palace, where they don't *never* come back. . . .

"Better answer him, Pancho," Bubba Lee Barnes was saying.

"Huh?" Esteban came back with a start. The other hands were beginning to loosen the piebald's straps.

"Where you been, boy?" Barnes grinned, and showed a few remaining teeth all stained a uniform tan by snuff juice. "Ole Terry has ta call ya again, he's gonna get a little peeved."

"Santiago!" Tucker's voice came from a large metal shed near the house, and Esteban realized it wasn't for the first time. He released his grip on the bridle to a bony character who called himself Waco, and started toward the shed.

"You got a call," said Terry Tucker. He was a fat young man, and when he got angry his neck puffed up like a frog's. "I thought I told you when you hired on, no personal calls on this phone."

Esteban's pulse kicked over. There were only two people who had the ranch number, and his parole officer never called anyone except a tout in Juarez who handicapped the greyhound races.

"Sorry." He averted his eyes, because he knew that was how Tucker liked Mexicans to act, and passed by him.

"Well, you make it quick, y'hear?" said Tucker. "You tell whoever that is you got work to do. No time around here for siestas."

"Who was that shouting?" David Delgado asked over the phone. The connection was scratchy.

He's in Juarez, thought Esteban. "That was Tucker. . . ."

"The Mean Motherfucker?" Delgado laughed.

"Yeah. He told me to get back to work."

"Well, you tell him to go piss up a rope, *mi amigo*. Your line of work just changed."

Esteban was taken across the river in a big Oldsmobile driven by a silent black man with long, braided dreadlocks. David Delgado sat up front with the man, who was called Angel, and Esteban rode in back.

When they crossed over, Esteban saw one of the Madrinas on the Mexican side wink at Angel. *La mordida.* As always, the bite was in.   •

It was all one country anyway, he reflected. La Frontera. It extended a hundred miles on either side of the meaningless Rio, and was really a third country between the other two. Its embassy was the *casa de cambio*, where dirty money became clean, its capital was El Paso–Juarez, two cities that were actually one, and its currency was *la mordida.* It was the meat in the sandwich, squeezed on one side by a country determined to keep it out and on the other by a system in financial chaos. When he'd left it as a child, twelve and a half pesos would buy a dollar. Today it took several hundred.

The hilly, northwestern section of Juarez had been a slum for years, and Esteban was surprised when Angel headed that way. He got no indication from Delgado, either. The boy had been unusually quiet since they'd picked up Esteban outside McKettrick's bar.

Finally, the Olds turned up a steep incline and passed between sandstone rocks and sage until the driveway leveled off outside a huge old adobe building. The sun was setting when they left the air-conditioned car, and Esteban felt the raw heat baking up from the ground beneath him, but still he got a sudden chill. *Entregar el espíritu*, his mother had called it. Giving up the ghost.

"He'll be back in a minute," said Delgado, in English, when Angel went in the building's open front door. "As far as I'm concerned, he can take his time."

"Angel?" Esteban shook off the atmosphere of the place. "What's the problem with him?"

"You name it. For one thing, he doesn't speak any English at all. The son of a bitch's Haitian, and all he knows is French and some damn voodoo language, and just enough Spanish to start a fight. He doesn't want you to talk *to* him, and if you speak English, he figures you're talking *about* him. He's touchy as hell—"

He broke off as the Haitian returned, followed by a skinny man in a dark jumpsuit that only made him look more emaciated. The man was nodding and gesturing, and a half-smoked cigarette bobbed in his teeth.

The man was the Coyote. Jaime Agustin.

Esteban straightened slowly. This would be the first test.

"Davie, would you tell this creepy bastard to load the trunk?" said Agustin. "He can't figure sign language, and every time I try English he looks at me like I just fell out of a dog's ass."

Esteban hid a smile. After all these years, the Coyote still hadn't learned Spanish.

Delgado turned to Angel. *"Pongo las maletas en el carro,"* he said. The Haitian scowled at him. *"En . . . el . . . carro."*

"El carro?" Esteban grinned.

The boy shrugged, then patted the trunk and began again.

"You're Esteban?" Jaime Agustin turned and put out his hand.

Esteban looked at the hand. It took all his concentration to keep his own from balling into a fist.

"Yes," he said, and shook the Coyote's hand.

"I've heard good things from Davie," said Agustin. "You were with his brother at Piedra Quemadura."

"And with Alejandro and the others."

Agustin shook his head. "That was bad. I hear Craddock's still hiding out somewhere along the Rio with some imported muscle. After the Wizard set you up at Piedra Quemadura, the old bastard doesn't trust the local talent anymore."

It was El Hechicero who sold them? Esteban remembered the Wizard dead behind the wheel of his Mercedes. Maybe. And maybe just another lie. He stored it for future consideration.

"I think I met you once," Esteban said. He stared the Coyote in the eye and pushed it to the limit. Better to find out now.

"Yeah?" Agustin looked him up and down. "When was that?"

"A long time ago, along the river. You were with a little blond guy. A Texan."

"Charlie." Agustin smiled through discolored teeth. "He was a pistol, that Charlie."

"Was? What happened to him?"

The Coyote shrugged. "He got a little carried away and killed a guy in a bar. Charlie always had a temper. Ended up in the Baz, and got wasted in a gang fight. You were in the Baz, weren't you?"

"El Pozo." Esteban nodded. "Me and a lot of others. I don't remember seeing him."

"Oh, you'd remember if you'd seen him. Cocky little fart. He used to burn his hands with the tip of his cigarette, just for the hell of it. Charlie was tough."

Agustin turned to Delgado, who was helping Angel load canvas bags into the trunk of the Olds. Esteban remembered the look and feel of those bags, and especially the smell. They were washed in lye soap and bleach to throw off the DEA's dope-sniffing dogs.

"Hey, Davie, I like this guy," said the Coyote. "He's little, but he looks plenty strong." He turned back to Esteban. "You must do a lotta weight lifting, huh?"

"Some."

"Some? Right. Well, there's this guy you're gonna meet you won't believe. All built up, like you, only he's a foot taller. I swear it."

Esteban felt his breath squeeze up into his chest. "I'll look forward to meeting him," he said.

But the meeting didn't happen right away. El Gavilán was gone on business, Delgado told Esteban. Gone to Colorado. Every six months or so he flew up there for a while and never said why, probably working on some import deal. Delgado grinned and winked when he said that part. El Gavilán always took Ware—that was the muscle man Agustin had mentioned—and his woman along with him.

Esteban pretended little interest in the information. That was the best way to keep Delgado talking, he'd found, by feigning indifference. Though a contrast in some ways to his older brother, the boy had the same desperate need to impress someone, anyone, and it was clear that neither Angel nor Jaime Agustin were likely candidates.

Were El Gavilán's trips because he'd already found the coins, Esteban wondered, or because he hadn't? Charlie Pellikern had been dead for some time now. A lot could have happened since then.

In the two weeks that followed, he watched and learned, and was amazed at the new refinements in border drug trafficking. The smugglers were nothing if not resourceful.

Marijuana and heroin were now taking a backseat to cocaine because the financial return was higher. Much of the cargo was still transported from places like the old adobe building and then loaded onto Cessnas and helicopters outside the city, but the level of security had risen exponentially. And, as El Hechicero had forecast, most of the networks were computerized.

"It's the goddamned DEA," said Delgado one night while they loaded the Olds outside the silent old building. "Those *cabróns* are everywhere, undercover all over Juarez, and they got their own computers. So it takes a new kinda smarts, tech-nol-ogy, *mano,* to stay ahead."

But some things hadn't changed in eight years. Cargo was still sand-muled into New Mexico near Los Palomas, or driven south to low-water crossings on the Rio where the bite was in. And the old operation of getting plasticine bags down a pay toilet and then retrieving them from the American sewer system was still called Shit Patrol.

"Innovation, man," said Delgado. "That's the key." He and Esteban had returned to El Paso at dawn, and the boy was still wired. "There are only the limits of imagination."

"I've seen that." Esteban nodded and lay on his motel bed. He wanted Delgado to leave.

"No, no, you ain't seen nothing, bro." The boy sat on the foot of the bed. "I'll tell you one you won't believe."

"Maybe I could just dream it." Esteban was thoroughly tired of both Delgado and the silent Haitian, and he was almost ready to get Agustin alone. Only the memory of Charlie Pellikern and the bloody cell in El Pozo stopped him. He couldn't lose control like that again. He was too close.

"No, listen. This is a true story, I swear." Delgado's dark eyes were sparkling with excitement. "This Anglo family crosses the river, *turistas* in a big station wagon, to go camping down near Monterrey, right? A fat-cat Texan and his wife and kids and his old mother-in-law. Well, first night out, the old granny goes to bed sick. Next morning, they find her dead in the tent."

"It's going to be a sad story, then." Esteban pulled a pillow over his head.

"No, listen. Now the Texan knows about the complications when an Anglo dies in Mexico. Forms to fill out, interrogations. It can take forever to get the body home, right? So he talks his wife into loading Granny on the luggage rack."

"I think I've heard this story. About three different versions, in fact. I think it was a 'Movie of the Week.'"

"No, you ain't, 'cause this is a true story, man. They hide the body inside the tent up top, right? They'll give it a Christian burial back in San Antone, blah, blah, blah. So they drive to Nuevo Laredo to cross the Rio. They're really sweating customs, as you can imagine, especially when the guys at the checkpoint pull them into a bay and do a search. Those Texans are about to chocolate their Fruit of the Looms, *mano*.

"But then they pass the inspection. They can't believe it. They drive off and stop at the first McDonald's, 'cause they *all* gotta hit the toilet, you dig. So they load up on Big Macs and go outside . . . and their car's gone."

Esteban opened one eye.

"Ah, got your interest, huh, man?" Delgado grinned. "So, they look all over, and that car is *gone*, bro. So what are they gonna do? Call the police? 'Yes, officer. It's a two-tone wagon, 1980 model, with a dead old lady on the roof. We lost her at McDonald's.' No way. All they can do is break out the plastic and catch a plane.

"Well, about a week later, the rich Texan gets a call. Someone's found his car, right there in San Antone. He walks up to the thing, and there's the tent, still on the rack. 'Let's see if anything's missing, sir,' goes the cop, and then opens it up."

"And Granny sits up and asks where's her french fries."

"No, no, man. The tent's empty, and Tex is lying in a dead faint on the ground."

"So what really happened?" Esteban asked.

"Don't you get it?" Delgado said. "Those *pendejos* at the river found Granny during the inspection, and they packed her solid with that synthetic shit, China White. They passed the car on and sent someone to follow it, then they stole it at McDonald's. They knew the Texans had to keep quiet."

"So what happened to Granny's body?"

Delgado shrugged. "Nobody knows, man. That's part of the legend. She's out there somewhere. That's just to show you what I meant. There are no limits, you see?"

"True story?"

"I swear it, bro," said Delgado. "Old Granny, she's out there somewhere."

In April, El Gavilán returned to Juarez.

TWENTY-THREE

"You're Esteban," said Ramon Carrillo in English. "I've been hearing about you." Even when he smiled, his eyes were flat and lifeless. "Jaime tells me you were with Alejandro at Piedra Quemadura. You're lucky to be alive."

Esteban tried to listen, to keep a calm expression that was slightly servile. What El Gavilán would expect.

But it was hard. So very hard. His breath was choking him, making him hyperventilate, because they were right there. Right there in the expensive restaurant, across the ornately carved table. The two of them. And, after all the years, El Hombre de Sambra finally had a name. Ramon Carrillo.

El Gavilán looked different than Esteban remembered, but he realized he'd never seen the man clearly. Only a shadow with a golden voice. He was a little taller than expected and wore a beard now, mostly gray, but the voice was exactly the same. His shirt was open at the neck, unbuttoned over a chest covered with a mat of hair. Hanging from a chain, nestled in the hair, was Pascual Santiago's coin.

Kill him. Kill him now. Reach across the table and put this silverware knife through his goddamned throat. Esteban's fingers trembled. He saw himself doing it.

". . . him someday," Ramon Carrillo was saying. "But there's nothing I can do at the moment. Wherever he is, I assure you his house is a fortress, filled with his foreign *mercenarios*. But we'll find him someday."

Craddock. El Gavilán was talking about Melvin Craddock. Esteban tried to cool the fire in his brain. He couldn't lapse now.

"I appreciate that," he said.

"Esteban . . . what?" said Joseph Ware. "You do have a last name."

"Santiago." Esteban made himself look at the man.

"Esteban Santiago." Ware's smile widened. "I'm very pleased to meet you, Esteban."

El Gigante Malo. Unlike the other man, Ware hadn't changed at all in nearly seventeen years. Most of all, Esteban remembered his smile.

"I heard you were in the Baz, Esteban," Ware was saying. "A friend of ours was there. Charlie Pellikern. He—"

"He never met Charlie," said Jaime Agustin from the end of the table. "I already—"

"—died in there," Ware continued. He looked suddenly amused. "A gang fight, they say."

Esteban studied a linen napkin by his hand. A hand he was proud to see lying rock steady. "It's a bad place," he replied. "A lot—"

"Am I late again?" The voice came from behind him. "As always, I apologize."

Carrillo was looking past Esteban, and his eyes were undergoing an amazing transformation. They came to life, shining with delight.

"Never apologize," he said, rising to his feet. "The later you arrive, the more you're anticipated."

"Más que galante," said the woman as she passed the head of the table. The others had stood—though Ware's smile was cynical and David Delgado was scowling—so Esteban did, too.

"This is Esteban Santiago, *mi flor,"* said El Gavilán, after lightly kissing her on the cheek. "Esteban, this is Engracia Torres."

"Como está usted?" She smiled.

"Bien," he replied automatically, feeling like the first page of a Spanish primer. "Thank you."

She wasn't strictly beautiful, he decided later that night when he was alone. Not in the classic sense. But he'd have a hard time convincing any man of that who was in her presence.

She was much younger than El Gavilán, probably near

Esteban's own age. Her hair was dark brown and hung, Indian style, straight and parted in the center, to the middle of her back. Her eyes were so black they didn't reflect the light at all; they swallowed it.

A man would always remember her mouth. She wore only a little pale lipstick because she needed nothing more. And there was a tiny scar, shaped like the letter *J*, on her upper lip.

She sat down and the rest of them followed, Carrillo glowing like a man given second life. She was bare-armed, and her nipples showed through a white, high-necked silk blouse.

She saw him staring at her breasts and smiled again. "It's the air conditioner in this place," she said. "It's always set one notch above solid goose bumps. Like being in the frozen north."

"Now there's a segue," said Ware, watching them both with his ever-present smile. "What if Rodgers and Hammerstein had named their play *'North' Pacific?"* He sang: "Some enchanted igloo . . ."

Only Agustin laughed. The girl, for whom the joke had apparently been intended, ducked her head to study a menu.

She's afraid of him, thought Esteban. There were cross-currents all around the table, too many for him to follow.

"North Pacific? *South* Pacific?" Ware was saying. He appeared amused rather than offended by the lack of response. "Ah, well, I suppose it's good I've kept my day job."

Agustin laughed at that, too. The waiter brought pitchers of beer all around and *cascos de guayaba con queso* for an appetizer, and the food temporarily stilled the conversation. Once, Esteban raised his eyes and found Engracia Torres studying him with an odd expression. Then she smiled and returned to her meal.

It was the next afternoon when she called him at the motel. She was picking up a new component stereo for her second-floor apartment, and she wanted him to help her carry it up.

"As strong as you are, that should be easy enough," she

said. "And I'm an Equal Opportunity Employer. I pay off in Carta Blanca and beer nuts."

He agreed immediately. Now that he'd found El Gavilán, the only holdup was the secret of Pascual's treasure. He needed to know what the man was doing in Colorado, whether he'd found the Strong Water and the Crown, and Engracia Torres was the only one who might tell him.

If he had any other reason for wanting to see her, he told himself, he wasn't aware of it.

She drove up in a Firebird convertible, gleaming black, with mag wheels and a throaty, rumbling engine.

"You like my toy?" she asked as he got in. "Ramon saw it, and he bought it. Just like that. He said it had my name written all over it."

She was wearing a white tank top, and a short leather skirt that revealed most of her tanned thighs when her feet shifted on the floor pedals. She saw him glance at her legs and smiled, but said nothing. The April day was hot and she was sweating slightly, and her smell—a mix of personal odor and light perfume—tightened a knot in his stomach.

"You don't talk much," she said, after they'd turned off onto Mesa Drive. "I like that. The strong, silent type."

Esteban wasn't sure where this was headed. El Gavilán's whore, Delgado had snorted contemptuously the night before. The boy had been offended at standing for the arrival of a high-priced *puta*. And now she was apparently coming on to Esteban. He decided to let her lead.

They walked into the air-conditioned coolness of a chain music store near a mall. She was tall and high-breasted, even when supported only by the thin tank top, and a passing Anglo businessman nearly ambled out into oncoming traffic while watching her go by.

She bought the system she wanted with a credit card, and Esteban loaded it into the backseat. When she leaned over the fender to be certain the sales slip was attached, she hooked an arm around his waist.

They drove northwest out of downtown, past the tramway cutoff, and then turned into a hilly area of expensive condos and apartments. Esteban noticed that by looking south he could see across the river into Los Colonias, the worst slum in Juarez.

Must be depressing, he thought. Up in the morning for your hand-blended coffee on the balcony, and you have to see those shacks across the border. Inconsiderate of them. And when the wind's from the south, you probably have to smell their outhouses.

"I've been noticing your chest," said Engracia, turning into a manicured cul-de-sac.

"Excuse me?" Esteban's anger gave way to an uncertain grin.

"My God, you're actually smiling," she said.

"Well . . ."

"Your chest. You prefer bench presses or flies?"

"Well . . . both, I guess."

"I figured." She glanced down at her breasts. "I could use a personal trainer. Some people don't realize there are disadvantages to having these *tetas grandes.*" She turned into a parking space.

Okay, thought Esteban. I'll play. "I'm one of those people," he said.

She laughed. "Until I hit thirty, I didn't either. Now, if I want to keep showing off in these tank tops, I have to work at it."

So she was older than she looked. Esteban unloaded two of the boxes from the backseat.

"It's right up there." She walked up a flight of outside stairs, the short skirt just in front of his face. "I have some exercise equipment in my bedroom. After we set up the—"

She stopped abruptly at the top of the stairs, and he nearly found his face flat against her buttocks.

"What the hell . . . ?" She whispered.

"What is it?" Esteban placed the boxes on the stairs.

"The door." Her voice was soft, and surprisingly calm. It bore no resemblance to her earlier chatter. "The door's open."

He saw it was. The door stood lightly ajar, and cold air was whispering out of the apartment into their faces. He put a hand against it.

"Be careful," she murmured. "Do you have a gun?"

When he shook his head, she pulled a small pistol from her handbag. Then she led him into air-conditioned coolness.

The apartment was even more plush than he'd expected. Thick carpet and expensive furniture. A huge aquarium fully six feet long sat on a raised platform against one wall. Its lights and bright colors, muted by swirling water plants, was the only illumination in the room except for the open door.

Engracia touched his arm. He looked back, surprised again by her calmness, and saw her point at the floor.

Blood. She mouthed the word without a sound.

The spots led away toward a French-style swinging door. He placed his mouth near her ear. "What's in there?" he whispered.

The kitchen. Again she mouthed it silently.

Esteban crossed to the door and heard, for the first time, another sound below the air conditioner's hiss. It was a sound he knew. He straightened and pushed open the door.

The two children had backed into a corner, as far away as possible. If the tiny window above the sink was larger, they'd undoubtedly have been gone.

The girl was perhaps six, the boy standing in front of her a little older. She was crying softly, the sound Esteban had recognized, and the boy was holding a dull-edged pocketknife toward them. His face was an equal blend of terror and defiance.

"Vengan!" he snapped in a shrill voice, staring at Engracia's pistol. *"No se mueva!"*

"No one will hurt you," Esteban answered, also in Spanish. "Put down your knife."

The little boy only shifted it to his other hand, and Esteban saw one of his fingers was trickling blood onto the kitchen's tile floor.

The refrigerator stood open, with an empty milk carton lying inside. There were torn packages of cheese and lunch meat, also empty, on the drain board, and a can of Hershey's chocolate with its lid gashed in. The girl had an uneven ring of chocolate around her mouth.

That's how he cut himself, thought Esteban. Opening

the chocolate for her. There's an electric can opener right on the counter, but it might as well be a sack of cat litter for all the good it'd do him.

"Puh-p-please." The little girl spoke for the first time. "Don't h-hurt us. . . ."

"Shut up!" hissed the boy, and flexed the knife.

The sound of her voice, the frightened stutter, hit Esteban like a physical blow. It was Jorge's voice. He felt his knees buckle, and he slid into a chair. All of them, all three, stared at him wide-eyed. Engracia lowered her gun.

"You've hurt yourself, my friend." He was unable to steady his voice, so he tried again. "If you'll let your sister —is she your sister?—have a sandwich, perhaps I can stop the bleeding."

The boy's eyes narrowed in distrust. "How do you know she's my sister?"

"Because you cut yourself to get her the chocolate. I . . . had a sister once."

The knife blade lowered a little. "If you try to grab us, I'll cut off your balls."

And this one said *cojones*.

"That's a dull knife, and I have enormous balls," Esteban answered. "You'd have a long gray beard when you were finished."

A quick grin crossed the boy's face. "She's my sister," he said. He lowered the knife, but he didn't drop it. "She talks funny. She can't help it."

The knot in Esteban's throat was nearly too thick to speak. "I have such a brother," he answered. "When he got older, he got better."

"I hope she does, too," said the boy. "Otherwise I'll sell her to some gringa for a maid, and buy myself a motorcycle."

He put his knife on the drain board.

The children were fed and the boy's finger was cleaned and bandaged. It would do no good trying to get him a tetanus shot because he'd never have gotten in Engracia's car. Besides, he'd be across the Rio in an hour and back into the filth of his daily existence. If the finger wanted to get infected, it would. At least he and his sister were well fed.

Esteban stood at the top of the outside stairs and watched them go. They moved quietly, staying in the shade, and when a car turned in, they cut down an alley. Neither had offered thanks or a name.

He turned back toward Engracia in the doorway and was surprised at her somber look.

"Was that true, what you said about your brother and sister?" she asked.

"Yes."

"You're not like . . . them, are you?" Her expression was unreadable.

"Like who?"

"Never mind." She pulled the door shut behind her. "I'll take you back."

And she didn't say another word on the drive back to his motel. No more flirting or casual touches, or flashes of her inner thigh when she shifted gears. She put on mirrored sunglasses and stared ahead at the road.

He stood outside his door and watched her gun the Firebird into traffic with a high-pitched whine of its engine. She roared through a yellow light, and an old Dodge pickup skidded sideways to avoid her.

What in hell . . . ? Esteban shook his head in bewilderment.

She was parked outside when he went for supper that night. She was leaning on the Firebird's fender.

He walked over to her. "Are you okay?" he asked. "This afternoon, you—"

"Come home with me," she whispered. "Please."

She was heat, and the velvet glide of soft flesh over muscle. He was on top of her, beneath her, next to her, and he was inside her. Her sweat oiled his skin, and her body pushed him past the limits of his endurance. Then she brought him erect again with her hands and her mouth, and explored him inch by inch. And each time he thought there was no more, she showed him he was wrong. There was always more. . . .

When he awoke, the digital clock by her bed read five minutes past one. He turned over and saw her, clearly outlined in the balcony's twilight. She was standing nude, out there in a slight breeze that ruffled her heavy hair. She was holding something to her breasts.

Esteban rose and padded across the room. When he walked onto the balcony, she turned.

"The night feels good," she murmured. "When I was little, I swore I'd get an air conditioner and stay under it year round. But I get tired of it sometimes."

"We're both going to get arrested out here," he said.

He saw the flash of her smile, and she led him back to bed. She held a small, ragged doll in her arms, and shifted it to one hand when she doubled a pillow behind her back.

"Her name's Carmelita," said Engracia, propping the doll on her flat stomach. "God, she's ugly, isn't she?"

Esteban's night vision was good enough to tell she was right. The doll was cheaply made, with a thick, shapeless body of stuffed cloth under a tattered dress and apron. The head was completely round, with most of its light-colored hair gone, and the eyes were wide and lidless with surprise. They caught and reflected what little light was in the room.

"She couldn't have cost more than two or three dollars American, even back then," said Engracia, fluffing the sparse hair. "But I thought she was beautiful. My mother scrubbed the kitchens of a lot of blond gringas to buy her, and . . . Shit. Forget it."

She turned to face him. There was faint starlight off the balcony, and its shadow hid her face.

"You're not like them, Esteban. Ramon and the others. I didn't realize that until I saw you with those children."

He felt a blush. "It was just—"

"Never mind. Thank whatever god you may believe in for those children, because they've probably saved your life."

"I . . . don't understand."

"You will, after I've finished. Just be still and listen." Her fingers worried the doll's head like catechism beads, and Esteban realized that was why it was so ragged.

"I came from over there, too," said Engracia. Her voice was a low monotone. "Over there on the heights. If I stand on my balcony and look in just the right spot, I can see a tin shed that was next to our house. If you want to call it a house."

"I'm sorry. . . ."

"Shut up and listen, okay? I know you have a sad story, too. We all have sad stories here. *Nos lamentamos.*

"But I was lucky, because I was pretty. I met Ramon when I was sixteen. He had a wife then, but he didn't care and neither did I. The first thing he ever bought me was a red, see-through nightie, but I had better taste than that, even at sixteen."

Her fingers plucked at the doll's hair.

"I made him give me the things I wanted. Not red underwear, but a savings account and a college education at UTEP. I have a bachelor's degree in business administration and an MBA in finance. Not bad for a dumb whore, huh?"

"One thing I never thought was that you were dumb," said Esteban.

"Just a whore," she said with a faint smile. "No, don't apologize again. Two things I really hate are apologies and regrets.

"I've been with Ramon for nearly fifteen years," she continued. "His wife left long ago because she couldn't take his paranoia. He's always convinced people are plotting behind his back. But I'm still here. Ware and I are always here."

She shivered, and pulled the sheet up over her breasts.

"Ware was a project of his, too. That's what he called us. His projects. Did you know Ware killed both his parents?"

"What . . . ?"

"No, of course you didn't. But now you do, is it such a surprise?"

Esteban lay still for a second, then he shook his head. "No," he answered.

"Ramon said Ware was this child prodigy as a kid back east. Probably would've ended up taking a Ph.D. at Stanford or MIT if he hadn't strangled his mother and father."

"Jesus . . ."

"Yeah. Seems the mother saw through that smile. Ever notice how he never stops smiling? She hooked him up with a shrink, who got so damned scared of him that he wouldn't see him alone. The psychiatrist wanted the mother to sign commitment papers, and she was going to, only Ware found out. So that night he strangled both parents, then propped them up in the family car and spent the evening cruising the main drag with them, waving at everybody."

"Jesus Christ . . ."

"Oh, he had that sense of humor, even back then. And before he left town that night, he killed the psychiatrist, too. Snapped his neck, Ramon said."

Her smile trembled. "So, that's us. Ramon Carrillo's projects. Ware and me. And it was Ware who sicced me onto you."

Esteban felt ice hit his spine where the sweat had dried. "Tell me what you mean," he said.

"It was all a setup," she replied. "All that short-skirt, show-you-my-squirrel bullshit in the car. And all that bedroom double talk, too. Ware told me to do it. I don't know why. Maybe he thinks you're DEA."

That's not it, thought Esteban. That's not it at all. He knows. Somehow he knows. . . .

"I couldn't refuse," she was saying. "Because Ware knows some things Ramon wouldn't like to hear. Other nights like this, when I tried to get free for a little while. I was supposed to . . . open you up, confirm whatever it is Ware suspects, then tell him. Just him."

"I . . ."

Engracia touched his arm. "I don't want to know what that is. I don't care. All I needed to know is you're not like them."

Esteban remembered Charlie Pellikern. "Maybe I'm more like them than you think."

"No, you're not. Listen, I don't have any illusions and I don't have many regrets. Like I told you, I hate regrets. And if I hadn't warned you, I think I'd regret it."

Esteban reached a decision. "Then I'd better tell you the truth," he said. "I wanted something from you, too."

"I could see that." She smiled.

"Besides that. I need to ask you something."

"Why not?" Her voice hardened. "I've already hung myself out to dry on this thing. What could make it worse?"

"I need to know about El Gavilán's trips to Colorado. You've gone with him. I need—"

Her laughter interrupted him. "You're kidding. Is *that* what all this is about? That fairy-tale treasure?"

"Then he hasn't found it?"

"Of course he hasn't found—" She stopped in mid-sentence. "Wait a minute. You're not saying those coins are really there?"

"Somewhere." He nodded.

"I'll be damned. I always thought that high-mountain stuff was just Ramon's own brand of masochism. He hates that country, and he hates flying up there because he's terrified of heights. And even when he took that old man into the Palace—"

"What old man?" Esteban sat up.

"Why . . . that crazy old man . . ."

"Soste Miel? El Gavilán has Soste Miel?"

"The Honey Bear. Yeah, that's him. He's crazy as a loon, that old man, and he must be over eighty. He can't string two intelligent sentences together, but Ramon swears he knows where the treasure—"

"You said the Palace. Which one is it? I've spent nearly every night drinking beer in one or another, waiting for Soste Miel to come in."

"Beer? You mean a bar? Esteban, the Palace isn't a bar. It's that old building up in the hills of Los Colonias. *El Palacio del Miedo*. The Palace of Fear. I'll bet you've been there a dozen times."

"That place?" He remembered the vague uneasiness he'd always felt outside its walls. "The Palace of Fear? Why do they call it that?"

"That shows you've never been inside." He was sure she shuddered. "It's well named. It was once used by the state police for interrogations. Back in the forties and fifties, I guess. People, mostly politicals, used to go in there and never be seen again. All the old people in Los Colonias know about it."

. . . gone to the Palace, where they don't never *come back . . .*

". . . has a series of basements down there, I've heard," Engracia was saying. "I've never been past Ramon's storage room on the main floor. It's bad enough. The whole damned place smells . . . well, that's just exactly how it smells. Damned."

"And that's where Soste Miel is?"

"If he hasn't died from the odor and the . . . Esteban, what are you doing? You're not going over there. . . ."

But he was already pulling on his clothes.

TWENTY-FOUR

There were night birds in the mesquites on the hillside, whistling to each other and following Esteban from tree to tree until he reached the top. Then they stopped and silently flitted away. No birds sang near the Palace of Fear.

The Olds was parked outside, along with El Gavilán's Chevy Blazer. Esteban used the vehicles for cover to reach the walls.

As always, the doorway stood open. It beckoned. Come in . . .

And, as always, the signals from the primitive nerve center at the back of his brain were the same. Get away from this place. *El lugar malo.* Get away.

For the first time, he stepped inside.

The room was large, with a low ceiling and no furnishings. The only light was a lantern sitting next to a cup and saucer on a spool of electrical wire. There was a folding chair next to it. A magazine lay facedown on the chair.

Esteban crossed to the spool and dipped one finger into the cup. The coffee was still warm.

He slipped a long-barreled Colt's .44 from his belt and checked its load. Five slugs, each nearly the size of his index finger.

El Gavilán had never offered a weapon to either him or David Delgado. They were sand mules, nothing more, doing the scutwork and having no need of a gun. Engracia Torres had her small .32-caliber pistol, but he had a feeling she might need it, so he'd hitched out to Terry Tucker's ranch. With a healthy sense of self-preservation, Engracia had offered the loan of her gun but not her car. Phoenix was in her plans, then Los Angeles.

"Wha'choo want with this gun, Pancho?" Bubba Lee Barnes had asked, watching him closely. "This is a kinda big shooter fer varmints."

"These are big varmints."

Barnes had nodded. "Always had that feelin' abou'choo, Pancho. Always figgered you's lookin' fer one varmint 'r another."

He handed over the old gun. "Kicks some," he said. "An' pulls a little to the left. But it'll knock a hole big enough t' run a stud roan's pecker through it. Take these truck keys—"

"I can't do that, Bubba Lee. You don't even know me."

"—an' leave the thing at the parkin' lot by the bridge, if it'll get that far 'fore it craters. I'll find it easy enough. Now, get on outta here 'fore ya wake up the Mean Motherfucker. He'd certainly feel compelled to do somethin' foolish."

Esteban crouched next to the electrical spool and closed the Colt's cylinder. There were two doors going out of the room, and he'd just entered one of them. The other led into darkness.

It turned out to be a hallway. On either side were doorways into smaller rooms. All stood open. He passed each one quickly, pausing against the dusty walls between. If there was someone inside even one, he'd be an easy target.

The smell, faint at first, was getting stronger. It was the smell of old earth, dry in his nostrils, and more. The smell of sweat, aged and rancid through the years. The odor of fear.

These were the interrogation rooms, he thought.

Ahead was a crack of light down low, the first closed

door he'd found. It was at the end of the hallway. When he reached it, he heard a faint sound. Voices. At least two voices, maybe more.

The door was metal. He felt hunks of peeling paint against the palm of his hand. The doorknob was greasy and slick to the touch.

They could be right on the other side. He cocked the hammer of the Colt to chamber a round and pulled gently on the doorknob.

And opened to a staircase, dropping down into a huge, dark area. The stairs were also metal and appeared to end on earthen floor below. The light and the voices came from somewhere far to his right. He could see enough to realize the ceiling was also natural dirt and rock. He was descending into the hillside behind the building.

One of the voices was El Gavilán's. Another sounded like David Delgado, but it was difficult to tell. It was muffled, distorted, like someone speaking through gauze.

Esteban reached the bottom of the stairs and looked around. The place was like a cavern, its ceiling sloping lower in all directions. There was no real floor, only layers of soft dirt that puffed up and then settled beneath his feet. The light source, to his right in the direction of the voices, reflected off the ceiling and threw shadows around him.

He went behind the staircase and found the earthen wall, then followed it toward the light. There were ragged abutments and depressions all along the wall, and with each step the odor he'd first smelled upstairs grew stronger. And now it was mixed with something heavier and older still.

There was an outcropping ahead, and the light was getting brighter. Esteban dropped into a crouch.

And stepped onto the leg bones of the first skeleton. They snapped beneath his weight.

He swore softly and stumbled aside. He put down a hand to steady himself. His hand went into the open rib cage of the second body.

Jesus y Maria. Sweet Jesus in heaven . . .

When he pulled his hand free, his thumb caught the rotten cloth of a shirt. It came with him and pulled the skeleton across his knee. From the darkness beneath the body he heard the familiar buzzing of a rattlesnake.

Mierda.

He rose carefully to his feet, and the snake's rattling rose in cadence with him. The body slid off his leg, and he heard something shift, slither away in the dark.

His eyes were adapting to the dim light, and he saw there were other bodies there. They were chained, some around the leg and others the neck. Some were dried into mummies by the arid atmosphere and others were only bones under strips of chewed flesh. And all around them were the whispers of movement, the occasional gleam of small red eyes. The mice chewed the carcasses, and the rattlesnakes came for the mice.

This entire place, this lower level, was like a medieval dungeon. A place of torture and death and fear.

El Palacio del Miedo.

He moved forward past the remains of a small naked woman. She'd been shackled at both ankles, her legs stretched wide apart by the chains, and her dress lay in tatters beside her. Esteban averted his eyes from what crawled in the dried, ripped flesh between her legs. He reached the outcropping and looked around it.

They were about fifty feet away, gathered around a big rectangular table. It was metal and there were three others like it nearby, covered with canvas sacks. A lantern glowed in the table's center, casting a shadow across the frightened face of David Delgado.

El Gavilán stood over him, hands folded behind his back. Agustin was there, too, looking lazily amused, and the silent Angel with his scowling face and long dreadlocks. Also another sand mule, a short, squat Zuni Indian named Patterson Peña. They were speaking in Spanish.

Delgado was the only one sitting down. The others stood around him in a loose semicircle. The boy looked nothing like the cocky, joke-cracking David that Esteban knew.

Old Granny, she's out there somewhere. . . .

"Enough crying," said El Gavilán softly. The sound carried in the cavernous chamber and prompted a faint echo. "Wipe your face, little faggot, and sit up." He used the term *"maricón,"* one of the deadliest insults in the language to someone who postured as macho as David Delgado.

The boy flinched, but didn't reply.

"You brought him next to me," Carrillo continued in the same flat, relentless tone. "This serpent. Close enough to strike me dead."

"I didn't know." There was a line of wet foam on Delgado's lower lip. "He was Chuey's friend. He was at Piedra Quemadura."

"Looking for me even then, probably. He was also in El Pozo, and Charlie died there. I'm beginning to doubt the coincidence. . . ."

Esteban pulled his head back. Somewhere El Gavilán had obtained the full story. From Engracia? No, she knew only what Ware had told her to do. From Ware, then.

And Delgado was taking the heat in his absence. If he'd been at the motel tonight, they'd have him, too.

Where was Ware?

There was nothing he could do for the boy. Not against four of them. Even the sand mule Peña was armed tonight. And Ware could be anywhere.

Delgado would probably survive with minor damage. He'd been no more fooled than the rest of them. The thing to do now was find Soste Miel. That came first.

Esteban crept back to beneath the metal stairs. His eyes had to readjust after looking toward El Gavilán's lantern. He stood still and listened, closing out the faint drone of voices, and realized the place had other sounds. Quiet shiftings, then echoes above his head. Bats. He heard the soft whirring of their wings.

He worked his way left along the wall. There were more bodies there. In this place there were always the dead. And the warning buzz of another rattlesnake.

And then, faintly in the distance, a different sound. Rising and lowering, then holding and repeating again. Someone was singing.

". . . goes out for a walk,
     Then comes the Rat, and he sings with a
     squawk. . . ."

It was *"La Araña,"* the old canticle from before the
Mexican Revolution. It had been Pascual Santiago's favorite song.

"The Rat and the Spider, the Rat and the Spider
   Are singing beside the Strong Water. . . ."

Even the last verse was altered to the way Pascual had
sung it. Esteban's throat ached at the sound, and the
memories it summoned. Then he moved through the
darkness more quickly, following the voice.

The wall swept gradually in an arc to his right, and the
ceiling continued to lower. His vision improved, and he
was able to step over the dried remains of the dead.

". . . the Rat and the Cat, the Cat and the
   Dog . . ."

The voice was very near, a clear tenor singing low.
Esteban stopped and whispered, "Honey Bear?"

". . . are singing beside . . . What is it?"

"Honey Bear, where are you?"
"Next to your foot, boy." The sound came from his left.
"And you're standing on my friend Naranjo."
"What . . . ?" Esteban crouched, and felt something
give beneath his weight.

"Aiee, such manners," said the fat man leaning against
the wall. "Where were you raised, boy? In Veracruz, I'll
bet. The sailors in Veracruz would piss on the dead."

"Your pardon, Señor Naranjo," Esteban whispered
quickly, and pulled his foot free of old cloth and trailing
bones. "Honey Bear, I've come to free you."

"From all this luxury? From these fine companions?
Who are you?"

The man's round face was indistinct in the darkness,

but Esteban saw a crown of white hair surrounding a bald skull. "I am Esteban Santiago," he answered formally. "I am the grandson of your friend Pascual Santiago."

"Pascual?" There was a flash of very white teeth. Dentures, thought Esteban. "Pascual Santiago? What a man. What a hero. Ask him for me if the Watchful One still guards the hilltop below the great dome. Ask him if her teeth are as sharp."

"We have to leave now." Esteban ran his hands along Soste Miel's arms and legs, looking for shackles. "This is a bad place."

"Sharp like needles, her teeth. Like the fangs of these snakes. The ones who eat the rats. In here, the serpents are my allies."

There was no chain. The old man sat in rodent droppings against the wall, surrounded by bones and leathered flesh. And all he had to do was stand up and walk out.

"Pascual, you say? Your father?"

"My grandfather." Esteban reached beneath Soste Miel's arms and pulled him up. The old man's body odor mixed with the smell of fresh excrement as he came to his knees. "You're heavy, old one. Can you help me a little?"

"Heavy, yes, but very strong," said Soste Miel. He seemed content to rest on his knees. "A man of immense power in my youth, like the honey bear of the mountains. Now, Valdes, he was the skinny one, Pascual. You remember how he stood in the center, above her teeth, to test the boards? And how you told him—"

"We have to hurry." Esteban pulled the man to his feet. God, he was fat. Honey Bear, indeed.

He'd turned Soste Miel in the direction of the staircase when a flashlight shone in his eyes, blinding him.

"Welcome to the Palace of Fear, Esteban," said El Gavilán. "You missed my invitation, but you came anyway. Thank you."

"The Cat and the Dog, the Dog and the Ox
Are singing beside the Strong Water. . . ."

Soste Miel sat in his chair and sang quietly to himself. He smiled and reached for the big Colt that lay in the center of the table.

"He's useless," Carrillo said in English, and stretched over the old man's shoulder to move the pistol out of his reach. "Worse than a child, because he can't be taught. Sit him in a corner down here and he stays without being restrained. He sings to himself. And I'm sure he knows where the Crown of Colorado is, somewhere down in that woolly old skull of his, but he doesn't know he knows."

He stroked Soste Miel's bald head.

Esteban didn't answer. He sat across the table, also out of reach of the gun. David Delgado and Jaime Agustin glared at him. Angel and Patterson Peña looked bored.

"And you, Esteban." El Gavilán's eyes were muddy yellow in the lantern light. "You don't know where it is either, do you? Or you'd have taken it long ago."

"Maybe I did." Esteban measured the distance to the pistol. The Haitian's sawed-off twelve-gauge would cut him in half before he could reach it. "Maybe I already found it. Maybe my only reason for being here is to kill you, pig. For the murders of my family."

Carrillo blinked at the insult, but then he smiled. "If I believed you, my friend, I'd have the answer before dawn. And it would give me a lot of pleasure. But it would also be a waste of time. If you had the coins, you'd never have gone to prison. Craddock bought his way out, and you'd make him look like a beggar by comparison. No, you'd never have wasted those years in El Pozo, Esteban. But you could tell me one thing. Did you kill Charlie Pellikern?"

Esteban smiled. "He died poorly, El Gavilán. He died without honor, crying and pissing himself and telling me everything he knew. I imagine you'll die poorly, too."

Carrillo's smile faded. "Then you'll have to be content with imagining it, won't you? It's a shame you wasted—what? Seventeen years of your short life?—on revenge. You could have gone your way, and I could have gone mine. Oh, well."

He nodded toward the Haitian. "Angel?"

The black man slowly brought up the shotgun barrel . . .

Dive for the pistol. Don't go out like a sheep. Dive . . .

. . . and pointed it at El Gavilán. "Drug Enforcement Agency," said Angel in clear, unaccented English. "You're under arrest, Mr. Carrillo. Tell your people not to move an inch, or I'll blow your fucking nose for you."

Esteban sat transfixed, one hand halfway toward the revolver.

"You too, pal." Angel glanced at him. "Back off that gun. I don't give a damn about your feud with these assholes. You're under arrest just like they—"

The last five seconds of light were a blur of movement. From Angel's left, Patterson Peña came up with his pistol and the DEA agent spun on him, emptying a load of buckshot from less than ten feet. Peña's head snapped backward as his legs buckled forward, and he landed sitting on his knees and draped back over his own heels.

At nearly the same moment, Jaime Agustin fired at Angel, hitting him in the side. Esteban grabbed the Colt just as El Gavilán knocked the lantern off the table.

The cavernous room went dark. More than dark, it went pitch black because all their eyes had acclimated to the light. Esteban landed on the dirt floor and rolled underneath the table. He heard a curse nearby and saw a muzzle flash. A boom of sound echoed with the chatter of flying bats.

"La Araña se sale a pasear . . ."

Soste Miel was singing in his chair. Esteban grabbed the old man by his belt and yanked him down just before a whizzing sound passed his ear and another muzzle flash.

"Esteban?" It was Angel's voice from somewhere out ahead. "You alive, man?"

"Yeah." Esteban rolled toward the wall, dragging Soste Miel with him.

"Okay. Us against them. Afterward, it's all square, right?"

"Like hell!" David Delgado's voice came from beyond

the table, moving toward the wall. "You ain't siding with no goddamn fed, bro!"

Esteban kept silent and pushed Soste Miel ahead of him. He knew generally where the stairs were, and he was beginning to distinguish shapes in the blackness.

"You hear me, *mano?*" called out Delgado. "You stick with . . . Aiiee!" His shriek cut the air. "No! No!"

And Esteban heard the clear buzzing of an enraged rattlesnake.

"No! *Fuera! Fuera!*"

A spot near the wall lit up with gunfire. One shot, two, then three. Esteban aimed for the muzzle flashes, but held fire.

"Oh, nooo . . ." The voice faded into silence, but Esteban still heard the snake. It's too quick for the poison, he thought. The poor little bastard must've missed the rattler and shot himself.

"Let's keep moving," he whispered in Spanish to Soste Miel. Then a whizzing sound burst into an explosion of dirt and rock above his head, and deafening sound echoed around them again.

"That was close, Pascual," the old man declared in a loud voice. "It's Huerta's butchers. Return their fire! Shoot them dead!"

Esteban dragged him lower as another bullet showered them with dirt. This time he saw its origin. A thin shape rose and crept forward. Jaime Agustin.

Esteban sighted in and waited for the shadow to go still. Pulls a little to the left, Bubba Lee Barnes had said. He allowed for it, then slowly squeezed the trigger.

Kicks some. Barnes was right about that, too. Esteban's hand and wrist went numb. The shadow screamed and flew backward onto the floor.

"Oh, God! Oh, God!" wailed the Coyote. "Ramon, I'm hit! I'm hit! Ramon . . ."

"Ramon's gone, pissant." Angel's voice sounded a little weaker. "He was up those stairs before it got good and dark. Nobody left down here but us peons. Hey, Esteban!"

"What?" Esteban moved Soste Miel to rest against the wall.

"Damn good shooting, my man. I was just drawing a bead on him myself."

"It was luck. How bad are you hit?"

He heard a laugh. "I've felt better, I guess. I'm not going anywhere in the next little bit."

"I am." Esteban sighted in on the writhing shadow a short distance away and fired a shot over the top of it. Agustin screamed and began crawling away. "Are you still interested in a deal?"

"Maybe," said Angel.

"Okay. I'm going to finish that trash over there, and then I'm leaving. I'll call help for you when I'm out, if you see this old man gets home safely."

"No!" the Coyote yelled. "You stay away from me! I have a gun!"

"What do you say, Angel?" Esteban asked.

"I've got no choice but to agree," called Angel. "Don't take too long, though. I've sprung a damned righteous leak over here. . . ."

"No! You can't do that!" Agustin fired off a wild shot. "You can't just let him kill me! You're the law."

"Then you better crawl over here and surrender while you can, pissant."

"I can see you, Coyote," said Esteban. "Move in that direction, and I'll put another one in you."

He reached out for Soste Miel's arm. "I have to go now, Honey Bear," he whispered in Spanish. "The other man, the black man, will take care of you."

"Be careful, Pascual," the old man replied. "Remember Huerta's killers, and how they tried to ambush us along the Sonora."

"I will." Esteban gently pressed Soste Miel's hand. "God be with you, my friend."

"And with you, my beloved old friend." Soste Miel's voice trembled. "It was so good to see you again. Do you remember how we were? We were the Sentinels. Young and brave and true for Madero."

"*Viva Madero,*" whispered Esteban, and then moved away in a crouch. "Remember your promise, Angel," he called in English.

"I hear you, man."

"I'm coming now, Agustin." Esteban went belly-flat and slid along the dirt floor.

"No! You stay away!"

"You'd better load your gun, Coyote. And while you do, I have some names for you. Pilar and Cesar. Are you listening? Rodolfo and Alicia and Señor Cuyas and Andres Rosario. And my grandfather, Pascual Santiago. Do you hear their names, coward?"

"No! Please don't! Oh, no . . ."

And, behind him in the darkness, that soft, clear voice. *"Viva Madero, Pascual. Viva Los Centinelos. . . ."*

Esteban leaked blood on the pickup seat. Bubba Lee Barnes would probably wonder about that, but he'd do it in silence.

He turned off past the tramway, then up into the wide streets and cul-de-sacs. He parked in an alley.

He checked the wound again. Clean entry and exit. It had hit no bones.

In the end, his whispered taunts as he crept ever closer had shattered the last of Agustin's nerve. In his terror, the Coyote had risen and charged, screaming hysterically. And he'd gotten off one lucky shot before he died.

Esteban stopped on the sidewalk. Engracia Torres's door was open, but her lights were off.

He went around to the back, to a parking lot below her balcony. Its concrete lip hung eight feet above the ground, ordinarily a simple thing, but not with a hole in his side.

He took three steps and jumped. The fingers of his right hand curled over the edge, then he grabbed on with his left and pulled up. The sliding glass door was unlocked, the bedroom empty. But there were voices in the living room.

One of them was El Gavilán. His voice was shrill.

". . . him! Goddamn him to hell!"

"Get control of yourself." The other voice was Joseph Ware's. "Remember the DEA agent. We can't—"

"No puedo evitarlo! No hay derecho."

"—stay here," finished Ware. "Calm down now. It won't do any good—"

"Damn him! Oh, damn him!" Then it sounded like Cuellar began to cry. Hoarse, snuffling sounds.

Esteban moved closer to the bedroom door. He was unarmed. The big Colt, empty after its last three slugs had torn through Agustin, was in the pickup's glove box.

"You knew all along, didn't you?" El Gavilán sounded on the edge of hysteria. "You knew who he was from the first time you saw him! It was another of your goddamned games, wasn't it?"

"Come to the car. There's a lot to be done, and no time—"

"*Matarife!* I swear by the Virgin he'll die!"

"Come along."

"And you!" The voices were moving away. Toward the front door by their sound. "I should kill you, too. Because you knew who he was, and you played with him. Your games. Your goddamned games . . ."

Esteban heard the front door close and rushed into the living room. If Engracia had left her pistol for him, she'd said she'd leave it hidden in the console drawer below the aquarium.

Why was El Gavilán crying? Screaming like a tortured child? If the gun was still there, Esteban would give that *cabrón* something to scream about.

The only illumination in the dark room was from the brightly colored lights in the water. He yanked open the drawer and rummaged through it. The gun was gone. Maybe she'd taken it after all. . . .

He stepped away, and his foot came down on something soft. He reached down and picked up Engracia's doll, Carmelita. Only Carmelita was no longer wearing her head.

Because it was floating in the aquarium, in there with the bright, colored lights. And it wasn't alone. There were two heads floating in the bloody water. Fish nibbled curiously at their vacant eyes. . . .

TWENTY-FIVE

The old man sat very still, painted first in tones of green, then red, by the light from his television set.

"C'mon in, boy," he said. "Expected you long before now." His voice was different than it had once been. Slurred at the edges.

"You're a hard man to locate," Esteban answered. "Are you drunk? Because if you are . . ."

Melvin Craddock's laugh was more like a gasp. It caught in his throat and caused him to cough.

"Then you want me to sober up, huh? So neither one of us'll miss any of it." Craddock coughed again, and spat next to him into a metal cuspidor. "No, I'm not drunk. Turn on the light if you want."

Esteban pushed a wall switch next to his shoulder, and the room went glaringly bright. He shifted his weapon, a .30-caliber hunting rifle, to his other arm.

"So, now the lights are on," said Craddock. "No secrets in the light. Like wha'cha see?"

It was difficult, but Esteban kept his face immobile. "What happened to you?" he asked.

"Stroke." The old man attempted a smile, but only one side of his face moved. "Ain't it the shits? Doctors all thought I wouldn't be nothin' but lunch meat, but I fooled 'em. I'm a tougher kill than ole Rasputin, boy. Santiago, that's your name, right?"

"That's right."

"I remembered. See, I may talk a little funny now, and I don't walk too straight neither, but there's nothin' wrong with my thinkin'. *Un hombre taciturno,* that's what Chuey called you that day."

"Congratulations." Esteban turned off the TV. The big man was a shock. He was mostly gaunt bone structure, his right hand atrophied and curling in his lap like a claw. This wasn't how it was supposed to be. "How long have you been a cripple?" he asked, his words intentionally harsh.

"Three years an' a month," Craddock answered. "An' twelve days. Doctor said it was the strain a hidin' out from all you Chilis who wanted me dead. Didja kill the boys outside?"

"They'll recover, I think."

"Appreciate it, although they're 'bout useless without the big Brit who ramrods 'em. Sent him off to San Antone on business today, worse luck for me." Craddock studied him keenly. "I heard wha'cha did to Carrillo. Killed all his men except that big son of a bitch Ware, I heard. Cut off his woman's head 'n left it floatin' in a fish tank. Savage little bastard, ain'cha?"

Esteban shrugged. So they all believed it. Not just El Gavilán, but everyone. Ware must be laughing himself silly.

"So," Craddock continued. "You gonna kill me, too?"

"Absolutely."

The old man nodded. "Wasn't me sold you that night, boy, although I do admit coverin' my ass at your expense later. So I guess you figger it's fair. What if I offer a swap?"

"I don't want your money." Esteban jacked a shell into the chamber.

"Didn't figger you did, but how 'bout this? How 'bout if I know where El Gavilán went? You been huntin' him over a year since that Palacio business. Ain't doin' so hot on your own, are you?"

Esteban's breath shortened. "That's interesting," he said, maintaining an outward calm. "And how about *this?* How about if I make you tell me, then I kill you anyway?"

"Jee-zus!" Craddock laughed and began to wheeze again. "Jee-zus, you changed some since I last saw you, boy."

"We all change, if we live long enough."

"Ain't it the truth? I'm proof a that. But looka here. You could probably make me talk, although I might have another stroke 'n go belly-up on you. You could even lie to me, then kill me later. But it strikes me that you got a tough row yet to hoe, and I got no love lost on Carrillo myself. Let me slide, an' you'll not only get the information, but I promise to back you later on if it comes to it."

"Your word, huh?"

"Yeah, you sarcastic little fart. My word." When Craddock got angry, his slur was worse and the dead side of his face began to twitch. "I'll tell you somethin', boy. I don't much like you Meskins, never have, but I'm a Texan, goddammit! We got somethin' around here we call a debt of honor. Ever heard of it? And, by God, I always pay my debts."

And Esteban realized he no longer had any particular desire to kill the old man.

"See that picture?" Craddock must have seen him weakening. "The one on top a the TV?"

Esteban glanced at a small boy. Dark hair, blue eyes. "I see it," he said.

"My grandson. He's ten years old, an' he thinks I'm all right. You imagine that, Santiago? He thinks his granpaw's all right. He's the main reason I'd like to hang around awhile yet. To watch him—"

"Calle la boca!" snapped Esteban. The story had hit too close to home. "Are you still a student of Spanish, *cabrón?* That means shut up. Shut up about all that and tell me where El Gavilán is."

Craddock struggled painfully to his feet. "I owe you, boy." He nodded. "More than just information, too. It's a debt of honor now. An' like I said, I always pay my debts."

He walked slowly toward a large table in the corner of the den, lurching awkwardly on his right side and his arm hanging limp. "There's a bottle in that bookcase." His mouth formed a half smile. "An' that big leatherbound folder beside it's my checkbook. Bring 'em both over 'n have a seat. *Sientese*, ain't that how you say it?"

When Esteban arrived in the southwestern Colorado resort town of Silvercat, El Gavilán had been there well over a year and was already established. It had all been so simple for him. Shave off his beard and change his name to Raymond Cuellar, then pay top dollar for a new, unimpeachable Social Security card. Everything else he'd needed flowed from that card and his ready cash. *Qué sencillo,* yes? Back on the Rio, Angel Christophe had run a nationwide computer search, with an emphasis on Colorado, but Ramon Carrillo had vanished without a trace.

Now the manhunt was turning south, toward Acapulco, and Mexico's cooperation was being sought.

Esteban had already been in Colorado the month after the Palace, jumping parole and hitchhiking to Durango, but his search had gone empty and he'd returned to Texas. Without Craddock's information and his check for ten thousand dollars, Esteban would never have tried Silvercat. It was no surprise to find his old enemy getting into local politics there. What a country.

The Colorado mountains were a revelation to him. Their coolness and high, bright beauty were like nothing he'd ever seen. He rediscovered his childhood love of climbing and found the company of others who felt the same. He grew his hair long and called himself Stephen James, dropping—aptly enough, he felt—the Saint from the title, and wondered wryly whether Brother Axton would've approved.

At the same time, he watched Raymond Cuellar's rise. The man made his own luck, Esteban had to admit. Political pundits in the area were suitably impressed and, before long, El Gavilán began making noises about the upcoming state congressional race.

Esteban knew Cuellar was at his mercy. He could have killed him on several occasions, or he could have simply contacted Angel. He wasn't sure why he did neither for the moment, unless it was some temporary lethargy, a respite from his own personal *Jornada del Muerto* that had driven him without release for eighteen of his twenty-eight years. Maybe it was a brief time of his own, for climbing the high walls and living his own life, before the inevitable final steps in that journey. Maybe that was why. It was a difficult question.

And then, one day in early autumn, he received the answer.

"Right there? That's La Brujería." Warren nodded to some closely grouped concentric lines on a topo map. "It means—"

"Witchcraft," said Esteban. "What's the rating?"

"Five-point-twelve on most charts. It's a good climb, got some caves in the face and the iron already hammered in. Doesn't matter, though. It's got a serious Moje on it, Stephen."

"Why's that?" The vernacular word was from a sixties beach term, a Mojo. It referred to a jinx.

Warren shrugged. "The usual, I guess. 'Some ropes got broked, and some Heads got croaked.'" He smiled to show he was only passing on gossip. "It's a fly-by now, and that whole basin's going to be underwater soon, anyway, unless the local tree-huggers can outfox the federal government. Hey, you remember when Tommy Eaton tried to flash Separate Reality last summer? I got some pictures here. . . ."

While Warren dug through a drawer, Esteban idly studied the map. The rockheads he knew around Silvercat were, by and large, as superstitious as a nest of *curanderos*—speaking of witchcraft—so he could either forget this particular wall or climb it alone, which was often a poor idea.

The ascent was formally titled Cupola Face, and was on a half dome in a basin of the same name. There was a pass, Mule Pass, going in, and a river, the Agua Fuerte, that fed out through a canyon. And across the river from the half dome was a hill called Riqueza Crown. A lot of Spanish names, not uncommon in the high San Juan. There had once been Spanish explorers all through the region.

Agua Fuerte. Strong Water.

. . . are singing beside the Strong Water . . .

Soste Miel. Esteban smiled at the memory of the fat old man and his song. He'd . . .

. . . ask him for me if the Watchful One still guards the hilltop below the great dome . . .

. . . died one night a few months after the Palace. Just went to sleep one night and . . .

The great dome. Riqueza Crown.

. . . and never woke up.

. . . beside the Strong Water.

Esteban's face went hot. *Riqueza* translated into English as "riches." Or sometimes as "prosperity."

The Crown of Colorado . . .

And Mule Pass, for the mules led by four young men in the autumn of 1914, carrying their burden and their promise to the crown below the great dome. Beside the Strong Water . . .

Jesus and Mary.

Warren was still talking, but Esteban didn't hear him.

He went in alone, driving a borrowed jeep up a twisting logging road to its trailhead. It was a long hike but easy enough, even with a shovel and pick strapped to his backpack, that finally brought him through the pass at nearly eleven thousand feet.

He stood at the edge of a boulder field and looked out over Cupola Basin. The Spanish word *cupula*—or cupola —meant "dome," and he saw the towering rock spire to the west. The basin was like a rare jewel, its setting the snowcapped peaks surrounding it. And below him was a rounded hill, topped in aspen and evergreens. It was a September afternoon, and the aspen dazzled the eye with the richness of their reds and golds. Riqueza Crown.

Esteban dropped to his knees in that same spot where his grandfather may once have stood. Help me, *abuelo*, he thought. Or maybe he whispered it.

On top of the Crown he selected the most likely spot, a clearing at its center, and began to dig. It was a slow process because years of falling leaves had created a wet humus that stuck to his shovel. After four hours of work, he raised his nylon backpacking tent and rested for the night.

It took much of the following day, seven hours of widespread excavation, before his shovel hit the hand-cut boards. It was midafternoon, and the sunlight turned the aspen leaves to flame. Another two feet below the boards he turned up an old leather sack, its edges cracking and mildewed. He was bending toward it, his heart pounding, when he thought the ground beneath him moved. But that was ridiculous, of course.

. . . *ask him for me if the Watchful One still guards the hilltop* . . .

He was probably standing just a layer of dirt above the other sacks, and they'd shifted . . .

. . . *ask him if her teeth are as sharp* . . .

. . . with his weight. He reached down, and his fingers touched the sack.

. . . *remember how he stood in the center* . . .

Esteban stopped dead still.

. . . *above her teeth to test the boards* . . .

Jesus.

He took a step toward the edge of the hole and felt something give. He dove onto the slope.

After that close call, it was easy. Esteban found the end to a second set of planks below the dirt and pulled them up onto the mound. They'd also been hand-cut, but in a slightly different way, shaved thinnest at their centers where a person would stand reaching for the leather sack. The bait at the mouth of the snare. He looked down into the pit beneath the hole.

La Vigilancia. The Watchful One. Sharp like needles, her teeth. That was what the old man had said.

Thank you, Soste Miel, he thought. For loving my grandfather through all the years, and for saving my life in this lonely place.

And it was standing there, looking down at the sacks stacked around the base of the sharp spikes, that an idea began to form in his mind. An idea so . . . *correct* that he knew at last why he'd waited. El Gavilán had killed Pascual Santiago nearly twenty years before. Now, Pascual would return the favor.

"Hay que tomar la muerte como se amante, asesino," he whispered.

But the waiting wasn't quite over. It took that autumn's remaining good weather to move the sacks into the big cave on La Brujería's face. That was essential. If the trap failed and things went badly, El Gavilán must never get his hands on Pascual's gold. The coins would be safe in the cave, at least for a while, because no one climbed La Brujería anymore. It was bad luck.

So Esteban waited through the autumn—a difficult time for the town of Silvercat, with a scandal at the ski resort, and the final implication of a prominent citizen in a years-old series of grisly murders—and then through the winter, watching his enemy's power and influence grow. Be patient a little longer, he thought. Just until spring.

As Pascual Santiago had shown him, every snare needed a lure. In early April, using a false name, Esteban took one of the Maderos into a Silvercat pawnshop. He pretended ignorance of its true value and let the owner cheat him because he knew that El Gavilán periodically sent a flunky, a blond man named Cooper, around to coin shops and pawn dealers in the region. He pocketed the two hundred dollars with apparent enthusiasm, then let slip he'd found the coin while hiking on a hilltop in Cupola Basin. Once within the basin, he knew El Gavilán and Ware would figure the rest out. They understood Spanish as well as he did.

He watched the shop for nearly a month before Cooper went in, and it came as no surprise when, shortly thereafter, the future candidate for state congress began to speak out against damming Agua Fuerte Canyon.

On the morning of May 15, Esteban hid the jeep a half mile from the Mule Pass trailhead and hiked into the basin, more heavily laden this time with supplies for two weeks. When the man who now called himself Raymond Cuellar brought his group through the pass five days later, Esteban was watching them from the top of the dome.

Sunday Afternoon
May 22

The Strong Water

A man gradually identifies
himself with the form of his
fate; a man is, in the end,
his own circumstances.
—Jorge Luis Borges

TWENTY-SIX

Beth lost control of the raft almost immediately. The wooden paddle was torn from her hands by the current when they slammed against a rock and leaned high on the right. She and Stephen lunged against that side to bring it down.

"It won't work!" she yelled above the river's roar. "Not if we get sideways! We'll capsize."

"Shut up and drive!" He tossed her the other paddle. She dug it into whitewater at the bow, and they straightened momentarily.

They emerged from forest and tore along between the high banks of a meadow. She saw Stephen's eyes widen.

"What is it?" She braced herself for another impact, but then he pointed to their left. She looked that way and felt her heart sink.

Joseph Ware was running through the high grass, angling to cut them off. His face was set in a fierce grin, and he carried his Mac-10 in one hand.

Beth dug in with her paddle, knowing as she did it was useless. The speed of the current would either carry them past him, or it wouldn't. He was running clumsily, one arm held against his side. He's been hurt, she thought. He's not bulletproof after all. . . .

The raft sailed between a series of outcroppings. Up ahead the canyon rose on both sides. To Beth it looked like an open mouth.

It was going to be close.

Ware's speed accelerated as he tossed the gun aside. He sprinted up a slight incline to a grassy bank. Beth felt Stephen yank the paddle from her hand. He fell sideways when they bounced over an obstacle beneath the surface.

Ware hit the edge and launched himself into a leap, timing the raft's speed. He hung in the air above them like a huge, grinning bird of prey . . .

. . . as Stephen swung the paddle over his head in an arc. The blade struck Ware across the chest and snapped apart. The big man's body dropped into the water.

And, almost instantly, his hand grabbed the rigging rope along the raft's side. Then his other hand was reaching for Beth.

She dove forward with a scream. Stephen was crawling toward her when they entered the canyon.

From the boulder field, Cuellar saw the raft emerge out of the trees. It tore along with the whitewater flowing toward the canyon. Two figures, tiny but distinct, moved inside it.

It was true, then, what Ware had said. Not a trick this time. Not another game.

Cuellar raised his weapon, then realized the futility. They were too far away, moving too fast.

Then he saw another figure running toward the riverbank. It was Ware.

"Disparar!" he screamed. "Shoot them! Shoot . . ." He saw Ware drop something. He'd dropped his gun. The man was insane.

Ware leaped from the bank at a spot where the river was hidden from Cuellar's view. Then he saw them again. The big man was pulling himself into the raft as the girl lunged away from him.

They rocketed into the canyon.

Cuellar wiped his face with a trembling hand. Then, as the realization reached him, he began to smile.

Dios mi, it was really true. They were gone, all three of them. Gone forever. Nobody could survive the whitewater hell that was Agua Fuerte Canyon after the storm. They'd drown in there, and their bones would be crushed on the rocks. The current would batter them beyond recognition.

Esteban Santiago was gone. Cuellar closed his eyes and breathed an Ave of gratitude. Engracia was avenged. Now she'd forgive him, and the horrible, continually repeating dream would end.

And Ware. Even more than with Esteban Santiago, Cuellar felt the weight of the big man's presence slide from his shoulders. One day, Ware would have killed him. He'd always sensed that. One boring day, when the monster had nothing better to do . . .

And the coins were almost certainly in the cave. Not an insurmountable problem. Find a climber, promise a share, then have the gold lowered to the ground. Climbers were always having accidents, especially on that wall. It was unlucky, they believed.

He'd have to leave the basin before he was seen, but not before some hard work on the hilltop below. There'd be hikers and maybe even survey crews during the summer, and every trace had to be gone from Riqueza Crown. The environmentalists would lose their battle against the dam project eventually, and then it would all be buried beneath an icy mountain lake, anyway. But, long before then, the coins would be gone, too.

It was going to be a tough afternoon, taking down the camp and filling that hole alone, especially with his wounded arm. Even wearing gloves, he'd surely get blisters.

Ah, well. As you once said, Joseph, *Qué puta es la vida,* huh?

He was smiling while he walked down the trail into the basin.

The raft hit a trough with a violent concussion, and Stephen saw Ware's grip loosen. If he could reach him in time . . .

The canyon rose on either side of them, and the river roared whitewater through its heart. There was no place to land, nothing to grasp except sheer walls. Huge underwater boulders created waterfalls, and backwashes where the torrent actually reversed. Each was a death trap.

The raft ricocheted between rocks. Water was everywhere, pouring over them, smashing them down. There was no air to breathe.

And Ware was slowly pulling himself on board.

Stephen slid past Beth, and a sudden impact flung him into the bow. Ware's arm hooked around his neck.

"Esteban . . ." Somehow he heard the voice above

the roar. The huge arm pulled him sideways across the bow. He slammed a fist into Ware's face, but the man's grin never wavered.

"Esteban. *Mi amigo . . .*"

Ware was half into the raft, pulling Stephen toward him. His legs hung out like a rudder and flew into the air when the raft glanced off an exposed tree limb.

Stephen hit at Ware again, but felt his strength failing. His lungs were heavy and on fire. Then the man released the rope and reached for Stephen's long hair.

"Esteban . . ."

Just as a slim arm came across his back. Beth's fingernails went into Ware's eyes.

The grip loosened, and Stephen levered his body around. He launched a kick that caught Ware in the right shoulder, and saw a grimace of pain. He kicked the same spot again as Beth continued to tear at the man's face.

Ware's arm came loose and his body went sideways. Then a huge rock was there, whitewater boiling around it, and Ware flew into its side, full force. Stephen heard the sound of the impact.

A bright streak of red laced across the gray granite. Ware slid down into a backwash.

Esteban . . . His mouth formed the word again, still smiling. Maybe he raised his arm. Maybe it was only the current pulling him under.

Then he was gone.

"Look out!" Stephen heard Beth scream, and rolled over.

Jesus and Mary.

In late summer it would become a narrow passage between high, jagged rocks. A bit of a squeeze, a bit of a drop-off.

But now the water went over the top.

He had an instant to grab for Beth, then the raft tore onto a protruding edge and ripped apart. Its front end caught and held. Its back flipped forward. Stephen felt himself fly into the air. For an impossibly long moment he hung above the river. He saw the high canyon walls. He saw the colors of a narrow band of sky. Then he dropped over the precipice and down, ten feet into a raging side channel.

He went under and, amazingly, hit no rocks. But then the current slammed him against one, and his shirt caught.

He couldn't pull free. The current bounced him back and forth. His elbow cracked against stone, then his skull. He was caught beneath the surface. He grabbed his shirttail, tried to wrench it over his head, couldn't. His breath was going, one lung heavy and full. The icy water had the musty taste of old snow. . . .

He wondered if Beth was alive.

He jerked backward, and his shirt came up around his neck. He fought his head through the opening just as another surge of the current literally yanked him free of it, and he exploded to the surface in a spray of bloody froth.

Just in time to throw up his hands and bounce off another rock. But he was in a side channel along the cliff, and the current was a little less fierce. After a while he grabbed the projecting piece of a tree, only its upper branches visible above the flood. He pulled to the side and crawled up onto a rock.

Beth worked her way along the canyon's east wall. There was a thin shelf about two feet clear of the water, and occasionally she was able to step out onto a boulder for better balance. She saw the shelf was going to peter out maybe a hundred yards ahead, and then she'd be stuck.

When the raft ripped apart and rolled over the precipice, she'd been flipped backward and to one side. She'd surfaced, certain she was about to follow, only to find herself in an eddy created by a downed tree. There were hunks of wood sticking out all around her, some sharp-edged and menacing. She thought of the aspen spikes in that pit. La Vigilancia . . .

When she'd tried to pull up, her legs were entangled in something. After another unsuccessful attempt she held her breath and ducked beneath the surface where brightly speckled cutthroat trout, drawn to the calm eddy, scattered away from her.

It was the climbing gear Stephen had been carrying when he came to the bridge. One of the jumars had caught on a limb. She freed her legs and started to leave it, then changed her mind. She was alone, and she might have to try climbing out of this canyon. It took some time and a great deal of breath to salvage the gear.

Now she moved downstream, one foot directly ahead of the other because there was no room to do otherwise. The rope was wound over one shoulder and below her other arm, crisscrossed with the Mac-10's web harness. She figured she probably looked like an ad out of *Soldier of Fortune* magazine. That, or freaking Mad Maxine.

The canyon was widening ahead, but the river was no less savage. She was almost at the end of the shelf, and there was nowhere to go from there.

She was alone. Ware was dead, which she could take some hard pleasure in, but Stephen was gone, too. Only she didn't want to think about him right now. If she did, she'd stop and sit down and quit. And then she'd die, too.

She'd known him intimately, and not at all. They'd spoken and touched, but she'd never really understood what was between him and those two men. Only that it was something old, and more elemental than any of them understood. Stephen had said he'd tell her someday. He probably didn't mean it.

She recited the four names and two places again and was surprised how easily they flowed from her memory. A promise, he'd said, and that thought brought a numbing tightness to her throat. She decided she'd loved him. And that maybe, in time, she'd have made him love her.

More trees along here, more driftwood wedged between boulders, and more . . .

She saw him lying facedown and shirtless on a broad rock up ahead. When water splashed his leg, she saw him pull it out of the way.

And, oddly enough, she didn't scramble down to him immediately. She just stood there and watched him while her eyes filled with tears.

She couldn't stop smiling.

TWENTY-SEVEN

The telling of it took a while, but she wouldn't leave it alone until he did. The river canyon was an odd backdrop for a story of the desert. But then again, maybe not, because it was essentially a story of two rivers, far apart in space and time.

Stephen made it as brief as he could, giving only enough details to string things together coherently. But he didn't soft-pedal any of it, not his family's deaths or El Pozo or the Palace. Or what happened to them all.

"So many dead." Her voice was soft and desolate, and he only heard her above the water's roar because she was near. "Every one of those damned coins is soaked in blood, isn't it?"

"But that's not what my grandfather intended. You can see that. It was for his country at first, and then later it was going to be a new life for us all."

"So many dead . . ."

"Do you understand now?" He asked it gently so she wouldn't stop holding him. He was very tired, and the sun felt good on his skin.

"As much as I ever will, I guess. Anyway, it's over. After all the years."

He shook his head. "We're not out of this canyon, and El Gavilán's still alive. It isn't over."

Her fingers were soft on his bruised face. "What do you think he'll do?" she asked.

"Cover his ass first, I'd say. Then come back to look for the coins. If he was still up in the pass, he may've seen us go into the canyon."

"Then he'll think we're dead now."

"We probably should be. And we will be if we stay here. All that rain's increased the speed of the snowmelt above the lakes. The water's going to get a lot higher in here before long."

He sat up, then struggled to his feet. His body felt

encased in lead and he needed badly to cough, but he didn't want her to see the blood.

The flat rock beneath them was about three feet out from the canyon wall and the tiny shelf Beth had traversed. That shelf dwindled away to nothing a little farther on. Above their heads was close to two hundred feet of cliff. It was nothing like La Brujería, but Stephen knew he had no climbs left in him. Not today, or for a long time to come.

Across the river, forty or fifty feet of boiling whitewater, the canyon's west wall was beginning to recede. They'd come through the narrowest part already.

"Is that the trail?" Beth shaded her eyes and pointed across to the other side. Stephen looked where she indicated, at a spot farther down where some terrain was above water. A tree-lined strip at the base of the west cliff.

"Looks like it. Looks like some high ground where the canyon widens."

"We landed on the wrong side of the river, didn't we?"

"If you were like me, girl, you landed wherever you damn well could." He estimated the distance. "But don't worry. Things are under control now."

"What does that mean?" She watched him uncoil the climbing rope, then smiled suddenly. "Wait a minute. You never told me you were Pecos Bill."

"Make that Pecos Guillermo," he corrected her. "I probably also never mentioned the time I spent wrangling horses in El Paso, either." He used one of the carabiners for his slide knot.

"Not as I recall." She stepped back onto the shelf to give him room. "Are you any good with that thing?"

"Taught by the best. There was this old hand named Bubba Lee Barnes—"

"Bubba Lee? You're kidding me, right?" Out of the corner of his eye, he saw her grin. "Not Jimmy Joe? Or Possum?"

"Nope. Bubba Lee. He was a good friend, as it turned out. Anyway, he used to say, 'Make a wide loop, Pancho. Throwin' a loop too small's like takin' a fart in a high wind.' "

"He called you Pancho?" she snorted. "And you let him? Jesus, he'd probably call me Little Lady and then try to pinch my ass."

She was getting her spunk back, Stephen noticed. For a while she'd gone on her considerable courage alone. Now she was beginning to believe they'd make it, after all.

If only he wasn't so tired . . .

"First try." He attempted to rouse himself by kidding her. "See that big stump? Over there by the base of the cliff? What'll you bet I don't nail it my first try?"

"It's a bet," she said from behind him. "Whoever wins gets to be on top when we bed down over in those trees."

He nearly dropped the rope in the river.

"What . . . does that mean?" he managed. He felt himself blushing, for God's sake.

"You know damn well what it means, Pecos Guillermo. Throw the rope."

He missed by five feet.

"All right! Care to try for a little bondage on the next toss?"

He pulled the wet rope out of the water and let out another loop before looking back at her.

"You have to let me concentrate on this, Beth," he said. "We have to get across." But he couldn't keep the grin off his face.

She was sitting on the rock shelf, leaning back, and her damp clothes clung to every line of her body. How beautiful, he thought at that moment. How truly lovely.

Then her smile went from provocative to something different. Something more tender. "You're right," she said. "Get us across, Stephen."

On his fourth try, the loop dropped over the stump. Stephen pulled it up carefully until the carabiner knot snugged against the base.

"Now, what?" Beth climbed back onto the rock beside him.

"Now we find something to tie off to on this side." He studied the cliff face behind them, and then the boulder they stood on.

"I don't see anything," she said.

She was right. The only nearby trees above flood line

were across the river, and the boulder's edges were too round. The rope would slip off.

Stephen considered the distance again, and then Beth's weight. *Como que no?* It would have to work. And it would, if he still had the strength.

"Okay," he said. "Here's how it plays. I was going to rig a tight-line, but there's nothing over here to tie onto. So, I'll hold this side instead."

Her fingers touched the mottled purple bruises along his side. "Stephen, I don't know if—"

"It's no problem." He made the reply as offhand as possible. "I'll just lean back and hold a hip belay like you did in the cave. How much do you weigh? About a hundred and fifty-five?"

He forced her to smile. "Maybe a hundred and two or three, dripping wet," she answered.

"Is that all?" He grinned. "I figured that mouth of yours weighed that much alone."

"And the thing I've admired most since we met is your gallantry. But, Stephen . . ."

"Like I said, no problem. And you will be dripping wet, all right. From this angle, you'll nearly be trailing your legs in the river. I hope you still have the super knife."

She dug the little Swiss army knife from a jeans pocket, and Stephen sawed a six-foot length off the end of the climbing rope and tied it in a double loop. She'd never used jumars before, so he attached them to the rope and showed her how to operate the safety gates.

"Couldn't be easier," he said. "Sit in the loop and pull yourself across with the jumars. Remember to hit the release each—"

"You haven't explained one thing. Who's going to hold a tight-line for you?"

He shrugged. "That can't be helped. The rope's anchored on the other side, and you'll be over there to give me a hand. I'll just have to get a little wet along the way."

"Stephen, your ribs may not take it if you hit another rock."

"I'll try to miss them." He pushed her to the water's edge. "Now get going."

* * *

Beth swung out over the river. Whitewater roared below, less than two feet beneath her dangling boots. Icy spray splashed her legs, and a thick mist billowed up around her. Before she was a quarter of the way across, she was soaking wet again. The weight of the Mac pulled her balance point backward.

Even double-looped, the length of rope cut into her buttocks. Reach with one hand, extend the jumar, then lock it. Do the same with the other hand, then pull across, the loop jerking along the main rope. Reach out and do it again. She raised her legs just in time as a dead tree swept past below her and then crashed against an outcropping farther down, scattering its debris.

She was halfway across.

She glanced back at Stephen leaning against the far slope of the boulder and holding her weight. His torso was covered with purple bruises, and his face was fatigued far beyond exhaustion. After she crossed, he'd have to go into the river with only his grip on the rope to save him. The time was long since past when she'd believed his strength was limitless.

She was raising her hand to wave, something to show him she'd kept her nerve and would make it across, when Joseph Ware came out of the water behind him.

"Esteban . . ."

The sound was an electric shock along his nerve endings at the same moment he heard Beth scream. Only the discipline of countless situations "on belay" enabled Stephen to keep his grip on the rope.

"So," he said, and turned his head to see . . .

Por el amor de Dios. For the sacred love of God . . .

El Gavilán called Ware the Deathmaster. And, dear God, it must be true because the man standing there *was* dead. Or should be.

Ware towered over him, dripping blood and water onto the boulder. His clothes hung on his body in tatters, and Stephen saw the pink and white of exposed cartilage and bone along the side of his chest. There was a gaping tear in the skin below his chin, with a pulsing, leaking artery visible in the puckered flesh, and his jaw was twisted to one side. That side of his face was purpling, his eye swelled shut.

"Esteban," he said again, and the jaw made him difficult to understand. "Do I look as bad as you do?"

"You look worse."

"Really. This has been a tough weekend for both of us. But fun, huh?"

Ware turned his head, and Stephen saw the exposed, bleeding tendons move in his throat. He was looking out at Beth, who hung immobilized in the makeshift harness. Whitewater splashed over her legs and swung her body up and down. Her mouth was an open *O* of horror.

"Let her go," said Stephen.

"Buh-Buh-Bette," said Ware. It looked like he was trying to smile. "She's a real warrior, that one."

"I know."

"The heart of a samurai . . ."

"Let her go," Stephen said again.

Ware stared out at her, and Stephen thought he saw something there, in the big man's face. Something he'd never seen before. But that was impossible. It could only be the pain of broken bones, of battered flesh. Nothing more. And he knew Ware saw the gun she was carrying. There wasn't a chance in . . .

"Okay." Ware said it so softly that Stephen wasn't sure he'd heard. "Why not?"

Stephen waved her across. "Go on!" he yelled.

"No! Stephen . . ."

"Go on, dammit! You're no good to me out there! Go on!"

She started up again.

Ware watched silently until she was above the opposite bank and Stephen let off the rope's tension.

"What's her name?" he asked. "Her real name."

Stephen watched her scramble up to the tree trunk. "Her name's Beth," he said.

"Beth . . ." The big man looked for a few moments longer, then turned back toward him. "Like you said earlier, so. We've come a long road, Esteban."

"Too long." Stephen tossed the rope aside. "I should have killed you years ago."

"Maybe." There was the grin again. Twisted and barely recognizable, but still the same Ware grin. "But then we'd have missed the end to the game. Tell me something, Esteban. You think we'll continue this in hell?"

It was Stephen's turn to smile. *"Yo no se,"* he answered.

From across the river, all sound drowned by its roar, it was like watching a silent film.

"Jump!" Beth screamed. "Stephen, jump . . ." But her voice was carried away downstream. And he wasn't listening, anyway. She saw him drop the rope, and the current pulled its end into the river. She saw the two figures, both more dead than alive, lunge at each other.

"No!" she wailed, but that was useless, too.

Stephen got in the first blows, hard shots to the torn flesh of the big man's chest that drove him backward. But then he hooked an arm around Stephen's waist and lifted him up and in. They fell across the boulder and rolled off its backside into an eddy below the shelf. Stephen's head went underwater. Ware seized the back of his neck and held him there.

"No! No, you son of a bitch!" The gun was in her hand before she realized it, and she was running upstream until she was directly across from them.

Ben, I'm sorry. . . .

She pulled back the cocking bolt, and only felt its hard snick. She didn't hear it, or anything else. Only the roaring of the river that had somehow gone inside her head.

Daddy, I'm sorry, but I have to. I'm sorry. . . .

Ware looked up at her just as she raised the gun. Their eyes met as she thumbed the conversion lever and squeezed off on full auto, and he was smiling. . . .

And the gun wouldn't fire.

It wouldn't shoot, goddammit! It was too wet or too battered or too some goddamned thing, and it wouldn't shoot. Ware's grin widened.

In that momentary lapse of concentration, Stephen broke free. He launched a kick up and into Ware's gaping chest wound, then rolled away, sliding out of control across the boulder. His legs went into the river and the current yanked them sideways. Ware dove after him, fingers locking in Stephen's hair. Both men rolled to the edge of the rock.

And the goddamned gun wouldn't shoot. Beth pulled the clip free, then snapped it back in and switched to semi-automatic. It wouldn't shoot.

Ware pulled Stephen partly onto the rock by his hair. The fingers of his other hand closed around the smaller man's throat.

Stephen was still fighting back, but Beth saw his blows were weakening. Then his legs began to drum a frenzied cadence on the water's surface.

She threw the gun across at Ware. It glanced off the boulder, and he looked her way again.

Stephen's body was convulsing under the pressure around his throat. His hands were sliding off Ware's shoulders. He was dying. . . .

"Stephen!" she screamed, and without conscious thought, she ran across the last rock and launched herself in a long, shallow dive toward the two men. She hit the water's surface and was bounced sideways, then she went under.

Icy water went into her nose and mouth. It smashed over her like a cold, hard fist. Her head broke the surface just as the current tore her away. She saw the astonishment in Ware's eyes, then the river took her down.

Ware shoved the dying man aside. He plunged into the water. His great strength, the pride of his life, was nearly gone, but not entirely. He surfaced and saw the girl's head bob up again. She grabbed the end of the rope trailing in the water as she rocketed past it.

She wasn't going to drown. He wouldn't let her. He wasn't finished with her yet.

She was losing her grip, her light body bouncing on the surface of the rapids. The current carried him right into her, and he grabbed the rope just behind her.

"Beth!" He hooked his left arm, the uninjured one, around her. "Hold on to me!"

Her head swiveled toward him, and he saw the horror in her eyes. She swung her fist, hit him across his broken jaw, but there was no longer any pain. Then she released the rope, and her fists rained blows onto his face.

"Damn you! Why don't you die, you goddamned monster!"

"Hold on to me!" He pushed her up the rope. The current swung them like a pendulum in toward the rocks, and he shoved her against a chunk of driftwood trapped there. "Grab on! Grab onto the wood!"

She was absolutely oblivious to her danger, swinging wildly, with her screams echoing above the river's roar.

"Damn you! Oh, damn you! *Why . . . don't . . . you . . . die!*"

And then her fist smashed through the ripped flesh in his neck. He felt a sudden pressure, and the water around them was sprayed bright red. Red over white, red into white into pink . . .

"Why . . . don't . . . you . . . die!"

The strength went out of him. He'd never felt it go like that. His fingers had no feeling, slipping from the rope, from her body. Everything went out of focus.

He was jerked loose, and the river took him. He saw her face . . .

. . . in the briefest moment before he went under the water and down into a rip flow of the current. Down and along and faster until he slammed into something, a tree wedged in the underwater rocks, and caught there. Large fish, trout pulled by the same current, swam past. One poked curiously at his open eye.

Which reminded him of something. Or someone. And he was trying to remember when things slipped away.

Beth climbed along the jagged piece of wood. Splinters cut her and the current tore at her, but she fought it until she won.

She scrambled onto the bank and looked back. The river poured past her, exploding in patterns of sound and motion, all power and menace. But *he* was gone. Ware was gone.

Why had he gone into the river after her? She would

never have had the strength to pull herself out with the rope alone. . . .

You know I'm the result of forces beyond my control. . . .

He could have killed Stephen and left her to drown. . . .

Stephen. In that moment she forgot about Joseph Ware. She ran upstream along the bank, carrying the end of the rope.

He lay on his side near the boulder's edge. He was forty feet away, across the river, and he wasn't moving at all.

"Stephen!" The roar carried her voice down the canyon. He still didn't move.

She tied the rope's end around her waist and climbed onto the highest rock on her side. Then she dove out into the river again, considerably farther than the last time. The water swept her past him, but there was an outcropping below, the spot where the dead tree had shattered.

She stretched for it, feeling the current tearing at her like giant hands, like *his* hands. She fought a surge of panic. He was gone.

No, he wasn't.

The big body broke the surface and lunged half out of the river. One arm flung wide before it splashed down and was swept into the outcropping.

Beth screamed, and choked on a mouthful of water. The current pushed her into Ware's body just as the rope hit its full length. She grabbed for wedged-in wood, but got his arm instead.

Ware hung in the debris, and she was entangled in him. His body spread-eagled onto the rock, half out of the water, and the wound in his throat gaped open like a second mouth.

He was smiling . . .

Buh-Buh-Bette . . .

. . . but he wasn't smiling at her. Only at the canyon and the river, and at the lifeless rock above him. His eyes were indifferent, glazed over and dead. He was dead.

She battled her panic and her churning stomach. She grabbed his shoulder . . .

. . . *felt it cold as marble under her fingers* . . .

. . . and climbed up over him. Her shirt had peeled back from the current, and her bare belly touched his face . . .

. . . rubbery and yielding and colder still . . .

. . . then she got a knee across the rock. She tumbled forward until the taut rope stopped her.

She thought she'd vomit, but she didn't.

She reached Stephen by half crawling, half swimming to the end of the narrow shelf. She untied the rope and held it taut as a balance point while she worked her way upstream to the boulder.

He still lay where Ware had flung him. He was moving now, coughing thick gouts of blood into a depression next to his mouth.

Beth turned him carefully and slid her leg under his head. Beneath the pattern of bruises, his face was a pasty gray.

I won't cry. I won't let him see me crying. . . .

"You're wet." His voice was a rasp. Blood trickled from the corner of his mouth.

"I'll dry." It came out unsteady. "How're you doing?"

A faint smile. "Not so hot. Where's Ware?"

"He's dead."

"He's . . ."

"Dead. He's dead, Stephen. This time for certain."

She was surprised by what crossed his face. A quick shadow, then gone. He nodded. "Dead. Like you said before, so many dead."

He opened his eyes, but they failed to focus. She realized he couldn't see her.

"Stephen, we've got to get out of here."

"Huh?"

Her throat locked shut. We've got to get out of here, she wanted to say. We've got to get help. But all she said was, "Stephen . . ."

His hand closed over hers, still strong in its grip, and she held him through the bloody spasm of another cough. "Ware's . . . dead?"

"Yes."

"El Gavilán?"

"Him too. I swear it. I swear—"

"Do you remember what I told you?"

And she recited the names and places.

He smiled. "That's good. You remember the names. I remember them, too. . . ."

"Stephen . . ."

"Listen, my love. I remember them, too. All the names . . ."

His voice faded to a whisper, a jumble of soft words, then the whisper to silence.

"I love you," she said, but she knew he didn't hear her.

Four people walked along the trail on Agua Fuerte Canyon's west side. They were fairly certain they couldn't reach the basin with the high water, but it was worth checking because it could save an extra five miles over Mule Pass. In their packs they carried hand-stenciled signs protesting the Cupola Basin Dam project.

It was their leader, a lean, balding internist from Durango named Donald Magill who first saw the body of the huge man in the river. The current tore at its legs, trying to pull it free of the rocks, and one arm flopped up and down when the water boiled over it. A greeting, of sorts. The hikers dropped their gear and stared, wide-eyed.

And it was the leader's equally angular wife who first looked across the river and saw the two people there. A small woman with long blond hair rocking a man back and forth in her arms and crying.

Betty Magill couldn't hear the blond woman's voice, but she saw her tears.

We can both get what we want. . . .

The man who'd renamed himself Raymond Cuellar dreamed of gold and the moon, of coins three-quarters of a century old, and the dream gave him a terrible headache.

Which was odd, because the coins had dominated his life through nearly twenty years of blood and hunger and death. But then, it was an odd dream all around.

The girl was in it, coming to him with a promise, it seemed. Or maybe it was only something connected to the girl. A message? She was quite lovely, the girl—*tez blanca,* her lightness a contrast to the dark beauty of his Engracia. Who wasn't in this dream at all.

A message from the girl, was that it? And there was a coin, one of the Maderos, and a promise of the rest. An exchange?

We can both get what we want. . . .

Then there was someone else in the dream, and a constriction in his breathing he recognized as fear. And there was motion. Motion, and then faint, whispering sounds against a moon that had motion, also. And a movement of air on his face that was . . .

The wind. It hurried across him in the darkness. It tugged at his clothes and blew his hair into his face.

Raymond Cuellar tried to sit up, but his head hurt too badly. It was the size of a basketball, the size of the moon.

Which gleamed in the darkness overhead. His fingers touched something soft, then hard underneath. He tried to sit up again, made it this time while the wind whistled around him. His head pounded waves of pain through his skull. He touched it, which only made it worse, but he could find no trace of an injury. Getting to his feet was absolutely out of the question.

"Painful, I'd imagine." A voice, friendly and conversational, came out of the moon. With a British accent, for God's sake. "Give it an hour or so. You'll be up and about."

"*Qué?*" He was suddenly nauseous and his ears were ringing, so he lay back on one elbow. "*Madre mi, hay mucho ruido! Donde . . .*"

"English, Mr. Carrillo. If you please." The moon moved across his vision, and he heard the faint, whispering sounds again.

"What's happening to me? Where am I?"

"You don't know?" There was a chuckle. "No, I suppose you wouldn't. Put out your hand. No, no, more to your left."

Cuellar's fingers went through thick softness, then found something firm. Closed over it.

"The . . . sacks?" The sound of his own voice drove pain into his temples. "The coins? It's the coins."

"Very good. Instead of bringing the mountain to Muhammad, we decided to do it the other way around, so to speak. I'm impressed, Mr. Carrillo. That cocktail's leaving your brain faster than expected."

The moon moved again—only it wasn't the moon at all, was it? Only a flashlight—and several figures silhouetted in the blackness. Cuellar saw three, maybe four. From the one closest, he had an impression of considerable bulk, and of a pale beard reflecting the flashlight's glow.

"Who are you?" He tried to rise, still couldn't because he was too dizzy. He slumped back and lay against something. The sacks. "What are you doing to me?"

A dark wind blew across his face.

"You don't remember?" The light blinded him, and he raised a hand to shield his eyes. A hand almost too heavy to lift. "It'll come to you. Remember the coin in the envelope? The offer to bargain for a share? How you went to . . ."

(*We can both get what we want*, the message said. . . .)

". . . the meeting outside town? I can well imagine your surprise that the girl was alive. And you went there to kill her, I don't have to imagine *that*. Of course, you didn't expect to find me instead, or my associates. It seems the girl was given some names to memorize, and my employer was one of them. She gave me—"

"Who are you, goddammit?" Cuellar's shout exploded a jolt of pain inside his skull. His mind formed a vague memory of a big man with a blond beard stepping quickly from behind him. "Tell me—"

"—the coin then, and she told me the story." The voice went on softly, relentlessly. "She said she stole it, which made the two of you just alike. A pair of thieves."

"Tell me what you're—"

"And you didn't expect a syringe of trichloroethylene cocktailed with halothane, either, did you? Powerful stuff. More bang for the buck, one might say. We had to dose you up once more along the way, I'm afraid. You'll probably walk awry the rest of the afternoon, not to mention puking up your socks."

"*Cabrón!* What are you doing? Where am—"

"Where?" The soft voice cut him off in midscream. "Where do you think? Do you hear the wind? The echoes?"

"Oh, my God!" The realization went through him. "The cave . . ."

"Do you hear the bats? When you shout, it scares them. You don't want to scare the bats away, Mr. Carrillo. Shall I tell you why?"

He tried again to rise, failed, and the ammonia odor of powdery bat guano puffed up around him.

"You were quite a burden to place in here, Mr. Carrillo. Dead weight, so to speak. But we're a hi-tech operation nowadays, and enjoyed the challenge. I was given a certain carte blanche by my employer, and I changed his original plans after the girl mentioned something interesting about you and high places that struck my fancy. You wanted the gold so very badly, after all, and I've always been a hopeless fan of poetic justice."

The meaning struck him then, through the numb edge of the drug, and it hit harder than any pain in his head. It rose to seal off his throat.

"Oh, no. You can't do this. Oh, no . . ."

"I admit we took a few of the sacks. For someone else's

agenda, so to speak. But you get to keep most of them.
For as long as it will matter to you, at any rate."

"You can't do this! You *cannot* . . ."

"You lived much of your life in Texas, Mr. Carrillo, so
you're probably familiar with its frontier ethic, are you
not? The concept of a debt of honor, for instance?"

"Oh, no. Oh, please . . ."

"My employer is. He values it more and more in his
latter days. And he speaks constantly of paying his debts
in full. I suppose one might call it an obsession. . . ."

By the time he reached the light, they were gone.

He couldn't go any farther. Not another step toward
that open circle of blue sky ten feet away. Or the empty
air that lay behind it.

Because if he did, he'd surely look down. And if he ever
looked down, he'd fall.

His head was clearing from the drug, and he stared at
the stone walls of the tunnel. Extending forward to the
circle of blue sky and the terrible emptiness behind it
that went down and down and down . . .

His stomach wrenched violently as his mind saw it. A
surge of bitter vomit touched the back of his tongue.

. . . and extending backwards, the walls, back into
darkness. Down to the hole, the tomb where the wind
howled across the leather sacks. Across his gold.

We can both get what we want. . . .

He screamed, and the pain in his head drove him to his
knees, but he did it again. The sound echoed along the
walls and several bats burst past him, blinded, and out
into the empty air. There was no one to hear him scream.

How long would it take? Months before the work crews
entered the canyon. Months before the shadow men
came back for the gold.

Climbers? No one climbed La Brujería anymore. It was
bad luck.

How long would it take? Long enough.

Until it got so very bad, *too* very bad. Then he might
close his eyes and run forward. Into the empty air . . .

His stomach wrenched again, a grinding pain that was
almost like hunger, and he suddenly understood what the

bearded man had meant. Why he wouldn't want to scare the bats away.

After a time, the birds gradually grew accustomed to the screaming and returned to their nests in the cliff.

EPILOGUE

[2]

—*June 24*—

Jorge wanted the little girl, Juanita Mares, to stand without her crutches.

"Be v-very still," he said. "No, don't hold on to me."

He took a step back, and then another. Juanita's eyes followed him, wide with panic, but he kept a smile on his thin face.

"Very good, Juanita. See how well you're doing? Okay, now. Two su-steps only. You c-can do it."

She looked down at her feet and missed the tightness in his face. Then she studied his outstretched hands. She slid one foot a few inches forward.

"Th-that's it. That's wonderful!" He wanted to help her, to reach for her, but he didn't.

She was among the *afligirs,* the afflicted ones. When the two governments sprayed their poison on the drug smugglers' mountain *plantios,* some had fallen on the crops of Bavispe's farmers. Juanita's parents had eaten the food—what was their choice?—and both she and her sister were born with what the doctors called the Open Spine. The sister had died as an infant, but Juanita held on.

"Good. Very guh-good. Another step . . ."

At the edge of his concentration, Jorge heard car engines outside. Two of them, it sounded like. The first was the tinny clatter of Brother Patricio's old truck, but the second had a heavier sound, somehow. More substantial.

"Now reach for my hand."

Brother Patricio had been called to Juarez that morning, even before Jorge rose for breakfast. He'd heard the priest on the phone outside his room, and the stunned thickness in his voice. Something about a debt of honor, and then something else Jorge missed at the edge of sleep.

Juanita's tiny hand closed over one of his fingers, and he lifted her carefully onto her padded seat by the wall.

"Jorge!" Brother Patricio's voice from the road.

He went to an open window. He saw the priest walking from his truck back to a large car parked behind it. A rich man's car, without doubt. Texas license plates.

Brother Patricio's face was creased in a smile, and Jorge tried to recall the last time he'd seen *that*. But it was a worried smile, and he suddenly remembered what else he'd overheard from his bed.

Something about the Greater Good, said in a voice that gave capital letters to the words. About the Greater Good for the mission and the town, and how far that outweighed a . . .

A deal with the Devil? Jorge must have dreamed that part.

A tall old Anglo got out of the big car's backseat. The man moved slowly, his right side lurching helplessly when he walked, and one arm dangling limp. Another of the *afligirs*, despite his obvious wealth, Jorge thought, and said a quick prayer for the old man.

A small Anglo woman with long blond hair emerged from the car and looked around her. Jorge saw the look of wonder in her face. And of sadness.

The car's driver, wearing an expensive-looking dark suit and sporting a thick blond beard, had opened the trunk and was hauling out two leather suitcases. He was a bulky man, and when he handed them to Brother Patricio, their weight jerked the little priest toward the ground.

Then Jorge saw the blond woman help someone else from the car. Drawn and pale, leaning on her for support. But smiling as he held her.

Sweet Mother of God . . .

"Esteban!" Jorge cried, and leaped through the open window.

"Jorge!" He heard the voice. "My brother . . ."

And ran toward the sound.

ABOUT THE AUTHOR

THE HIGH SAN JUAN is the second novel by Kristopher Franklin. His first, SILVER-CAT was also published by Bantam. Kris and his wife live in Colorado.

Now there are two great ways to catch up with your favorite thrillers

DON'T MISS
THESE CURRENT
Bantam Bestsellers

☐	28390	**THE AMATEUR** Robert Littell	$4.95
☐	28525	**THE DEBRIEFING** Robert Littell	$4.95
☐	28362	**COREY LANE** Norman Zollinger	$4.50
☐	27636	**PASSAGE TO QUIVIRA** Norman Zollinger	$4.50
☐	27759	**RIDER TO CIBOLA** Norman Zollinger	$3.95
☐	27811	**DOCTORS** Erich Segal	$5.95
☐	28179	**TREVAYNE** Robert Ludlum	$5.95
☐	27807	**PARTNERS** John Martel	$4.95
☐	28058	**EVA LUNA** Isabel Allende	$4.95
☐	27597	**THE BONFIRE OF THE VANITIES** Tom Wolfe	$5.95
☐	27510	**THE BUTCHER'S THEATER** Jonathan Kellerman	$4.95
☐	27800	**THE ICARUS AGENDA** Robert Ludlum	$5.95
☐	27891	**PEOPLE LIKE US** Dominick Dunne	$4.95
☐	27953	**TO BE THE BEST** Barbara Taylor Bradford	$5.95
☐	26892	**THE GREAT SANTINI** Pat Conroy	$5.95
☐	26574	**SACRED SINS** Nora Roberts	$3.95
☐	28436	**PAYMENT IN BLOOD** Elizabeth George	$4.95

Buy them at your local bookstore or use this page to order.

THRILLERS

Gripping suspense...explosive action...dynamic characters...international settings...these are the elements that make for great thrillers. Books guaranteed to keep you riveted to your seat.

Robert Ludlum:

☐	26256	THE AQUITAINE PROGRESSION	$5.95
☐	26011	THE BOURNE IDENTITY	$5.95
☐	26322	THE BOURNE SUPREMACY	$5.95
☐	26094	THE CHANCELLOR MANUSCRIPT	$5.95
☐	28209	THE GEMINI CONTENDERS	$5.95
☐	26019	THE HOLCROFT COVENANT	$5.95
☐	27800	THE ICARUS AGENDA	$5.95
☐	25899	THE MATERESE CIRCLE	$5.95
☐	27960	THE MATLOCK PAPER	$5.95
☐	26430	THE OSTERMAN WEEKEND	$5.95
☐	25270	THE PARSIFAL MOSAIC	$5.95
☐	28063	THE RHINEMANN EXCHANGE	$5.95
☐	27109	THE ROAD TO GANDOLOFO	$5.95
☐	27146	THE SCARLATTI INHERITANCE	$5.95
☐	28179	TREVAYNE	$5.95

Frederick Forsyth:

☐	05361	THE NEGOTIATOR (Hardcover)	$19.95
☐	26630	DAY OF THE JACKAL	$4.95
☐	26490	THE DEVIL'S ALTERNATIE	$4.95
☐	26846	THE DOGS OF WAR	$4.95
☐	25113	THE FOURTH PROTOCOL	$4.95
☐	27673	NO COMEBACKS	$4.95
☐	27198	THE ODESSA FILE	$4.95

Buy them at your local bookstore or use this page to order.
